P9-EEU-398

SWAMP SPIRITS

A Miss Fortune Mystery

GHOST OF A CHANCE?

NEW YORK TIMES BESTSELLING AUTHOR
JANA DELEON

Copyright © 2022 by Jana DeLeon

All rights reserved.

No part of this book may be reproduced in any form or by any electronic or mechanical means, including information storage and retrieval systems, without written permission from the author, except for the use of brief quotations in a book review.

Design and composite cover art by Janet Holmes using images from Shutterstock.

❀ Created with Vellum

MISS FORTUNE SERIES INFORMATION

If you've never read a Miss Fortune mystery, you can start with LOUISIANA LONGSHOT, the first book in the series. If you prefer to start with this book, here are a few things you need to know.

Fortune Redding – a CIA assassin with a price on her head from one of the world's most deadly arms dealers. Because her boss suspects that a leak at the CIA blew her cover, he sends her to hide out in Sinful, Louisiana, posing as his niece, a librarian and ex–beauty queen named Sandy-Sue Morrow. The situation was resolved in Change of Fortune and Fortune is now a full-time resident of Sinful and has opened her own detective agency.

Ida Belle and Gertie – served in the military in Vietnam as spies, but no one in the town is aware of that fact except Fortune and Deputy LeBlanc.

Sinful Ladies Society – local group founded by Ida Belle, Gertie, and deceased member Marge. In order to gain membership, women must never have married or if widowed, their husband must have been deceased for at least ten years.

Sinful Ladies Cough Syrup – sold as an herbal medicine in Sinful, which is dry, but it's actually moonshine manufactured by the Sinful Ladies Society.

CHAPTER ONE

RONALD, IDA BELLE, GERTIE, AND I WERE ENJOYING AN afternoon in my hot tub, along with a round of frozen margaritas, when my former CIA partner, Ben Harrison, rounded the corner of my house, tugging his fiancée, Cassidy Williams, as fast as her shorter legs could manage. He had that look I'd seen so many times when we'd done a mission together—part intensity, part excitement.

"Who'd you kill?" I asked as he approached.

He frowned for a moment, then grinned. "Oh, yeah. Old times, right? No one today and I'm really hoping no one anytime soon."

"You haven't even been here a month," Ida Belle said. "Give it time."

"Or we could introduce you to Celia and cut that down some," Gertie said.

Ronald clinked his glass against Gertie's.

"Who's Celia?" Cassidy asked.

"Our nemesis," I said.

"She's that bad guy on every sitcom," Ida Belle said, "who's constantly trying to get one over on the hero, but just ends up showing her butt instead."

Gertie grinned. "And she means that butt part literally."

Harrison grimaced. "Yeah, YouTube is filled with Celia's butt shots. That woman should really stick to pants."

We all nodded.

Harrison gazed around, then checked his watch. "Is this really what you guys do on a Tuesday at 2:00 p.m.? I thought you were PIs. Well, one of you anyway."

"Hey, it's a chilly sixty-two degrees, and we had leftover margarita mix from the holidays," I said. "Frozen drinks don't get warm in here like beer does."

"You're just not drinking the beer fast enough," Harrison said. "But still, Hot Tub Tuesday?"

"In their defense, they did catch a murderer a few weeks ago," Ronald said.

"And saved a father and daughter from prison," Ida Belle said. "Prompted an engagement *and* cleared the way for a woman and her disabled daughter to land a serious money deal with a television producer."

"And I had to wear a dress," I said. "An itchy, tight, uncomfortable dress and a padded bra."

"Facts," Ida Belle agreed.

"How long are you going to milk that whole queen thing?" Gertie asked.

"The whole month of January at least," I said. "Maybe the first quarter."

"As well you should," Ronald said.

Cassidy smiled. "It sounds like you've earned the drink and more."

"Oh, there's more," Gertie said. "We haven't even dipped into Nora's stuff yet."

"Who's Nora?" Harrison asked.

"You don't want to know," I said. "And I mean that—the less you know about Nora, the better. You're not put in the position of arresting beloved locals if you don't know what they're up to."

"But if you like sketchy, middle-aged women hitting on you, look her up," Gertie said.

I laughed. "Carter crosses the street if he sees her coming."

Harrison cringed. "I'll take a pass on Nora."

"We all do, honey," Ronald said.

I shot a glance at Ronald but wasn't about to ask.

"So what's up?" I asked. "I know you didn't drag Cassidy across my backyard just to see what we were doing. And you have that look like you just assassinated a drug lord."

"The good ole days," Harrison agreed. "But not this time— we found a house!"

"That was fast!"

"Congratulations!"

"Good for you!"

"Great news!"

We all cheered at once and Harrison beamed. Cassidy looked far less excited.

"Where is it?" I asked, wondering why Cassidy wasn't as thrilled as my former partner.

Since Harrison would be serving multiple towns as a flexible deputy, he'd been trying to locate something central to all of them. No matter what, it wouldn't be too far from Sinful because that was one of the towns he'd be covering when needed. Cassidy, who was as smart as she was gorgeous, had put herself through medical school while working as a nurse in the ER and then later for a pediatrician when she'd had to shift to part-time hours in order to concentrate on school. She'd recently graduated and had easily secured a residency at the hospital up the highway. ER doctors weren't easy to come by.

There were a ton of homes in more rural areas and Cassidy wanted horses, so I figured they'd found an old farm somewhere and would soon delve into upgrades, repairs, and fencing. Maybe she was already dreading dealing with contractors. I couldn't blame her on that one.

"It's sort of in the middle of all my coverage areas," Harrison said. "It sits on a bayou and comes with twenty acres, so plenty of room for Cassidy to have horses. There's even a nice stable and a training arena already, and they're both in decent condition."

"Sounds perfect," Gertie said.

"It's so big," Cassidy said somewhat hesitantly. "I'm a bit concerned about repairs and maintenance."

"With the price of real estate down here, you should be laughing all the way to the title company," Harrison said. "The profit on the sale of our condos in DC will cover the price of the house *and* the repairs. We'll have a new start with no debt. How many people get to say that?"

"Very few," Ida Belle said. "What kind of repairs are needed?"

"It's been sitting empty for a long time," Harrison admitted. "It looks rough, but the structure is in excellent shape. The plumbing is working okay. Since it's so far out, it's got a well, and the electricity isn't on, but the inspector said he didn't see any cause for alarm. I think it mostly needs a good cleaning and some updating—the kitchen and the master bathroom are first on the list. And then just changing things out to our taste, but we can do that a little at a time. Not like we need ten more bedrooms anytime soon."

I spit out my margarita. "Ten *more* bedrooms?"

Gertie sucked in a breath and shot a worried glance at Ida Belle.

"You didn't buy the Leroux estate," Gertie said.

4

Harrison nodded. "That's the one. I couldn't remember the name."

"Did you sign something already?" Gertie asked.

Harrison frowned. "Yeah, why? Does it flood or something, because the Realtor said it had never flooded. Crap! With all that stone, the place looks like a castle. I knew there had to be a reason it was unoccupied and so cheap."

"That's not why," Gertie said. "It's empty and cheap because it's haunted."

Harrison, Cassidy, and I stared at her. Ronald and Ida Belle just nodded and kept drinking.

"Haunted?" I asked.

Gertie nodded. "The story goes that the house was built about ninety years ago by a French count, Lucien Leroux."

"Sounds like a stage name," I said.

"The general consensus was that he was good-looking enough to be on the stage," Ronald said. "The rumor was that he was kicked out of France because he had an affair with the wife of a marquis who was also a cousin of a prince. Those pretty boys are always trouble."

"Leroux landed in New Orleans, like a lot of French did," Gertie said, "and proceeded to take up with the very young daughter of a powerful voodoo priest."

I whistled. "This guy knew how to pick them. So I guess he was 'asked' to leave New Orleans as well."

"Yes, but not before the daughter got pregnant," Ida Belle said. "The daughter, Lovelie, was shunned by her father and sent into exile with the count. The count had plenty of means, so he built the house for his bride, hoping to bring her the glamour and richness of the city she loved and had to leave behind."

"Did it work?" I asked.

"Sadly, no," Gertie said. "The bride missed her city and her family and fell into a deep depression, which only worsened after her daughter, Celine, was born. She never recovered."

"That sucks," Cassidy said. "Today, we'd call that post-partum and give her a pill and counseling, but back then, women were expected to get on with things, regardless of how they felt."

Ida Belle and Gertie both nodded.

"You 'sucked it up,'" Gertie said. "One of my mother's favorite phrases to throw out to me when I was complaining about womanhood requirements."

Cassidy smiled. "I see that you didn't take your mother's advice."

"To her great dismay," Gertie said, then shrugged. "She couldn't comprehend my choices any more than I could comprehend hers. But we loved each other despite all that. And at least I had Ida Belle. We always knew we weren't going to toe the line in regard to societal expectations. It would have been a lot harder on my own."

"Somehow, I think you still would have managed," Ida Belle said, and we all laughed.

"So what happened to the bride?" Cassidy asked.

"Depends on who you ask," Gertie said. "Some say she committed suicide by walking into the bayou and drowning. Others say her father, enraged over her betrayal to her family, dragged her into the bayou and killed her. Celine wouldn't have even been ten years old yet."

Cassidy's hand flew over her mouth. "Oh my God. And that's who's haunting the house?"

"The house isn't really haunted," Ida Belle said. "That's all local drama and hooey."

"You don't believe in ghosts?" Cassidy asked.

"You do?" Ida Belle asked. "You're a doctor—a scientist."

Cassidy nodded. "And I've seen a lot of things I couldn't

explain. I don't know. I mean, if you believe in God and an afterlife, then why not spirits who are stuck in between?"

"Exactly," Gertie said.

"It's a big fear of mine," Ronald said. "I mean, what if you're stuck wearing what you die in forever? That thought hit me one evening, and I spent the whole night shopping for designer pajamas and the highest-quality fabric I could find for underwear—chafing, you know? I started wearing shoes to bed for a while there, but finally decided a good pedicure would cover me."

"I found these super-soft shorts that are also boxers," Gertie said.

Ronald shook his head. "Honey, you can't just go around dangling for centuries."

"What happened to the count?" I asked, getting back to the story. "And Celine?"

"The count went into seclusion for a couple years after his bride's death," Ida Belle said. "Then he turned up again in town, which, according to rumor, thrilled the local ladies, as most of the men were off at war."

"He had servants the entire time, of course," Gertie said. "And they reported that the count and Celine were well cared for, even during his seclusion. After he emerged, locals called at the home from time to time, but no one ever laid eyes on Celine. She had a private tutor and never left the estate."

Ida Belle nodded. "Until the count died."

"Then Celine—who was probably twenty by that time—came out into New Orleans society at a huge charity gala," Ronald said. "The heavenly red-haired one. That's what her first and last names mean in French, and by all accounts, it was an accurate description."

"They just left out the deadly part," Gertie said.

Cassidy's eyes widened. "Deadly?"

"Celine Leroux was a voodoo priestess," Gertie said. "Some say her power was greater than that of Marie Laveau."

Ronald nodded. "The stories say that she even went to Haiti for her initiation. And that the day she returned to the country and took that first step on American soil, her grandfather—the man who'd disowned her mother—fell to the ground dead, and snakes burst out of his belly."

"Oh my God!" Cassidy said.

"Fascinating," I said. "Harrison and I have seen and heard some stuff—the remote ends of the earth contain stories that are sometimes uneasy to explain—and the snake thing is one of them. It's a curse of some sort, I think."

"A curse?" Cassidy asked, paling a little.

"Don't worry," Ida Belle said, cluing into Cassidy's growing fear. "This is all tall tales and flat-out gossip that have been handed down from generation to generation and told fiftieth, sixtieth, and seventieth hand. The reality is that no one knows if Celine ever left Louisiana, much less the country. After that one supposed appearance at that big charity event, she was never seen outside the house again. And you know how people are—in the absence of facts, they'll just make something up."

"Especially in places like Sinful where scandal is king and not much else is happening," Ronald said.

"But why come out for that one event and then disappear again?" Cassidy asked.

"Maybe she didn't like what they were serving," Harrison joked.

"More likely that she got her first big dose of the general public and wasn't impressed," I said.

Ida Belle nodded.

"Did she die in the house?" Cassidy asked.

"No one knows," Gertie said. "One morning, the one housemaid who was left came downstairs and couldn't find her.

Nothing was missing from the house and there was even a warm cup of coffee on the sitting table in the parlor. But Celine was nowhere to be found and was never heard from again."

"How old was she when she disappeared?" I asked.

"Oh, that was only a month or so after the charity ball, so young," Gertie said.

"Surely the house hasn't been empty all that time," Harrison said.

"No," Ida Belle said. "Apparently, Lucien hadn't been paying the taxes on the house, so the bill was quite high when he passed. Lovelie's family wouldn't or couldn't pay the back taxes after Celine disappeared, so the taxing authority seized everything and auctioned it off. It's had several owners, but none of them stick around very long. People around here won't buy it, even if they had the money. Some probably fear the rumors, although they wouldn't admit it, but most don't want to deal with the upkeep on a bunch of space they don't need."

"And living remote and without regular services available isn't for everyone," Ronald said. "A lot of city folk think they'll leave the smog and crime and dance in fields of flowers at their country estate, but then reality sets in and they head back to the concrete jungle."

"Not me," I said. "But then, my house isn't haunted, and I've got good internet service and a bakery I can jog to."

"Did you know any of the previous owners?" Cassidy asked.

"Not that I remember personally," Ida Belle said. "I have a vague recollection of people who've stopped in the General Store or the café and said they had bought the place, but they've never been around long enough for me to put the effort into getting to know them."

Ronald laughed. "You're just getting to know me, honey,

and I've been here for decades. You're not exactly a people person."

"True," Ida Belle acknowledged. "But if you're really interested, you could stop by the store and ask Walter. And Francine usually knows everyone who breezes through here."

"You should stop by the Catholic church as well," Gertie said. "You're going to want to get the place blessed."

"I thought you guys were Baptist," Harrison said.

"Baptists don't deal in that sort of thing," Gertie said. "We stick to fishing, casseroles, and lying about drinking."

Ronald nodded. "You have to know your lane."

Cassidy looked up at Harrison. "Maybe we should look at more properties."

Harrison sighed. "Where else are we going to find that much square footage and acreage on the water for that price? Not to mention the stables and training arena already in place. And the place comes furnished. I know a lot of it will go, but there are some really nice pieces that can stay—like in that office you loved so much."

Cassidy looked conflicted.

"Cassidy has in mind that one day she'd like to open a rehab facility for special needs kids," Harrison said. "The kind where they come and stay for months for intensive therapy."

"That would be incredible," Gertie said.

Harrison nodded. "And that house is perfect to house patients and parents, and there are rooms over the stable for live-in staff if we ever had them. All we need to do is put in a pool."

Cassidy sighed. "That's true. It really is perfect in size and space and existing structures."

"We're not going to find anything else even close," Harrison said.

"He's right on that part," Ida Belle said. "There's nothing

remotely comparable in the area. I keep an eye on the local market."

"You and Walter already have one house and one camp each," Gertie said. "How many more places do you need to sleep?"

"Depends on how much he annoys me," Ida Belle said. "But if you must know, I'm looking to diversify my portfolio and have been looking for some good real estate investments."

"I think you should buy an island in the Bahamas," I said. "Just so I can visit."

Ronald held up his drink. "Hot tanned men in barely nothing gets my vote. Come to think of it, hot tanned women in barely nothing get my vote too."

"Anyway," I said, refusing to go down the rabbit hole that was Ronald, "I guess congratulations are in order. And when you close, I want a tour of this place. I've always wanted to see a haunted castle."

CHAPTER TWO

It was early Thursday morning and I'd barely started a cup of coffee when I heard my front door open then someone running down the hallway. A couple seconds later, Gertie burst into my kitchen, guns blazing. I dropped my cup and jumped up from the table, drawing my weapon and scanning the room for the threat. Gertie looked confused and lowered her arm.

"What the heck was that about?" I asked.

"Sorry." She grabbed some paper towels and started cleaning up my coffee mess. "I got woken up by a text from Ida Belle saying to get over here. Said it was an emergency. You weren't on the text, so I thought maybe someone had a gun on you."

"The only person who's had a gun on me this morning is you. And if someone had managed to get the best of *me*, do you think you would have taken them out by coming through the front door and running down the hall? Ronald probably heard your footsteps next door."

She tossed the wet paper towels in the trash and flopped

down in a chair. "You're right. I should have grabbed my AR-15 and sneaked around the back."

"*Or*...you could have called."

"Hmmm. Maybe I need some coffee."

"What you need is to stop watching those forensic shows before you go to bed. And Ida Belle needs to stop sending cryptic texts before you wake up."

"So what's the emergency?"

I shrugged. "No idea. I haven't heard from her, but if she told you to get over here, then I'm assuming she's on her way."

"Do you have any baked goods? All that running lowered my blood sugar."

"You ran all the way over here?" I asked.

"Well, from your front door..."

I shook my head and snagged a plate of cookies from the counter, then poured her coffee and set it all in front of her. In the meantime, Merlin had set up a howl at the back door, then stormed in and apparently decided since Gertie was eating, it was time for his breakfast as well.

"Between you and the cat, I'm never going to get a cup of coffee," I said as I prepared Merlin's morning meal and placed it on the floor.

Finally, I poured another for myself and figured since Ida Belle was on her way, I'd better make another pot because one cup was definitely not going to do it for me. I was just scooping up the grounds when the front door opened again and I heard Ida Belle call out.

"In the kitchen," I yelled back and looked over at Gertie. "You see, that is how you enter a house."

"Sure, when people aren't being held at gunpoint."

I heard scrambling on my hardwood floor that wasn't human and froze. A second later, a bloodhound puppy came bursting into the kitchen, took one look at Merlin at his bowl in the corner, and let out a howl before running that way.

Gertie jumped up from her chair right as Ida Belle ran into the kitchen after the puppy. Merlin took one look at the charging hound and did one of those ejector seat moves that only cats can perform and flew straight up in the air. He clung to the curtains for half a second before doing a spring bounce, flinging himself completely sideways across the kitchen. Ida Belle ducked and he hit Gertie right in the stomach, dug his claws in, and ran straight up her body and perched on top of her head.

Gertie yelled as if she were being tortured. And as someone who'd had those claws across my forehead more than once, I couldn't blame her. She whirled around, arms over her head, trying to pull Merlin off as you would a hat, but he wasn't budging. The puppy was jumping at her legs, making her dance even more.

Ida Belle was scrambling for the puppy, who thought the entire thing was a game. Unable to think of anything else to do, I grabbed a pitcher of water from the refrigerator and threw every drop on them. At the same time, my back door burst open and Carter flew in, pistol drawn.

Merlin, seeing an open door, leaped from Gertie's head to Ida Belle's, then did a rebound off Carter's chest before bouncing out the back door and slamming right into Ronald, who shrieked as though it was end-times and discharged the pistol he was toting into a patio chair, sending stuffing flying everywhere, including back into my house. Merlin disappeared into the bushes, and I figured he was halfway to Mississippi. The puppy decided pursuit was too much effort and started drinking water off the floor.

I took one look at my kitchen, which the housekeeper had

just cleaned the day before, and threw my arms up. "Why is everyone waving guns around here today?"

"She was screaming bloody murder," Carter said. "I could hear her when I pulled up in my boat. I mean, I get it. That cat was attached to her head and I've been there before. But how was I supposed to know that until I got in the room?"

Ronald gave us all an exasperated look and pulled the sash on his shiny silver robe. "What he said. I lost my good slippers and my tiara coming through those bushes. If you're going to make this much racket so early, I'm going to start taking my coffee inside and with the stereo on really loud. This kind of stress is bad for the skin."

Ida Belle scooped up the howling troublemaker and kissed him on top of the head. "You're having an excellent morning, aren't you?" she said as she petted him.

"I'm glad someone is," Carter said.

Gertie shrugged. "Hey, I got breakfast, cardio, and a shower in one location. How often can you say that? So I take it this is the big emergency?" She waved a hand at the wriggling puppy.

Ida Belle beamed. "Yep! I took him off Scooter's hands this morning. Pick of the litter because Scooter was wanting to keep a female. I wanted a prize male."

"*Everyone* wants a prize male, honey," Ronald said.

I had to admit, the puppy was incredibly cute. His ears were as long as his body and he was currently licking Ida Belle's chin and wearing an adoring expression as he gazed up at his new owner.

"I'll help you clean up," Ida Belle said. "But isn't Rambo the cutest thing?"

Carter raised his eyebrows. "Rambo? How appropriate."

"He's definitely cute," I agreed.

"You should get one too," Ida Belle said.

I stared. "I'm pretty sure my cat is off to call social services on me. I couldn't manage a dog."

"Wait until you have kids," Ronald said.

Carter let out a strangled cry and I stared at Ronald. "Yeah, because what this situation is *really* lacking is a baby in the room."

Ronald looked around. "Valid."

"Well, since there's not a crime being committed," Carter said, "I'm going to grab my laptop, which I forgot this morning, and head back to work."

"And since there's nothing for me to shoot, I'm going to go comb the bushes for my lost wares," Ronald said. "Then I need to find a replacement cushion for your chair. At least I didn't accidentally shoot the cat."

I waited until the men left, then stuck out my arms. "Okay, now that the guys are gone, hand me that puppy."

Ida Belle grinned. "Don't want Carter getting any ideas?"

"Not about me getting a puppy," I said. "Merlin barely allows me to live here. I can't handle a dog."

"Well, yeah," Gertie said. "But Merlin's a cat. They're like crackhead toddlers."

I brought the puppy up to my face and inhaled. "Puppy breath."

He licked my face and I smiled.

"He really is adorable," I said. "But I'm not ready for this level of responsibility. What does Walter think?"

"The old softy is thrilled but trying to act manly," Ida Belle said. "It's been a long time since either one of us had a dog. I'm not looking forward to the housebreaking part but I'm excited about the other training. I'm going to test him when he's older and see if he'll make a good cadaver dog."

"We don't need any help finding dead people," Gertie said. "We just leave the house and they appear in our path."

"Yeah, let's not tell Carter that you're planning on deliberately trying to find corpses," I said. "He *just* got some more help. We can't increase his caseload at the same time."

But my mind was already whirling with all the possibilities that a good bloodhound provided. Marge's bloodhound, Bones, had come with my house when I arrived in Sinful, but the aging hound was happier living out his retirement with Marie, who had plenty of time to spoil him.

"So what are you going to teach him first?" I asked. "Besides the basics."

"I think you should teach him to chase Celia," Gertie said.

Ida Belle grinned. "There's an idea."

———

AFTER WE DOCTORED UP GERTIE'S AND IDA BELLE'S foreheads to stop bleeding from the cat tracks, we spent the rest of the day working and playing with Rambo. We'd train for a while, and then Rambo and Gertie needed a nap, then we'd train some more. Finally, we'd called it a day and all headed for our respective showers. Now, Carter and I were on his couch—mostly because we were scared to stay at my house because Merlin had returned—and we were enjoying beer, Molly's crab dip, and a *Terminator* marathon when my phone rang. As it was close to midnight, Carter raised one eyebrow.

"Under normal circumstances, I should be the one getting late-night phone calls," he said. "But with the company you keep..."

"It's Gertie."

"That can't be good."

"Hey, what's up?" I answered.

"Help!" A man's voice sounded over the phone.

I bolted up from the couch. "Who is this?"

"It's Jeb. There's a situation over at Gertie's house and I need help."

"Do you need the paramedics or the fire department?"

"Uh, neither, I don't think. If you could just get over here—"

"On my way."

I shoved my phone in my pocket and motioned to Carter. "Emergency at Gertie's house. We need to get over there."

Carter started pulling on his tennis shoes. "What kind of emergency?"

"The kind that doesn't require paramedics or the fire department—at least, not yet."

"I notice you didn't offer up the police."

"Gertie would never call for the police at her house. The medical examiner and some body bags, maybe."

"If only that statement didn't hold so much truth. So what do you think the problem is?"

"With Gertie? How can you ever know? Jeb didn't say I needed a chain saw or a fire extinguisher, so hopefully it's not bad."

Carter glanced over at me. "Those are the only options—chain saw or fire extinguisher?"

I shrugged. "I'm not exactly the girlfriend you call when you're out of flour or hair spray."

"At least Jeb's there. It can't be too bad, right?"

People in Sinful really had to stop making those sorts of statements.

When we walked out the front door of Carter's house, I could see Gertie's porch lights were on. There were lights on inside as well, but from what I could see through the blinds, it looked like a disco in there.

"Oh no!" I said and ran for the front door, pretty certain I knew what the emergency consisted of.

The music was blaring with some thumping beat that made the front door rattle and I pounded on it, hoping I could be heard inside. If not, I was going to have to shoot my way in. I was just about to reach for my gun when the door swung open and I locked eyes on Jeb.

Good God. The things in this town that you couldn't unsee.

CHAPTER THREE

JEB WAS DRESSED. OF SORTS. BUT THE BATMAN SPEEDO AND
mask he wore were almost as scary as the stack of ones he
clutched in his hand. I heard a strangled yelp behind me and
figured Carter had gotten an eyeful. Without even looking into
the living room, I already knew what had happened.

"Oh good!" Jeb said. "You brought Carter. Not that you're
not strong, but he's taller. This will be easier if someone can
lift while someone else stands on the stool."

Jeb moved over and I stepped inside and got my first official look at the emergency. And it was a doozy.

Gertie had gone for the whole matching costume theme
and had on what I was sure she'd refer to as sexy Catwoman. I
was going with confused streetwalker and unhappily stretched
plastic. The zippers were practically screaming out complaints,
and the entire outfit looked as if it had been walked through a
thresher before she put it on. The out-of-place red scarf tied
around her neck was the biggest solid piece of covering on her
body except for her boots.

And the entire disaster was hanging upside down on a

stripper pole, the safety strap apparently leaving her stuck at the top, as the strapped ankle was up at the ceiling. The other leg had given in to gravity and currently her knee was resting about where her boobs should have been. Unfortunately, the top of the costume wasn't all that tight at the top, and gravity had won the boob battle as well and they were tucked up under her chin.

"Great," Carter said. "More incidences with cats and stripper poles. Just what I was missing in my life this week."

Since Carter had caught the brunt of a cat-stripper-pole situation at Nora's New Year's party, I understood his dismay. But that wasn't going to fix the situation.

I noticed Francis in the corner, swaying dizzily on his perch, and yelled, "Turn off the music and the lights."

"I don't know how to work that stuff," Jeb said.

"Then shoot the stereo," I said.

"Or," Carter said, "unplugging it works."

He pulled a surge protector from the wall and the room went almost to normal—except for the whole Gertie half-dressed on a pole thing.

Francis started rapping about liking big butts and not lying about it and promptly fell off his perch. Fortunately, he landed on an ottoman, then stood up and ruffled his feathers, pretending he'd done it on purpose.

"Can you please get me down before I pass out again," Gertie said. "All the blood is rushing to my head."

"That's not all that's rushing that direction," Carter mumbled.

"I heard that," Gertie said.

"What are you going to do about it?" Carter asked cheerfully.

"Just lift," Gertie said. "I don't need Jeb passing out again, either. This hip won't last forever."

I glanced over at Jeb and could see the blush on the non-masked part of his face as he scrambled onto the stool and shakily rose up. I wasn't about to ask.

"Carter," Jeb said, "if you'll lift her up, I'll undo the strap."

Carter looked at Jeb's Speedo, which was just about face level now, and shook his head. "No way. Let Fortune up there."

"I don't know," I said. "I think I should film it. You know, for a warning and all."

"Sexy seniors on YouTube," Francis said.

I stared at him in dismay, because the bird only repeated what he heard.

"No film," Carter said. "Get off that stool before your spine snaps in two, Jeb."

I gave Jeb a hand and helped him step onto the couch before I hopped up on the stool. "Okay," I said, my hands ready on the strap.

Carter lifted and I released the strap from her ankle.

"Incoming!" I yelled when she dropped.

Carter had a decent grip on her, but dead weight was still a hard thing to balance, especially when you were trying to work around a pole and a stool with me standing on it. As she shot down, her loose knee caught him on the top of the head, causing his grip to shift, and they both pitched forward, then fell onto the couch, right where Jeb was sitting.

Carter sprang up as if he'd fallen into a fire while Gertie and Jeb lay there, giggling as though they were twelve.

"If no one needs the paramedics, we're going to go home," Carter said.

"We might need them later," Gertie said and winked at Jeb.

"The paramedics have oxygen if things get wild," Francis said.

Jeb grabbed some of the bills still clutched in his hand and tried to hand them to Carter, who ran out the front door.

"Do *not* get on that pole again," I said. "And keep that music down. If Carter has to come back, you're both going to be sitting in jail half naked on principle."

"I owe money to half the people I've put in jail tonight," Francis said.

"Sitting in jail half naked sounds like the start of a sexy movie," Gertie said as I hurried out after Carter.

"If Gertie and Jeb try to get arrested," I said as I caught up to him on the sidewalk, "do *not* fall for it."

He gave me a pained look but wasn't about to ask.

"Why have that woman's joints not collapsed?" he said. "I know Special Forces guys who couldn't take the level of abuse she does."

I nodded. "I know. It completely vexes Ida Belle since Gertie rarely works out, eats crap, and refuses to take supplements. Ida Belle says she must be Gumby in disguise."

"Semper Gumby," Carter said.

"What?"

"Nothing. Military stuff."

"Cool. So what do you say we get back to our night? Those movies aren't going to watch themselves."

Carter looked over at me and grinned. "I was thinking maybe you needed to take some clothing tips from Gertie."

"I am not wearing a shredded Catwoman suit."

"I was talking about the red scarf and the combat boots."

"Would you settle for one of your red-and-white plaid dish towels and tennis shoes?"

"I could probably make that work."

———

SINCE THE STRIPPER POLE ADVENTURES HAD THROWN OUT Jeb's back again, Gertie had a full week of hip and leg recovery before Harrison and Cassidy closed on their house and we were up for move-in duty. Investigative work had been light lately, and Rambo could only take so much training at one time, so it had been a really slow week. I was excited to see the new place and still couldn't believe that they'd moved to Louisiana. I really hoped they were happy with the house and their jobs so they'd stick around. It was strange how I used to think I didn't need anyone but myself and my own competence, and now I wanted more of the people I cared about close by. Granted, it was a small number, but they made up for it with quality.

Carter was working, so Ida Belle, Gertie, and I had packed up sandwiches, chips, a pie, Ally's cookies, and a cooler of drinks and headed out that morning after breakfast. I had directions from Harrison and so far, we'd turned off the paved road onto an unpaved road, then onto another unpaved road, and we headed deeper into the swamp. Maybe so deep we had entered an alternate universe.

I wondered if the driver from the moving company would be able to find the house. The directions I'd gotten from Harrison included a lot of statements like 'turn right at the blackberry patch' and 'left at the burned-out barn where Lou used to keep his prize heifers.' But Ida Belle, who hadn't been to the area the house was in for years and had asked Harrison for a refresher, didn't seem remotely worried about it. Since she was driving, I figured the worst thing that could happen was we'd end up lost but with plenty of ammunition to hunt for food once we polished off our lunch. Plus, we could probably survive for a week or better on whatever Gertie was carrying in her purse. I wasn't even going to consider her bra.

I'd expected the house to be big. The place had eleven bedrooms, after all, and Harrison had already told me it clocked in at over 12,000 square feet. That didn't include the stables with additional living quarters, the garage, or the 2,000 square feet of porches. Even the front entry was impressive with massive stone columns on each side and an iron gate that was open. Given the clumps of weeds growing through it, I don't think it had been closed in a long time. I thought I was prepared for what I was going to see, but when Ida Belle rounded a corner and I got my first look at the monstrosity, I actually gasped.

"Good Lord!" I said. "It looks like something out of a Stephen King movie."

The house really did look like a castle. It was made of various shades of gray stone and even had turrets at each end. The house itself stretched out so wide that I was pretty sure we could hold a hundred-yard dash inside. The exterior was surrounded by enormous trees—pine, magnolia, cypress, and some others I didn't recognize—and an assortment of hedges that had gotten so out of control they sort of looked like trees. As we approached, I spotted a huge fountain in the middle of the circular drive, but it didn't look as though it had contained water for some time.

The mass of trees made it hard for sunlight to get through onto the grounds in front of the house, but when I looked up, I saw that dark clouds from an incoming cold front were already arriving. Still, I could see why the rumors of ghosts had persisted. The appearance of the house alone was enough to cause the mind to shift to creative mode. With the Old World architecture, unkempt grounds, and gloomy weather, it was the thing scary stories were made of.

"And we're going to walk around here like it's just another day," Gertie said, obviously still apprehensive about the whole thing. "I should have stayed home and baked something. Baking is far less dangerous."

"You set an entire bag of groceries on fire last week and blew up your microwave," Ida Belle reminded her. "Besides, you already baked something. You're carrying a pie. There's a bigger risk of an asthma attack from the dust in there than seeing a ghost."

"I'm more worried about getting lost going to the bathroom," I said as Ida Belle circled the decommissioned fountain. "Can you use GPS in a house?"

"I'm more worried about using my gun in the house," Gertie said.

"Really?" Ida Belle said. "You're going to shoot a ghost?"

"I brought a crucifix as backup," Gertie said.

"We're Baptist," Ida Belle said. "What the heck are you going to do with a crucifix? Throw it at them?"

"I'm sure no one will have to shoot anything or throw crosses," I said. "But I might leave a trail of bread crumbs when we do the tour—just in case."

Ida Belle pulled through a porte cochere and off to the side so that the moving truck had plenty of room to park close to the massive front entry doors. I stared up as I climbed out of the SUV, shaking my head. It looked twice as big up close as it had from the gate.

"This is just...wow," I said.

I'd seen some palaces during my time in the Middle East, but it was a whole other thing to come across something that looked straight out of King Arthur in the middle of the swamps of Louisiana. It was completely out of place and yet somehow fit in the thick backdrop of trees and darkness. Maybe it would look more pleasant after a good landscape clearing and under sunny skies.

The doors were a mass of wood with a giant metal dragon that spanned both of them, splitting in two when the doors were opened. Ida Belle pressed the doorbell and I wondered if it was even in working condition, but a couple seconds later, extremely loud chimes rang out through the house.

"Good Lord, I could hear that back at *my* house," Ida Belle said.

"At least it's a pleasant tone," Gertie said. "From the look of the house, I was expecting something foreboding—you know, like dark opera music."

"I think the theme to *Jaws* would be amusing," I said. "Harrison should put benches up here. No telling how long it will take them to walk to the front door."

"Are you going to keep calling him Harrison?" Gertie asked.

"Huh?" It took me a second to understand what she was asking, then I shrugged. "He's been Harrison since I knew him. To be honest, I'd feel strange calling him Ben."

The door opened and Harrison grinned out at us. "And I'd feel strange being called Ben. Plus, if you yell Ben at me somewhere, I'm likely to keep walking. Harrison is fine—preferred, even."

"Okay," Gertie said. "But I'm not going to start calling Fortune 'Redding.'"

"You could always call her by her given name," Harrison said, giving me a sly look.

"We've seen her in action," Ida Belle said, "so even if we knew the name her parents gave her, we still wouldn't use it."

"Nice try," I said and looked at Ida Belle and Gertie to explain. "The only person who knows my birth name is Morrow. The file is even sealed in HR. Only Morrow can have it opened. Harrison was just fishing to see if I'd told you."

I turned back to Harrison and smirked. "So, are you going to invite us in or what? We have food, and Gertie's knees might go before she gets to the kitchen. It's probably in the next parish."

"At least we won't starve on the way," Gertie said as we followed Harrison into the house.

We all stopped short in the front entry and gazed around. It was just as overwhelming on the inside as the outside. The floors were white marble and two enormous curving staircases rose up in front of us, scrolled metal railings leading up to a second-floor landing that looked into the entry as well as the back of the house. On each side of the staircases at the bottom stood full coats of armor, taller than me. In the center of the circle that the curved staircases made was a table with a vase as big as a person sitting on it. The whole thing looked like a movie—tapestries, rugs, vases, paintings, furniture. Even if it hadn't been expensive when purchased, one would think they'd be worth something now just due to age.

"Lord have mercy!" Gertie said and even Ida Belle looked impressed. "This place is like a museum. You need to have an appraiser come out here. You could probably sell off the stuff you don't want and cover some of your remodeling."

"I bet Ronald could give you an idea on things," Ida Belle said. "He's a real history and antique connoisseur."

"I'm surprised he isn't with you," Harrison said, still grinning. "He seems to have grown quite attached to Redding."

"I asked him," I said. "He said there wasn't enough Versace in the world to get him in here. However, he also said if Versace was haunting the place to give him a call."

"I have a feeling if Versace was haunting this place, Cassidy would keep him to herself," Harrison said. "She has shoes that cost more than some of my guns."

"You should price out a Birkin bag," Gertie said. "I thought about upping my style game, but my purses blow up too often to spend that much on them. No use spending decent bass boat money on something that will probably go up in an exploding shower of sandwiches and glitter."

Harrison stopped walking and looked at Ida Belle and me. "Do I want to know?"

"Probably not," I said. "And you definitely don't want to search her handbag."

He shook his head and started down the hallway again. "People around here seem to spend a lot of time intentionally not knowing things."

"Self-defense," Ida Belle said.

Gertie, who was half jogging to keep up with our longer strides, huffed out a breath. "Where are we going—Texas?"

Harrison laughed. "Feels like it sometimes, but we're headed to the kitchen, where Cassidy is walking back and forth between rooms, trying to figure out whether she wants to unpack kitchen stuff in the actual kitchen or put it in the dining room so we don't have to move everything again when the kitchen remodel starts."

It felt as if we'd walked a block before we finally went through a huge archway and into the biggest kitchen I'd ever seen. I was pretty sure even hotels weren't working with this kind of space. I looked around and whistled.

"Wow," I said. "What are you going to turn this into—a runway with a kitchen?"

"Movie theater would be cool," Gertie said. "Or bowling alley."

"I think my boat would look good on display in front of those windows," Ida Belle said. "You could easily fit a moat in here, then you could grab your beer, hop in your boat, and motor out for fishing without stepping outside."

"I definitely vote for a moat," I said.

Cassidy came out of a door next to an antiquated stack of ovens and laughed.

"I don't want the mosquitoes," Cassidy said. "They're lethal here. But earlier, I did cartwheels in the master bathroom just because I could."

I had to admit, even outdated, the entire place was sort of spectacular. The kitchen had stone walls that matched the outside of the house and an island in the center that could seat all the Knights of the Round Table plus their dates. And even if all the seats were full, they might still need a conveyor belt to pass the ketchup. The kitchen was open to a living area, the back wall of which was floor-to-vaulted-ceiling windows.

Someone—probably Lucien—had the forethought to clear out the trees, so the view went all the way to the bayou at the rear of the property. On the negative side, the lawn was currently a mess of weeds a good three feet high, and the kitchen appliances looked as if they'd been installed around the last time Elvis released an album. But still, I could see how it would all be magnificent when they were done.

Ida Belle stepped up to one of the windows and looked outside. "Once you get the lawn in shape, it will be a beautiful view."

"I agree," Cassidy said. "And I can't wait to get everything done, meet more people, and have a huge party."

"You might want to just go ahead and have that party before you get to know everyone too well," Gertie said. "Otherwise, the guest list could run pretty short."

We all laughed.

"So are you feeling better about buying the place?" I asked.

"Yes," Cassidy said, somewhat hesitantly.

"But?" Ida Belle asked.

"We slept here last night," she said. "Today is official moving day, but yesterday after closing, we started cleaning the rooms we were going to use and ran way into the night. We'd brought a change of clothes and the water heater is working, so we figured the couch would do for one night and save us the time spent driving back and forth to the motel."

"Well, the house was probably just as clean as the motel," I said. "Even before you started working on it."

"And just as sketchy," Gertie added.

"There were a couple of weird things..." Cassidy said.

Harrison waved a hand in dismissal. "It's just an old house making noise. The wind whistles through the turrets and sometimes sounds like shrieking. Who knows how bad the seal is on all the doors and windows. Old pipes bang and moan. You know these things from those ghost-hunting shows you watch. More of those people end up proving it isn't ghosts rather than deciding it's something they can't explain."

Cassidy frowned. "And the glowing woman I saw walking into the bayou?"

Ida Belle, Gertie, and I stared.

"That one can't be explained away by pipes and the wind," I said.

"But it can be explained by exhaustion, stress, the bottle of celebratory champagne, and an overactive imagination due to the stories about the house," Harrison said.

"You're working just as hard as I am and drank more of that champagne and you didn't see anything strange," Cassidy said, sounding a bit testy. "And I'm an ER doctor not some silly shrinking violet."

"I didn't mean—" he started but she interrupted him.

"I know you and Fortune probably saw more on one mission than most of us see in a lifetime, but my job isn't exactly the pinnacle of sanity and low stress," she said. "I don't break under pressure, and I know when I'm physically challenged and when I'm not. It would be unfortunate if I was uneducated on the subject of my own health, given that I'm telling other people what to do with theirs."

Harrison looked instantly contrite. "I'm sorry. I wasn't trying to be dismissive. I just think it was a trick of the lights or something. Like the moon reflected on fog coming off the bayou... What's that thing you told me about? Pareidolia? Where you think you see something in other objects like clouds?"

"Trust me, I'd love nothing more than a logical explanation." Cassidy looked at Ida Belle. "Is there such a thing as swamp gas or glowing fog?"

"Sure, there's both," Ida Belle said. "But they don't much resemble someone walking. I suppose if there was mist or fog creeping low and a gust of wind got it, it could swirl it around a bit and maybe resemble a ghostly figure. If the moonlight was coming down on it, it could look like it was glowing. Maybe it was a combination of that and being overly tired and perhaps slightly unnerved by this place."

"I'd be more than slightly unnerved if I saw something like that," Gertie said.

"Look," Harrison said. "I talked to the Sinful priest this morning, and he's agreed to come bless the house even though we're not church members—well, I might have bribed him with wine."

Ida Belle, Gertie, and I nodded.

"And we're getting a security system on the entire perimeter installed by Fortune's guy as soon as the equipment is in," Harrison continued.

"Mannie?" Gertie asked.

He nodded. "That guy looks like a combination of the Terminator and a serial killer. If he says he can secure the place, I believe him."

Cassidy finally managed a small smile. "He *was* rather impressive," she said.

"I was impressed," Harrison said. "And man enough to admit it. Where did you find that guy?"

"That falls under more things you don't want to know a lot about," I said. "Mannie is the right-hand man for Big and Little Hebert—father and son bayou Mafia guys who run the local stuff—gambling, loan-sharking, and the like. They're nonviolent, within reason, and have taken a liking to me because I clean up the really bad guys from the area."

Harrison stared. "You have reasonably nonviolent Mafia guys backing you? That's seriously hard-core."

"And rather a sticking point between her and Carter," Gertie said.

"Yeah, I can see how it would be," Harrison said. "Hey, you know me—I'm all about eliminating the dangerous ones from polite society, and if the bayou Mafia wants to help, then I have no problem looking the other way. We were CIA, after all. We're pretty much trained to do that."

Ida Belle snorted. "I can see why you two were partners."

"This house," I said to Cassidy, "is incredible. And we want you and Harrison to be happy here. If Mannie says he can secure the place, then bet your life on it. So what can *we* do to help? I'm horrible at domestics, but even I can dust and mop."

"Says the woman who just won a cleaning lady from us," Gertie said.

"I had to wear an itchy dress and a bra ten sizes too small to get that cleaning lady," I reminded her. "I'm still not convinced it was worth it, so you best start looking for another queen for next year."

Gertie gave Cassidy a critical eye. "You're tiny and gorgeous. And that whole saving-people's-lives thing would work well for you. The Swamp Bar crowd spends a decent amount of time in the ER."

Cassidy, who *did* resemble a reduced-height runway model, stared at Gertie in surprise.

"Oh no," she said. "I couldn't—"

"Sure you could," I said. "I did. And trust me, once you meet Celia—the local villain running the competition—you'll get why. Then you'll be stuffing your boobs up in a bra with more padding than a good recliner and figuring out where to strap your weapon so it doesn't chafe your thighs."

Harrison laughed. "Just like the old days."

"So what can we do to ensure you're here next New Year's?" Ida Belle asked, studying Cassidy as though she was assessing her for an evening gown.

Cassidy looked a little uncomfortable with the scrutiny, then checked her watch. "The moving truck is supposed to be here soon. They've got two guys to unload, but if you could pitch in and help me unpack, then that would be great. We've cleaned all the areas we'll be using and can work on everything else a bit at a time as we figure out what we're doing with all of it."

Gertie patted Cassidy's arm. "You'll feel better once your stuff is in place. Then it will start becoming home. The house needs to get used to you, just like you need to get used to the house."

Ida Belle nodded. "And I'm going to give Walter a call and have him send Scooter over with his tractor to mow the grounds. It will just be shorter weeds, and they'll have to bring a hay baler after, but you'll feel better about the view, and it will cut down on bugs and the snakes that are after them."

"That would be great," Cassidy said, her eyes widening at the word *snakes*.

I heard a horn in the distance and Harrison's phone signaled an incoming text. "The movers are here," he said.

"Then let's get this move started," Gertie said.

They all headed back toward the front of the house, but I lingered for a few seconds, staring out the back windows. It really was going to be pretty when it was fixed up, and the house was beyond impressive, even cluttered with old stuff. But there was something else...something I couldn't quite put my finger on but didn't like.

And I was certain Cassidy felt it too.

CHAPTER FOUR

Since the house had come fully furnished, Harrison and Cassidy had sold most of their furniture except a couple of inherited decorative tables Cassidy wanted to keep. Their washer and dryer, televisions, and mattresses were the largest items, and the movers made quick work of them. The rest of us started hauling the boxes into the rooms designated on the tops and about an hour later, the delivery guys closed up the back of the truck, thanked Harrison and Cassidy for the tip money and our help, and headed off.

"Good thing all the rooms the boxes went to were on the first floor," Gertie said.

Cassidy nodded. "I'm still pretty sure I heard my Fitbit protesting."

"That was probably my thighs," Gertie said.

Cassidy laughed. "Now the real work begins. But before we start unpacking, do you guys want a tour? We didn't have time before the movers showed up."

"Definitely," I said. "The inside of the house, at least. We can see the stables and grounds when there's not boxes to unpack."

The downstairs of the home contained the kitchen, dining room, and three different living areas, including the one open to the kitchen. Ida Belle explained that the different areas were for different stations of people—those who lived in the house versus close relatives and friends and then the callers you had to take but didn't really want to. Based on her explanation, what I got out of it was that the farther past the front door you got, the more important you were to the family. The front parlor was the place Celia and her kind were limited to, assuming they were allowed in the gate.

Those rooms made up most of the north wing of the house, along with two bathrooms and a butler's pantry I could fit my entire kitchen into. The south wing of the downstairs contained the master suite, which consisted of a bedroom, sitting room, dressing room, bathroom, and two enormous walk-in closets. There was a claw-foot tub in the middle of the master bath that Cassidy said would remain, although the rest of the room was slated for an update.

The south wing also contained two more bathrooms, an office, and two other rooms that could be anything they chose to make them. But my favorite room was the library. It was at the end of the hall on the south side of the house and spanned from the front of the home to the back. As the second floor of the home cut off before reaching the library walls, this room had ceilings at least twenty feet high. There was more square footage in this one room than in the entire downstairs of my house, and it was magnificent.

When you walked in, there was a huge sitting area with floor-to-ceiling bookshelves covering the entire south wall of the house, including a curved niche area at the front of the house where the turret was. Ladders on wheels were attached to rail bars that ran the length of the bookcases, making it possible to access the highest shelves, all of which were still

packed with books and other decor. An enormous stone fireplace stood just off to the right of the entry and created a
barrier between the large sitting area and a maze of cubbies
and nooks that ran almost all the way to the back wall of the
house. It reminded me of a university library with all the separate areas for privacy.

Most cubbies held at least one chair for reading, and one
was large enough to hold two. One had a desk and a chair, and
they were all staggered on each side of the walkway, so none of
them faced each other. And every wall was composed of ornate
woodworking with series of moldings that made geometric
shapes on every wall, even in the smallest cubbies. The wall on
the rear of the library, which faced the bayou, was floor-to-
ceiling windows with enormous drapes pulled back on each
side, allowing the natural light to bathe the back side of the
sitting area in warmth—well, when the sun was out. I immediately decided that if I was ever homeless, I was moving into
this room.

The upstairs was a vast stretch of bedrooms and bathrooms that Ida Belle said had probably served as children's
rooms, nursery, guest rooms, and nanny's quarters depending
on the needs of the current owners. One room still had old
wooden school desks and a chalkboard. The furniture was all
old but good quality, and some of the wardrobes in the rooms
had excellent craftsmanship. Ida Belle said they could probably
get a good price for some of them, but all I could wonder was
who the heck would carry them downstairs. They looked like
they weighed as much as a car.

Cassidy said that they would address usage room by room
but probably wouldn't get to the second floor anytime soon
except to give it a good cleaning to improve the overall air
quality in the house. But ultimately, she said, unless they hit
the lottery, adopted ten kids, or had all of us move in with

them, the upstairs probably wouldn't see much usage until she could open her rehab facility. Fortunately, there were thick pocket doors at the north and south entrances of the hallways and each wing was a separate zone for HVAC, so the wings could be closed off with only minimal utility usage until needed.

Tons of decorative items and paintings had been left behind. Most of it was a mishmash that reflected different eras of ownership, where people apparently decided to simply leave behind what they didn't want to bother moving. Styles and periods often differed vastly from room to room and often within the same room. Cassidy said a lot of it didn't fit their vision for the house at all, but I was willing to bet the hodge-podge of items contained some hidden gems and thought it was smart that they'd planned to hire an appraiser to come out and take a look.

"I just love all the built-ins and walk-in closets," Ida Belle said. "Such a surprise given the era of the house and bookcases in every room with all that ornate scrolling. And then those wardrobes on top of that. So nice."

Gertie nodded. "Between the frame, the built-ins, paneling, and molding, there's probably an entire forest in this house."

"I can't even imagine," Cassidy said. "I was a bit surprised by all the storage as well, but a lot of it chops up the rooms. You definitely know it's old-school design compared to today, when you can walk in a room and see all of it."

Ida Belle nodded. "I'd hate to see that wood torn out, but you might want to simplify some of the rooms at some point."

"I think we will," Cassidy said. "And some of them are small, so we might turn them into larger rooms that can hold two beds so parents can bunk with their kids or so older kids staying alone could bunk together. And I'd really like all the rooms adjacent to bathrooms to be connected. Only the two end rooms have a dedicated en suite."

"My guess is those two were constructed to handle babies and a night nanny," Ida Belle said. "And placed on opposite ends of the house so that one crying baby didn't wake another."

"I hadn't thought of that, but you're probably right," Cassidy said.

"It looks like a couple of the other bedrooms were retrofitted to include another access door to the hall baths," Ida Belle said. "You could probably find a way to do some more."

Gertie nodded. "And even if you combine some of the small bedrooms into larger ones, you've still got a ton of room here."

"And there are living quarters above the stables as well," Cassidy said. "They're very basic but still, there's four bedrooms, two bathrooms, and a small kitchen and living area. I wonder how many people Lucien employed."

"Have you found any of the old house records?" Ida Belle asked.

"Not yet," Cassidy said. "But the attic has so much stuff in it we might not live long enough to go through it all. The only thing we've had time for is walking it to check the roof."

"Where do you enter the attic?" I asked. I hadn't seen a pull-down door in any of the rooms or the hallway.

"Oh, it's so clever," she said and pushed a section of the paneled wall in the hallway. It opened to reveal a staircase.

"That is way cool," I said and stepped inside. "Anyone else coming?"

We all tromped upstairs and stared.

"Wow," I said. "You might be able to host the Olympics up here."

The attic appeared to span the entire length and width of

the house. And Cassidy hadn't been exaggerating about the contents. It looked as if a hundred years of Costco inventory had moved in.

Ida Belle looked around and shook her head. "I don't think anyone who's ever lived here got rid of anything."

"I know," Cassidy said. "Like the house and the grounds aren't enough on our plate. I did walk up here with the roof guy, but I haven't been back since. I'm sort of trying to forget about it because it makes my hands sweat."

"But there might be valuable stuff in all of this," Gertie said as she wandered off. "You see those news stories all the time about someone finding a Picasso rolled up in an underwear drawer in some forgotten attic room."

"Well, if there's one up here, it's going to be a while before it's found," Cassidy said. "But if it's been surrounded by old underwear all these years, it's probably safe."

I opened a drawer on an old dresser but it was empty. No Picasso. Still, this place was like an amusement park for someone interested in history and old things in general. I was just starting down the narrow strip between stacks of stuff that Gertie had disappeared into when I heard her yell, and then— God forbid—there was a gunshot.

"It's got me! The ghost got me!" Gertie yelled.

I ran through the piles of stored items, scanning as I went to see where Gertie had disappeared to. I was almost to the end of the house when a stack of boxes hit me and launched me backward into an empty storage bin. The top dropped and I heard the latch fall into place. I pressed on the top, but it didn't budge.

"I'm going to kill you when I get out of here!" I yelled and pounded on the bin.

"Maybe we should leave her a while," I heard Gertie say.

"And you think that will make things better for you?" Ida Belle asked.

I heard the latch release and the top popped open. All three of them were staring down at me. Ida Belle was trying not to smile. Cassidy and Gertie didn't even make an attempt.

"What the heck is wrong with you?' I asked Gertie. "You discharged your weapon."

"I thought the ghost was after me," Gertie said.

"And you thought you could shoot a ghost?" I asked.

"It wasn't a ghost," Cassidy said. "But no one will be using that dress mannequin for a display—not unless it becomes fashionable to have a large bullet hole through the center of the head."

"Nice shot though," Ida Belle said.

I held my hand out toward Gertie. "Give it."

"But I might need protection," she argued.

"The only protection any of us needs is from your purse," Ida Belle said.

She pulled a bag of beef jerky out of the handbag, then handed it to me.

"And whatever you have in your bra," I said.

Cassidy's eyes widened, and Gertie groused but dug around in her bra and pulled out a small-caliber pistol and a baggie of sunflower seeds.

"You can keep the food," I said and shoved the spare gun into her purse.

"How is that remotely comfortable?" Cassidy asked.

Gertie shrugged and popped some sunflower seeds into her mouth. "You get used to it."

Cassidy sneezed and I waved a hand toward the exit.

"Let's get out of here before we all die of collapsed lungs," I said. "This place needs a good airing before anyone even attempts to clean it."

Cassidy nodded. "Or masks. Thank God we moved while it was cool. I've been wearing medical masks to clean."

"Smart," Ida Belle said as we headed downstairs. "Did you get a chance to ask Walter or Francine about the previous owners?"

"Yes," she said. "But neither of them could remember anything of consequence. Just that they'd met people who lived here and neither one could remember seeing the same owners more than twice. I looked at the tax roll and people have owned it for years at a time, but apparently, no one actually lived here long enough for the locals to know them."

Ida Belle nodded. "I figured as much. I can't recall anyone ever showing up at church or local organizations and the like, although the place is closer to Mudbug, so that could be part of it too. That nightmare of an attic might hold more information about the house than the people who lived here do. If you ever decide to tackle it, give me a call. Several of the Sinful Ladies are part of the parish historical society. I've already asked them about the house, but they don't have anything on it. However, they'd probably jump at the chance to dig through any records you might have and see about preservation."

"That's a great idea," Cassidy said. "When we're all settled, I'll definitely give you a call."

We had just walked back into the kitchen and poured some iced tea when Harrison came running into the room from the front of the house. His stiff shoulders and set jaw put me on high alert and I pulled out my nine.

"What's wrong?" I asked.

"I heard the shot and ran upstairs to find you guys. I was in that end bedroom and saw someone standing in the backyard looking inside the house," he said. "Right into this room."

We all whirled around and looked outside, but the only thing I saw was weeds swaying in the breeze. I headed for the back door, Harrison right on my tail. We exited and immediately took up proper formation and started clearing the backyard just as we would a military compound.

"All clear," I said when we reached the dock.

"Yeah," he said. "He must have gone into the woods. Was someone upstairs?"

"No. Gertie thought she saw a ghost."

He stared.

"Don't worry, I took her purse away. I don't hear an engine—so he's not leaving by boat or any land vehicle. At least not one close by. And unless there are good trails in those woods, he's not on horseback."

Harrison shook his head. "There's a new one to consider."

I shrugged. "At least horses are easy to track and not nearly as fast in dense terrain. Quite frankly, I've had more problems with water pursuits than anything else since I've been here. The alligators throw a big curve that asphalt doesn't have."

"Yeah, maybe we don't mention that one to Cassidy just yet. I'm trying to work all the obstacles in a little at a time." He looked around and blew out a breath. "So what do you think—lookie-loo? Poacher?"

"Hard to say. Were there any signs of squatters when you moved in?"

"No. There were footprints in the dust, but then, Realtors, inspectors, and maintenance people have been in and out, and for all we know, others might have looked at the house to buy."

"More likely just out of curiosity, but no food wrappers, signs of building a fire, or the like?"

"Nothing like that. And all the bed mattresses were dusty as heck and had no bedding. I suppose someone could have used them anyway, but you'd think we would have found other signs of life."

"Maybe, but if someone was squatting, they would have

moved on when activity started. And the Realtor would have cleaned up any signs of it. It's not exactly a selling feature."

"You're frowning and I know that look. What are you thinking?"

"That it's really far out for a squatter to live. Unless he's hunting and fishing, acquiring food is a hike, not to mention other living essentials or things like doing cash work or cashing Social Security checks."

"And why come back here when the property's been sold?"

I sighed. "Maybe I'm overthinking it. Maybe someone just took advantage of a huge empty house and set up here for a while. He could get into town by boat and it wouldn't be a huge expense compared to a car."

Harrison nodded. "Then he was 'evicted,' per se, with all the activity and maybe came back to see if the house was available again."

"I think that's plausible."

"You think we have anything to worry about?"

"Well, squatters here aren't any different than in the city— they want to remain out of sight. Even if the guy's on the run, the last place he's going to stick around is the house a cop just moved into. And that information will be easy to get, even for a stranger."

"How is that?"

"All he'd have to do is pop into the Swamp Bar and bring up the house. I'm sure all the regulars already know you bought it. A new cop, much less one that bought the haunted Leroux estate, is big news in a place like Sinful. They'll all be talking about it."

"Okay, then the evicted squatter is the theory I'm going with when we tell Cassidy. I don't want her worrying about this. Unless you think we need to."

If it had been anyone else, I probably would have told

them things would be fine and moved on. But this was Harrison, my former partner. He'd know if I was hedging.

"Based on the evidence, I don't think there's anything to worry about," I said.

"But?"

"But there's something here I don't like. An undercurrent. Doesn't mean you'll have problems. More likely, there was trouble here before and it's moved on now that you've taken up residence. Maybe I'm picking up on lingering bad energy."

He nodded. Harrison knew better than anyone not to dismiss my intuition.

"So don't worry, but be aware," he said. "I'm pretty sure you and I are aware in our sleep.

"Cassidy will be fine, too. She's an ER doctor so very observant, and if she thinks something is off, she'll let you know. And hopefully Mannie will get the equipment in and install it soon. That should give you both some peace of mind. This is a lot of ground to cover with no help from technology."

"True. And just seeing cameras keeps most people away."

We headed back to the house, both of us scanning the woods as we went. It was habit and it was a deeply ingrained one. Likely, we'd both be casing our environment when we were lying on our deathbeds. But that wasn't necessarily a bad thing. Because something was definitely off here.

I just hoped it didn't come back to haunt them. So to speak.

CHAPTER FIVE

IT TOOK US SEVERAL MORE HOURS TO GET THE ESSENTIALS unpacked, but at least by the time we left the house, Harrison and Cassidy had dishes, bathroom supplies, bed linens, and clothes they could access. They'd pared down their belongings before they left DC, which helped with the volume, but even with five of us working, there was still a lot of time involved with unwrapping all the breakables, giving the dishes a hand-wash, and hanging the clothes. We were all happy to be headed home for a shower and our respective recliners.

"I'm glad Cassidy decided to put all her kitchen stuff in the dining room for now," Gertie said. "I know it's kind of inconvenient running back and forth, but she'd have been hating life if she'd put all that in those cabinets then had to pull it all back out to have them painted."

"I'm not sure I've ever seen that much china in my life," Ida Belle said. "And I'm saying that as a Southern woman of a certain age."

Gertie nodded. "Cassidy told me she inherited every set from a different aunt, great-aunt, grandmother, great-grand-mother, and so on."

"And she can't get rid of it, or she'll feel guilty, right?" Ida Belle shook her head. "This is why I'm glad I don't have any china to pass on or kids to burden with it."

"At least she's got plenty of room for it," I said. "Once she decides where all those hutches will go, she can probably put it all on display. I mean, if she wants to."

"That brown and yellow set could scare away intruders," Gertie said. "They could probably just skip Mannie's security system and place them at strategic entry points."

"Speaking of security," Ida Belle said, "it was a real treat to watch you and Harrison work the backyard earlier today. I can see why you made such a good team. You're really in sync."

I nodded. "We had each other's backs a lot of years and in a lot of high-stakes situations."

"So what do you think about our Peeping Tom?" Ida Belle asked. "I know what you told Cassidy, but I got the feeling that wasn't everything."

"It's everything tangible," I said.

"But you have a gut feeling," Ida Belle said.

"Yeah," I admitted. "Something is odd about the place, but I'm sure it doesn't have anything to do with Harrison and Cassidy. And if anything shady was going on before, or if anyone shady was using the place, I think they've checked out. The Sold sign is up and our peeper would have seen all the moving boxes inside, so he knows it's occupied now."

"You think that will be the end of it?" Gertie asked.

"I think so," I said.

But I wasn't certain.

———

CARTER WAS ON DUTY THE NEXT COUPLE DAYS AND I PICKED up a couple insurance cases that Gertie, Ida Belle, and I made quick work of. According to updates from Harrison, all was quiet on the Leroux estate front, which pleased me to no end. The puppy training was also going well. Rambo was housebroken and picking up something new every day. I was really enjoying learning how to train a dog from Ida Belle, especially since it was occupying a lot of our downtime. Today, Ida Belle, Gertie, and I had spent the entire afternoon stomping around the woods, teaching Rambo to track. Because we were both tired, Carter picked up dinner at the café and the two of us took up residence in my living room, planning on spending a relaxing evening on the couch.

And it had started out that way.

Now I stood in my living room, arms crossed, eyes closed, shaking my head. Ronald was in front of me holding up his laptop, which was the reason for the stance, the shaking head, and the closed eyes. It was close to 10:00 p.m. and he'd been at it for two painful hours already. I'd thought by standing and refusing to look at the screen anymore, he would get the hint and give up. But so far, it wasn't working.

"I'm not paying a lot of money for some scraps of lace," I said. "I'm not Celia—fanning my underwear around town. They don't need to be fancy and definitely don't need some designer logo on them."

"This designer is the pinnacle of high-end women's lingerie," Ronald said. "Their quality and craftsmanship are superb."

I opened my eyes a tiny bit, and they almost popped out when I saw the price. "A hundred bucks for a pair of underwear? And I might add, I have more fabric in the headbands I wear when I run."

Ronald turned the laptop toward Carter, who was sitting in my recliner and enjoying my exchange with my nosy neighbor way too much.

"Surely a man of your taste and discretion can see the value here," Ronald said.

Carter grinned. "I'm far more concerned with what she's *not* wearing than what she is."

Ronald collapsed onto the couch, a crestfallen look on his face. "The two of you are hopeless."

"Or," I said, "we're perfect for each other."

"I bet Harrison's lady has elegant undergarments," Ronald said, trying another avenue.

"She's a doctor and can afford them," I said. "Plus, she's removing bullets, not running from them, so that lace string up her butt wouldn't come into play."

Carter perked up. "Let me see those again."

I picked up a sofa pillow and whacked him so hard the recliner flipped over and he rolled out into the hallway, laughing.

Even Ronald had to smile. "I have to admit, the two of you are really cute together. Almost as cute as Ally and that massive hottie she's dating. They edge you out on the cuteness with the whole size disparity. Well, and you have that fear factor as well, given that both of you can easily kill people. Although I'm pretty sure Ally's man can as well. However, I'm equally as sure Ally has never killed anyone."

"Some people might die of diabetes now that she's opened her bakery," Carter said as he stood up and righted the recliner.

"Anyway," Ronald said. "I'm officially giving up on trying to convert you to finer things."

"It's not that I don't appreciate the effort," I said. "But it's just not me. I only wear finer things to win bets against people like Celia. Except for my weapons of course. They're always the good stuff."

Ronald gave me a look of dismay so intense I had to smile.

"You'll have to find someone else to do a makeover on," I said. "Ida Belle and I would love it if you could get Gertie into things more age-appropriate. Or even legal to wear outside her house would be a step up lots of times."

Ronald waved a hand in dismissal. "Gertie is the only one of you three with any creativity. I wouldn't personally go for her selections, but I can't fault her for being bold and adventurous, can I?"

Given some of the choices Ronald made with his own wardrobe, I could see why he'd defend her. My cell phone rang and I glanced at the display and frowned. Why would Harrison be calling me this late?

"What's up?" I answered.

"I'm taking Cassidy to the hospital," he said, his voice elevated and strained.

I immediately understood that he wasn't giving her a ride to work.

"What happened?" I asked.

"I don't know. I was working a late shift in Mudbug, and when I came home, I found her unconscious at the bottom of the stairs. Her vitals are strong but there's a lump on her head and I can't get her to wake up."

"We'll meet you there."

I shoved my cell phone in my pocket and saw that Carter, ever observant and who knew my tone, had already grabbed his truck keys and our jackets and was ready to go.

"Cassidy took a fall," I explained to Ronald as we all hurried out. "Harrison's on his way to the ER with her."

"Oh no!" Ronald said. "Keep me updated."

We jumped in Carter's truck and as he drove, I filled him in on what Harrison had told me.

"That blows," he said. "I hope it doesn't make her regret moving here and buying the house."

"Me too. I think they'll really be happy here if they can get settled, and that house is enormous but perfect for her long-term plans of having the live-in therapy practice. And you should have seen the place. It's incredible, and you know I'm not usually impressed by that kind of thing."

Carter nodded. "I was in it once years ago."

"Really? You never told me that."

He shrugged. "Didn't see much. It was late at night, and some guys hunting snakes reported seeing lights moving around in the house. As the electricity was off at the time, I figured it was vandals, so I rode out to take a look."

"Did you find anyone?"

"No. They probably took off before I got there. But the weird thing was all the doors and windows that I checked were fine. Nothing was tampered with and there were no footprints in the dust around the entries."

"Maybe the snake hunters were drinking more than they were hunting."

He nodded. "Always the likely answer around here."

"And you never had another call to the house?"

"Not a single one. But then, I doubt anyone but old locals and people who fish this bayou even know it's out here."

I sighed. "I hate that they're dealing with something like this. I know Harrison probably wouldn't like the invasion of privacy, but maybe they should have Mannie set up some interior cameras in some of the main areas so that he can check on her when he's working night shifts."

Carter laughed. "You want a former CIA operative to agree to putting security cameras—tied to the internet, no less —*inside* his house?"

"Yeah, I wasn't thinking."

I wasn't sure what it would take for me to put cameras inside my own house, but I was pretty sure it would be something extraordinary. I'd be more likely to move if something was wrong with my house than live under the potential of constant scrutiny. We were silent the rest of the drive and at the hospital, the nurse sent us straight back to the ICU. One of the advantages to having Carter with me.

Harrison was sitting next to the bed in Cassidy's room, and I was relieved to see her awake and talking. She was definitely pale, and the dark circles under her eyes indicated a good level of exhaustion and lack of sleep. But I didn't see any body parts bandaged, so that was a plus.

"She woke up on the way to the hospital," Harrison said, and I could tell he was relieved as well but still seriously stressed.

"Are you all right?" I asked Cassidy as we stepped up to the bed.

"I have a pounding headache," she said. "They're going to get me back for some tests to make sure it's not serious, but I think I'm okay."

"What happened?"

She glanced over at Harrison, and I could tell she was hesitant to say. Finally, she sighed and said, "I saw something upstairs on the landing that startled me. I whirled around to run downstairs but tripped on the runner. It must have come loose."

"And you fell down the stairs," I finished.

She nodded.

"What did you see upstairs that startled you?" I asked.

She bit her lower lip and looked down at her hands, which were currently rolling the edge of the blanket over and over.

"A ghost," she said softly.

I could tell Harrison was worried about the situation but wasn't about to buy into a ghost story. I couldn't really blame him. People were bad enough with the trouble they caused.

We didn't need to add the undead to the list of things we had to worry about.

"What did the ghost look like?" I asked.

I didn't believe Cassidy had seen a ghost, but I absolutely believed she'd seen something that scared her enough to cause her fall. And since Cassidy wasn't the type to jump at the slightest little thing, I figured it had to be something substantial.

"It was a woman," Cassidy said. "She had long red hair and was wearing a white nightgown—the old-fashioned kind that came to the floor."

"Did you see her face?"

"No. When I stepped onto the landing, I saw her walk into the bedroom at the end of the north hall." Cassidy frowned at Harrison before turning back to me. "I'm not crazy. I went upstairs because I heard a bang, like something big dropped or metal clanged. And since I'm not stupid, I took my gun. After I saw the woman, I went to that room and looked everywhere, but there was no one there."

"And you're sure that was the right room?" I asked.

She nodded. "The doors to the other rooms were closed. That one should have been as well, but it was open. When I was about to head downstairs, I thought I heard something from the south side. I took a couple steps closer then decided I should probably get out of the house and call Harrison, when the door to the bedroom at the end of the hall flew open and I saw red eyes staring out at me from the dark."

"That would have been enough to make me retreat," I assured her.

"You would have opened fire," Harrison said.

Since I'd shot holes in my roof when I'd first moved there —all because of a raccoon who'd moved into my attic—I couldn't really argue. But then, Harrison didn't know about the raccoon, so...

"I prefer to identify my target before I shoot," I said.

"That's not what happened with the raccoon in your attic," Carter said.

I shot him a dirty look. "Since nothing was supposed to be in my attic, I felt justified in firing. But I don't advise it. The repair wasn't cheap, and I could have accidentally shot Marie."

"Why was the mayor in your attic?" Harrison asked.

"It's a long story," I said. "Anyway, my point is, it sounds like someone is accessing your house, which obviously isn't cool, but that doesn't mean you want to deal with the fallout of shooting them."

"That's why I decided to leave and call Harrison," Cassidy said. "Until I saw those red eyes. Then all I could think about was running. They were down too low to the ground to be a person, unless they were on all fours. But anything brave enough to enter a house with people is brave enough to attack, right?"

I looked over at Harrison, who put his hands up.

"I don't know what to think," he said. "Obviously, she saw something, but I just scooped her up off the floor and hauled butt here. I didn't take the time to check anything out, but then, I didn't know I needed to until she regained consciousness and told me what happened."

"Do you want us to take a look?" Carter asked. "An intruder is police business."

"Oh man, I don't know that I want our names to jump right into a case log," Harrison said. "But if you want to check it out, I would appreciate it. If you feel we need to file a report, then we will. Otherwise, I'd rather keep it on the down-low."

I nodded. "It's better if it doesn't get out. You know how

things get overblown in Sinful. If people heard you had a ghost, you'd have everyone from the ghost hunter nuts to the religious crazies camped out in your front yard. I caught hell when I first arrived, and all I did was move into a house where a dog dug up a guy who'd been dead since long before I got here."

"There was a dead guy in your lawn?" Cassidy asked.

"Another long story," I said.

Carter sighed. "Unfortunately, what Fortune said about the locals is accurate. Let us check out the house—see if we can find any sign of entry, footprints, something—and I'll keep it quiet unless we find enough to start an investigation and you okay it."

Cassidy looked relieved as Harrison passed his keys to Carter. I gave her shoulder what I hoped was a reassuring squeeze before we exited the room.

"I don't know Cassidy well," Carter said as we left the hospital, "but she doesn't seem like the type who frightens easily."

"I don't think so either. And I have no doubt that whatever frightened her was very real."

Carter nodded, looking worried. "I'd almost prefer a ghost."

CHAPTER SIX

THE LIGHTS WERE ON ALL OVER THE DOWNSTAIRS OF THE house when we pulled up, and I wondered if Cassidy had been rearranging things and unpacking more boxes or if she'd been uneasy being there alone at night and had left the lights on. Carter frowned as he parked and I figured he was thinking the same thing I was, but he didn't say anything.

He handed me a flashlight and grabbed another for himself, and we checked the ground surrounding the front door. But the weeds were too thick to allow footprints, which was the same problem Harrison and I had with the Peeping Tom. The front door was still locked and showed no signs of tampering, but if someone was going to break in, there were many other easier options than the giant doors of heavy wood and metal. And a lot less obvious ones than strolling in the front entry.

Carter unlocked the door and we stepped inside. There didn't seem to be anything amiss in the entry or the parlor, so we headed upstairs. There was a spot of dried blood at the bottom of the stairs, and I assumed that was where Cassidy had ultimately landed. It was a long way to fall.

"Good thing the stairs are carpeted," Carter said. "She could have been a lot worse off."

I nodded and stopped at the top of the stairs and checked the carpet on the landing. It was easy enough to see where Cassidy had tripped. A piece of the runner was bunched up right where the landing met the stairs.

"Old carpet," I said. "I don't remember it being torn when Ida Belle, Gertie, and I were here before, but it might have easily been pulled up if they were rearranging things."

Carter squatted down and pulled up the edge of the runner. "Except it looks like this has been cut, not torn."

I looked down at the clean slice and frowned. "Why would someone cut the carpet that way? It wasn't Harrison or Cassidy. They wouldn't have been foolish enough to create a tripping hazard right by the stairs."

Carter frowned and rose up. "Let's take a look at those bedrooms."

We headed to the room where the 'ghost' had been seen but didn't find anything out of order. All the windows were securely latched and there were no doors connecting that room with any others, so the only way out was the way we'd come in. We checked the other rooms as we worked our way back down the hall to ensure the windows were all secure but found nothing amiss, so we headed to the other side of the landing.

"Anything look off to you?" he asked.

I shook my head. "As far as I can tell, the rooms look the same as they did when we did our tour, except they've been cleaned."

Carter nodded and we began our check of all the bedrooms on this wing, but the result was the same. Nothing was out of place. No windows were unlocked. We headed back downstairs and went through the entire house, checking every door and lock before finally heading back to the kitchen and sitting at the counter.

"I don't get it," I said. "Someone had to be in here, but every window was latched, and all the doors were dead-bolted. Even if someone had left through a window and come back after Harrison left with Cassidy to lock it from the inside, they couldn't have drawn the dead bolts from outside."

"I know," Carter said.

I could tell he was unhappy with the lack of explanation, and that made two of us.

Scooter had been by the day before to mow the grounds surrounding the estate, so visibility from the house was definitely improved. But he hadn't baled the weeds yet, so a thick layer of them sat on top of the turf. It would be impossible to determine whether someone had passed across the lawn.

"I want to walk the outside before we leave," he said. "I know we won't be able to see footprints, but I wouldn't feel right not doing it."

"I agree."

We headed out, locking the front door behind us, and started around the house, each of us scanning to our sides as we went. But the only thing we found were some thorny bushes, several snakes, and far too many spiderwebs.

"Where did Harrison see the Peeping Tom?" Carter asked.

I pointed to the windows off the living room. "He was looking into the living room-kitchen area."

"And Harrison was upstairs when he saw him?"

I nodded. "He went up looking for us when he heard the gunshot, but we must have gone down while he was in the other wing."

"Gunshot?"

I waved a hand in dismissal. "Gertie."

"I don't want to know."

I frowned.

"What's wrong?"

"I was thinking in the hospital that Cassidy said she heard a bang upstairs but not footsteps. And when Harrison came down from upstairs that day, he ran down, but I never heard footsteps either."

"Then the place is built solid, and with that runner on the upstairs hallway and stairs, and all the runners and rugs downstairs, it would mask a lot of sound."

"Sure, which makes it easier for someone to roam around undetected. But then the intruder must have dropped something heavy for Cassidy to hear it. We didn't find anything on the floor that shouldn't be there, so they must have put it back afterward."

"Or took off with it after she fell."

"But we still don't know how they managed to get out and lock up behind themselves," I said. "Do you want to check the stables?"

"No. It's too dark to see much of anything and I doubt the lighting in there is great. I'll come back tomorrow and go over everything with Harrison and Cassidy, if they release her. I didn't see any obvious gaps where something was missing, but we don't know what all was in there."

"I don't think anything upstairs belonged to them originally, so they probably don't either."

He nodded. "Let's head back to the hospital and give Harrison the keys and tell him what we found."

"You mean *didn't* find?"

As I climbed in Carter's truck, I looked into the woods at my right and saw a light moving. I bolted out of the vehicle and dashed off into the woods. I heard Carter yell, but I knew he'd follow, and I didn't have time to explain. Not if I wanted to catch whoever was out there with that light.

When I got to the spot where I thought I'd seen the light, I stopped and looked around. I couldn't see the light anymore, but I heard the sounds of something moving through the brush away from me and toward the bayou. Carter burst into the small clearing, and I pointed.

"Someone's moving that way," I said.

We set off through the woods, scanning as we went to find the markers of passage—broken branches, stamped-down marsh grass—and eventually, we came out of the woods near the bayou. The moon was completely hidden by clouds, so there was no light other than our flashlights. I could hear water lapping against the bank, but no boat engine. We shone our lights up and down the bayou, but it bent not far from the house in both directions, so we had a limited view.

"If he came by boat, he rowed out," Carter said.

"But he could have just as easily taken a right and gone deeper into the forest. He had a good jump on me. You want to walk the bank?"

"We won't catch them on foot. The forest is too dense and we don't even have moonlight to help. Besides, he's got a getaway vehicle stashed somewhere and is probably halfway to it by now."

"I don't like it."

"Neither do I, but there's no way to know if that was the person who scared Cassidy."

"Maybe not, but just how many people do you think are roaming around out here? This can't be a coincidence. But what really makes no sense is that this house has sat empty for years, and, according to Harrison, the Realtors have never reported issues with squatters or burglars. So why break into the place now when it's occupied?"

Carter shook his head. He didn't know any more than I did. And he didn't like it any more than I did either.

———

IT WAS ALMOST 2:00 A.M. BEFORE CARTER AND I GOT BACK to Sinful, and we were both exhausted. Cassidy had finished up her tests by the time we returned to the hospital, and everything looked good. They were going to keep her until morning just to make sure the swelling was going down, and then she'd be released with instructions to take it easy for a couple days.

They were disappointed that we were unable to come up with a good theory about what had happened and were clearly worried about the carpet runner, which they both swore had been in good condition before Cassidy's fall. Harrison promised to call Carter when they were back home, and Carter and I would make another trip out and walk the entire property with them in the daylight.

We'd done everything we could for the time being, but still, it felt as if we'd accomplished nothing.

Trying to sleep yielded no great level of success either.

I must have sighed when I slumped into a seat at my kitchen table early the next morning, because Carter put a cup of coffee in front of me and sat with his own.

"Frustrated?" he asked.

"How did you know?"

"That sigh is familiar. And I've issued it myself a couple hundred thousand times."

"Something is going on at that house, and we have to figure out what it is. Cassidy could have been seriously injured or even died from that fall."

"I know. But even if Harrison wants me to launch an investigation, I have next to nothing to go on. I can get a forensics team out there, but I doubt they'll come up with anything. Something like that doesn't just happen. It has to be planned and planned well. The noise that prompted Cassidy to go upstairs, the disappearing ghost, the red eyes, the cut carpet... none of that was spur-of-the-moment."

I took a big sip of coffee and narrowed my eyes at him.

"Are you going to tell me to stay out of this if it becomes police business?" I asked.

"No. There's no point anyway as you never listen, but just to cover all of our butts, I'd recommend you have Harrison sign a client agreement and pay you a dollar. At least then, the sheriff's department can't come down on either of us when things happen."

"What do you mean 'when things happen'?"

"Mostly Gertie things."

Given that we'd rescued her from a stripper pole the week before and she'd shot a mannequin just the other day, I saw his point. And it wasn't as though Ida Belle and I failed to pull our weight in creating a scene. I'd already shot more people in Sinful in the time I'd been there than the sheriff had during his entire career—a fact that the ADA had made a point to fill me in on. Given that he only knew about the ones that had become part of an official record, I didn't bother to get in a discussion on the matter. And since I'd only shot bad guys, I was still okay with the ADA, but I had no doubt he was keeping an eye on me.

It wouldn't hurt to attempt a lower profile. I'd been within my rights to take the shots I had, and some of the time, I'd been within my PI jurisdiction to be in the position to need to take those shots. But other times, the stories explaining my involvement were elaborate and better fiction than I read in books. The last thing I wanted was for my actions to create fallout for Carter—and now Harrison—and I'd already pushed that envelope more than once.

"Do you have a plan for the search today?" I asked.

"Not really. I just figured we'd walk the entire property

with Harrison. And Cassidy if she feels up to it. Then we can get feedback as we go as to what they've changed, moved, and so on and if they notice anything missing. When I finish this coffee, I'm going to head up to the sheriff's department and pick up an evidence collection kit, then I'm going to go home and grab some old clothes that I don't mind tromping through the brush and grime with. Did you have anything on your schedule today?"

"Breakfast with Ida Belle and Gertie. Believe it or not, Gertie's thinking about buying a new car. We were going to decide about going car shopping, but obviously Harrison's situation takes precedence."

"Gertie's going to buy a new car? Is she going to get new glasses?"

"Not that I know of, but it's her insurance, right?"

"Yeah, but it's everyone else on the road with her. Make sure Ida Belle doesn't pick out a car more suitable for Ida Belle."

"If Ida Belle were picking, Gertie would keep driving that beat-up Cadillac and we'd bury her in it. Ida Belle sees a door ding in a new automobile as a personal affront. I'm not even going to discuss the fact that the last wax Gertie's car has seen was when Gertie set a box of candles on fire in the back seat."

Carter smiled. "I know there's no point in asking you not to fill them in on Harrison's situation, but I'd prefer that only you and I go back out there today for the assessment. Any evidence that might be there is already at risk of being compromised with just the four of us. Additional people walking through there just muddies the waters even more."

"Gertie doesn't like the place anyway. When we helped unpack, Ida Belle took full advantage of Gertie's unease and jumped out of a doorway at her whenever the opportunity arose."

"I'm surprised you didn't have a heart attack or a shooting on your hands."

"Given the things she's walked away from, Gertie's heart is obviously stellar. And I took her purse and made her empty her bra after she shot the mannequin, so she didn't have anything to shoot Ida Belle with."

"I'm not even going to ask."

"Smart."

He rose and rinsed out his cup and put it in the dishwasher, then he leaned over to give me a kiss. "Let me know as soon as you hear from Harrison. I'll be ready to roll whenever."

I nodded and he headed out. As soon as he left, I polished off my own cup and sent a text to Ida Belle and Gertie that I was on my way to the bakery and I had news. Ida Belle got up before the chickens and was ready to tackle the day as soon as her feet hit the floor, but Gertie liked to sleep late and drag around a bit in the morning. The added part about having news would get her perked up quickly.

I hurried off to the bakery as soon as I sent the text, hoping to get a couple minutes of conversation with Ally before Gertie got in the mix. Specifically, I wanted to ask her about how dating Mannie was going. I knew they saw each other a couple times a week—at least that's what the local gossip train said. I hadn't wanted to get into her business before she'd had some time to feel things out, but it had been over a month now, and that was long enough to determine whether she wanted to continue seeing him at least.

I lucked out and the last patron was leaving the bakery as I pulled up. Ally's new assistant, Lillie Mae, greeted me as I walked in and called out to Ally, who was back in the kitchen.

"Fortune's here," Lillie Mae said and nodded in my direction. "I can finish icing those cupcakes. You take a break. You haven't so much as paused since we got here this morning."

Ally gave her a grateful look and grabbed a bottle of water.

"You want anything?" she asked.

"Not yet," I said. "I'm meeting Ida Belle and Gertie. Just figured we could get a chat in before they arrived."

"Oh?" she said as she sat across from me. "Is anything wrong?"

"Not at all. I wanted to see how things are going with you and Mannie."

Her blush and shy smile said everything. She glanced back to make sure we were alone, then said, "It's going great. He's such a gentleman, which I wasn't expecting given his, uh, employment. But then I guess a lot of that goes back to how he was raised."

I nodded. "Parents and the military both provide the skills needed to navigate well among society, and to be honest, the Heberts are very classy guys. For criminals, they have a strong sense of propriety. I think that's one of the reasons they like Mannie so much."

Ally twisted the hem of her shirt, her expression pensive. "I'm glad you came by and brought up the subject because I've been wanting to ask you something. I know the Heberts do illegal stuff, but just how illegal? I mean, I like Mannie a lot and Lord knows he's hot, but I can't let things go any further if he does horrible things for his job. I'm not capable of being one of those silly mob wives who pretend to not know anything, and this town wouldn't let me anyway."

I'd been expecting the question eventually but was a little surprised that it was coming up this soon. That must mean Ally really liked Mannie and she didn't want to get too attached if there was no chance of a future.

"Obviously, I don't know all the specifics of Mannie's job or everything the Heberts are involved in," I said, "but according to Carter, they're not in the business of violence. That's not to say that they don't solve problems with violence sometimes, but then so do I."

"But what you're doing isn't illegal. I mean, mostly it's not illegal."

Since I had probably broken the law a thousand times since stepping foot in Sinful, and Ally was completely unaware of most of it, I didn't address her statements. She was far better off not knowing, but then we were friends, not dating. A romantic relationship was a whole other kettle of fish.

"If you're asking if I think Mannie is breaking kneecaps when people owe the Heberts money, then my answer is no," I said. "*If* they had him collecting—which I also doubt because it's way beneath his pay grade—my guess is all he'd have to do is show up and people would find the money."

Ally blew out a breath. "I know people are starting to talk. Sometimes I approach a table to refill coffee and they go silent, and I feel like people are assessing me, you know?"

"I definitely know what it feels like to be under the Sinful microscope. Listen, I can't assure you that everything Mannie does is on the up-and-up, but I also have some suspicions about the Heberts and Mannie that I've never shared with anyone, not even Carter. I'm going to tell you because you're dating Mannie, but you have to promise me to never repeat this and definitely don't discuss it with Mannie. If I'm right, it could cause a lot of problems for him and the Heberts."

Ally frowned. "I would never repeat something you asked me not to."

"I know. I just need to impress on you how serious this could be if my suspicions got around. I'm talking potentially life-threatening."

"Now you've got me worried."

"It's not bad. It's actually good. For you anyway." I looked around to make sure Lillie Mae hadn't come back out of the kitchen. The room was empty, but I still leaned forward and lowered my voice. "I think the Heberts are federal CIs—confidential informants."

Ally's eyes widened. "Seriously? Oh my God. But then, that makes total sense, right? I mean, how they never seem to have problems with law enforcement."

I nodded. "My guess is the Heberts have been feeding the Feds information on the hard-core criminals for years. So along that line of thinking, I think Mannie is their handler."

"So he doesn't work for the Heberts?"

"Honestly, I'm not sure how it would work in regard to regular stuff like payroll and benefits. But my guess is Mannie works for the Heberts, but also makes sure they're staying in the lane the Feds want them in."

"Do you think they know what he's doing?"

"Absolutely."

"And Carter doesn't know?"

"Carter's no fool, so my guess is he's formed the same opinion I have, which is why he tends to look the other way when the Heberts' names crop up. But we've never discussed it and we never will. We both know the risks of exposure."

Ally sat back in her chair and shook her head. "I'm having a hard time wrapping my mind around it all. But it's such a perfect fit for things. How did you figure it out?"

"Well, I don't know for certain, but I've just noticed some things and I know how the Feds work. Anyway, if this got out —even as a rumor—it would be as good as drawing a target on their backs for every criminal in south Louisiana to see."

"No one will hear a word of it from me, but thank you for telling me."

"Does it change things?"

"I think it might."

"You know the person you really need to have this conversation with is Mannie. Ultimately, if he really wants a future with you, he'll be willing to change some things to make sure you don't take the heat. It's one thing to date casually, but if people are already gossiping behind your back, then they already think it's more than a fling."

Ally sighed. "I know you're right. I keep thinking 'tonight is the night I'm going to broach that conversation' and then I chicken out. But now that you've given me a different perspective, when the time is right, I think I'll start asking some questions."

"Don't expect the same answers I gave you. If I'm right, you'll never get that information out of him. He'd never expose you that way."

She jumped up and ran over to hug me. "Thank you so much! You coming to Sinful is one of the best things that's ever happened to me."

"Me too."

CHAPTER SEVEN

THE BELL ON THE BAKERY DOOR RANG, AND WE LOOKED over to see Ida Belle and Gertie walking in. Well, Ida Belle was walking. Gertie was limping.

"Don't tell me you've been on that pole again," I said as they sat down. "I would have thought you'd learned your lesson last time."

"I'm still waiting on a part for the winch," Gertie said. "I don't understand why such important items aren't kept in stock, but that's just the state of our society."

Ida Belle stared. "Because parts for stripper pole winches should be on aisle nine of the grocery store next to toilet paper and water?"

"Anyway," Gertie said, looking a little too excited for my taste. "There was this accident with the handcuffs Jeb bought."

"Nope!" Ida Belle said. "Unless Jeb was arresting you, this sounds like sexy-time talk and you know the rules."

Gertie grinned. "Well, he *was* taking me into custody..."

Ally laughed. "Before this discussion becomes more suited for the Swamp Bar than my bakery, let me get your order."

We requested pastries and coffee, and Ally hurried off, still smiling.

"She's in a good mood," Gertie said. "Must be that hunk of a man she's dating."

Ida Belle shook her head. "Why does a woman always have to be thinking about a man if she's smiling? Maybe she's thinking about how well her bakery is doing, or buying a new bass boat, or how ammunition is going to be on sale next Tuesday."

Gertie rolled her eyes. "Anyway, Fortune said she had news. Is Ally getting married?"

"Probably someday," I said. "But my news doesn't have to do with Ally. Cassidy took a fall last night down the stairs and ended up in the hospital. She's going to be okay, but there's a bigger problem."

I filled them in on what Cassidy had told us in the hospital and what Carter and I had discovered in the house. When I finished, they glanced at each other, clearly worried.

"I know Cassidy had her reservations about the house," Ida Belle said. "I don't know her well, and I know she buys into the spooky stuff on some level, but I don't think she's imagining what she saw. And she certainly didn't cut her own carpet."

"I know," I agreed. "So we're left with two alternatives—either ghosts are real and they want to live alone in the house or someone is entering the property for whatever reason and doesn't like owners being in the way. I don't suppose I have to tell you which theory I'm going with."

"But why would someone want in there?" Gertie asked. "The place was full of stuff for years. Surely if someone was going to steal things, it would have happened before now."

Ida Belle nodded. "And one would think Carter would have been aware if the burglary was obvious. Likely, there's been random theft throughout the years, but Realtors would have noticed an entire shelf of stuff disappearing and reported it."

"Exactly," I said. "Which is why I'm at somewhat of a loss. Carter and I are going back over there today when Harrison and Cassidy get home from the hospital. Carter wants to walk the property with them—or Harrison, at least—and see if he notices anything off. Carter doesn't want you guys there for this search."

"Of course he doesn't," Gertie groused.

"This first one might end up being official," I said. "He's bringing an evidence kit and if Harrison wants him to start an investigation, it has to go on record."

Ida Belle nodded. "And more people just contaminate any evidence he might find."

"Yes," I agreed. "But he knows I'm filling you guys in and there's no way I'm staying away from this. He suggested I draw up a contract for Harrison and collect an advance—just so everyone is covered and there can't be any issues with anyone's employment if things go sideways during the investigation."

"I'd be more surprised if something *didn't* go sideways," Gertie said.

"That's because you *are* the sideways," Ida Belle said.

"I get things done," Gertie argued.

"That's one way of putting it," Ida Belle said. "So what can we do?"

"I want to know more about the house," I said. "Obviously, there's something in there attracting an intruder, and unless we catch the intruder or figure out what it is that they want, we're not getting rid of them."

"Which means Cassidy won't feel safe," Gertie said. "I really want her to be happy here. She's such a nice young lady and if she isn't happy, then Harrison will leave for her sake. And I really want Harrison to stay. Carter has needed qualified help for a long time, and Harrison is perfect for the job."

"That's a lot of 'reallys' and 'wants,'" Ida Belle said. "But I agree with Gertie. The house has a not-so-pleasant history, but after helping over there the other day and talking to Cassidy about her long-term goals for the rehab facility, I can't think of any other place in the area that would work. And the house has good bones."

"Probably not the best description in this case," Gertie said.

"As long as it doesn't have any human bones, we're fine," Ida Belle said. "Gertie and I told you everything we knew about the house, but there's a woman who's an amateur historian of sorts who lives in Mudbug."

Gertie shook her head. "I know you're not suggesting we talk to Scary Mary."

"Who's Mary?" I asked. "And why is she scary?"

"Mary is a bit of a hermit," Ida Belle said. "So the gossip train has run wild with stories about her."

Gertie raised her eyebrows at Ida Belle. "Selling it a little short, aren't you? Mary makes Nora seem lucid and Celia seem nice. She hasn't been seen outside of her property for decades now, and I heard that one time when the postman started to deliver a package to her house, she shot at him."

"Lucky for the postman—and for us—she's a bad shot," Ida Belle said. "She's also the only one who might know details about the house when Lucien and Lovelie lived there."

"That's because she was alive then," Gertie grumbled. "Hence the 'amateur historian of sorts' comment."

"How old *is* this woman?" I asked.

"Four thousand eighty-two," Gertie said. "Or let me put it this way—she looked old when I was a kid."

"I'd put her at a hundred or close," Ida Belle said. "But she would have heard the gossip firsthand, versus second, third, fifth, or tenth, which is what you'll get from everyone else around here. And there's a possibility she personally crossed paths with Lucien or Lovelie at some point."

"Well, I guess this is why I bought bulletproof vests on the company credit card," I said. "Find out if Mary is still alive and still has an itchy trigger finger."

"I'll pull out a casserole," Gertie said. "You can't call on women in Mary's generation without an invitation and not bring an offering."

I nodded. "And I'd like to know her last name. Given her age and the whole Southern rules thing, I can't call her by her first name, and Ms. Scary doesn't bode well either. Is there anyone else you can dig up from around that time?"

"Anyone else from around that time would literally *have* to be dug up," Ida Belle said.

"Then it looks like Mary's our girl," I said. "Sorry, Gertie, but I can't swing car shopping today. I want to be able to jet as soon as Harrison calls."

"No big deal," Gertie said. "We can go another time. It's not like I have to replace my car today or even this year."

Ida Belle looked up and mouthed 'thank you' and I smiled. You had to love a woman who preferred accosting someone with a penchant for firing at strangers to car shopping with her best friend of a million decades.

Ally arrived with our pastries and coffee and placed them on the table.

"Sorry this took so long," she said. "I was making a fresh pot of coffee but also wanted to bring you guys my new raspberry-cream cheese croissants right out of the oven, and they needed a few more minutes."

"Raspberry cream cheese?" Gertie repeated. "That sounds delicious. It's official. I'm going to have to buy a treadmill."

Given Gertie's ability to run into problems with even the most basic of mechanical items, I wasn't sure a treadmill was the best option, especially after she'd managed to set fire to one at a doctor's office during a previous investigation.

"How about you just splurge on a good pair of tennis shoes and walk outside?" Ida Belle suggested, obviously on the same page as me.

"That's a good idea," Gertie said. "I can go running with Fortune."

Ida Belle snorted. "Sure. You can half jog to the end of your driveway. By that time, she'll be rounding the corner at the end of the block, and that's the last you'll see of her."

Ally laughed. "I've seen Fortune 'jogging' and it looked like someone was chasing her. I'm going to stick to yoga and only hang out with Fortune when she's doing leisurely activities, like pretending to fish."

Gertie stared at Ally in dismay. "How in the world do you stay so thin doing only yoga and owning a bakery?"

"Her metabolism is about a hundred years newer than yours for starters," Ida Belle said.

"I'm sure that's the biggest part," Ally said. "But the truth is, I only eat my own stuff to get the recipes down, and then, it's only a taste."

"You're surrounded by all this goodness 24-7 and don't eat it?" Gertie asked, sounding so upset I wasn't sure if she was going to try to talk some common sense into Ally or just start praying for her right there at the table.

Ally laughed. "I don't have a choice. If I eat everything, then I won't be able to stand all day baking and selling it. Then I'd be a sad, out-of-shape woman with no bakery."

Gertie looked slightly mollified. "Well, I appreciate that you're making all those sacrifices so that I can enjoy this croissant that is so excellent you could serve it to Jesus."

Ally beamed. "I'm glad you like it. I'm going to test it today."

I took another bite and shook my head. "I don't think you need to test it. Just put it on the menu and let it rip."

"Agreed," Ida Belle said. "No freebies. Start charging for it now."

Ally bounced off to adjust her menu and Ida Belle sighed.

"That girl has a gift," she said. "Which my taste buds highly appreciate and my thighs do not. But I'm glad to see her doing so well. She deserves a break after giving up school to come home and care for her mother."

"Someone else who needs a break is Cassidy and Harrison," Gertie said. "So besides lining up to be shot by a crazy woman, what else can we do to get this situation fixed?"

"Nothing else that I can think of until we know more," I said. "I want to talk to the Realtor, so I'll get that info from Harrison. If the Realtor wasn't overseeing the property while it was empty, then he should know who was. I know there wasn't much of anything being done, but someone had to be checking on it periodically to keep squatters, vandals, and our unknown someone away."

Gertie gave me a pointed look. "Or some*thing*."

———

HARRISON CALLED ME WHILE CASSIDY WAS SIGNING HER discharge paperwork and Carter and I headed out. We arrived right after they did. Cassidy sounded fine when she opened the door but she was a little pale. The worried look was still firmly in place. Harrison, on the other hand, was doing what I would have done—strapping on another weapon and mumbling choice words. He upped the ante on cussing from mumbling to an outright yell when we showed him the sliced carpet runner.

"Obviously, we didn't do that," Cassidy said. "Not intentionally or accidentally. All we've done up here so far is clean. The only thing I've carried up here is cleaning supplies and the vacuum, and I am certain I didn't snag anything on the runner."

"Something snagged on it would have made a jagged tear anyway," Carter said. "This didn't separate at a seam. It's been deliberately cut."

Cassidy blew out a breath. "But why?"

"So you or Harrison would trip on it and fall down the stairs is my guess," I said. "What else could it be? It's not like there could be some treasure hiding under the runner. It's not thick enough, and the floor beneath is marble and we're on a balcony landing with a pass-through beneath."

Carter nodded. "Someone wants you out of the house."

"I don't get it," Harrison said. "All this stuff has been here for years. Why does someone care about it now?"

"I don't know," Carter said. "But I want to find out. I'd like to go through every inch of the estate and see if anything stands out."

"Like what?" Cassidy asked.

"Missing objects," Carter said. "I don't expect you guys to have memorized the contents, but sometimes a blank spot indicates something used to be there if that makes sense. How many of the rooms have you cleaned already?"

"Everything but the attic and the stables," Cassidy said.

"When you cleaned, did you notice any obvious gaps on shelves or wall hooks with no paintings? Anything that would indicate something used to exist there but was now gone?"

"Not that I recall," Cassidy said. "But I can't say for certain that I would have noticed. Some shelves had things clustered in bunches and others had them evenly spaced. I swept the walls, but it's possible I missed a nail, and I definitely could have missed a nail hole. There's so much hardwood on the walls and the lighting isn't the best in a lot of rooms, so they won't show easily."

"Okay," Carter said. "Then let's just start upstairs where you saw the woman and work our way across the entire second floor. If anyone sees anything they think is off, then say so. And Cassidy, if you just have a feeling that something isn't right, I want to know. Fortune, Harrison, and I are used to trusting our instincts on this sort of thing. I know you have great instincts as well or you wouldn't be a good fit for the ER, so don't be afraid to speak up if something strikes you wrong. It doesn't matter why or if you can even explain it."

Cassidy nodded and I could see some of the tension leaving her body. Disbelief was the worst thing that could be thrust at victims or witnesses. And even though it was true that lots of times their feelings were misdirected or quite simply inaccurate, it was still better to work with all information, even if some of it wasn't correct. I'd rather sort through ten things looking for the one that mattered than have nothing to work with.

"Are you going to make this official?" Harrison asked.

"I would like for you to, so we have full access to investigative tools, but for now, I'm going to let you make that call," Carter said. "I understand if it makes you uncomfortable to have something like this with your name on it right after starting your deputy job here."

Harrison nodded. "At the hospital, I was thinking I'd just wait and see what happened, but the carpet runner and you guys chasing someone through the woods last night changed my mind. I want it on record so that you have everything we can use at our disposal. I know I can't be on the case officially, but—"

Carter held up a hand. "I know there's no way you're going

to stay out of it. I wouldn't either. And I'm going to make another suggestion that you never heard from me—you should hire Fortune. She has methods of accessing information that you and I don't."

"You mean can't," Harrison said.

Carter nodded. "But she's also got two old ladies working with her who remember who broke wind in church back in 1943 and if they don't know something, they can find someone who does. Those people often have a problem talking to cops, but not to two unassuming seniors."

"Ha!" Harrison let out a strangled cry. "Those two are not remotely unassuming. But I guess appearances are everything."

"And long ties to the community," Carter said. "People trust them, and they trust Fortune because she's their friend."

"I guess if people won't talk, she can always get her Mafia friends to make them," Harrison said.

Carter gave him a pained look.

"Oh, sorry," Harrison said when he noticed Carter's expression. "Touchy subject, I guess."

"More importantly," Carter said, "one I need to remain ignorant on. Are you guys ready to get started?"

We all nodded. Showtime.

CHAPTER EIGHT

It took all afternoon and into the evening to cover the house, the stables, and the surrounding grounds that weren't wooded. We shifted to outside after covering the upstairs before we lost daylight, then moved back inside once we were half frozen and ready for something to drink. Cassidy, who'd headed back inside to rest after the stable search, had tea waiting for us along with a tray of sandwiches. We recharged, then searched the downstairs.

I took at least a million pictures with my phone, since I never knew what might turn out to be important. But ultimately, the entire thing was a bust. The sliced carpet was the only thing indicating a human being had been in the house, but we still had zero idea why.

The one thing we all figured, though, was that he'd be back.

I got the Realtor information from Harrison, but it was too late to contact him that day, and besides, I wanted Ida Belle and Gertie along for that ride. Since he was from the area, chances were they knew him or his mother or aunt or someone else they could throw into the introductions that made him feel more comfortable or as though he had to tell the truth.

I could tell Cassidy was anxious about night approaching, as she kept looking outside every couple minutes as the sun started going down. I offered to stay but she and Harrison declined, just as I figured they would. With nothing left to contribute, Carter and I called it a night and headed out, making them promise to call if anything happened.

We were both silent for several minutes of the drive, then he looked over at me.

"You're worried about them," he said.

I nodded.

"So am I," he said.

"Someone's going in that house, and we don't know how or why. Those are two critical unknowns. I could even wait a little on the why if we could figure out the how and block them."

"Yeah. But the place is solid. All four of us looked at every window and door. Heck, a lot of those windows wouldn't even raise because they've been painted over so many times. Harrison changed all the locks the day they closed on the house, and he did the work himself, so no one is running around with a key."

"Do you think someone is crazy enough to come down a chimney?"

He blew out a breath. "It's been done, but all the doors and windows were locked from the inside. If he's coming in that way, he's going out that way as well. And carrying whatever he's stealing—assuming that's what is going on here."

"That would mean at least two people. One to collect and another to hoist things up."

He nodded. "But it doesn't feel right. And even if someone were doing that, where did that woman Cassidy saw appear from and where did she go? There's no chimney in that room."

"Don't forget the red glowing eyes. I know things can be done with cameras and mirrors and the like, but we saw no signs of that. And I know we just walked down the center of the attic, but there were no track marks on the stairs or around the entry to it."

"Or any smell that indicated an animal was occupying it."

"Someone could have collected their goodies and vacated after Cassidy fell, but that still doesn't explain *how* they got out and locked everything behind them."

"The only thing I can figure is someone has a key."

"But how?"

"They were already in the house, lifted one while Cassidy and Harrison were sleeping, and generated a copy with a 3D printer."

I frowned. "You know, technology has made our jobs both easier and more difficult."

"Yeah. Mannie's got the cameras coming, right?"

"Yeah, but that's only outside, remember. Harrison told me he did ask Mannie to order a couple interior cameras that he could move around, but Mannie said his supplier can't get them here for probably another week. I thought about picking up something cheaper in New Orleans."

"The quality has gotten a lot better on the off-the-shelf stuff, although the bigger problem is the satellite internet out there. It's not a bad idea though...at least until Mannie can get them the military grade hardwired."

I slumped in my seat, feeling defeated. "The whole point of them moving here was not needing military-grade cameras in their home."

"You have them in yours. I think the unfortunate thing about your and Harrison's past is that you're probably never going to feel safe without a certain level of protection around you. You've been here over a year and a half, and you still shower with the door locked and your gun within reach."

"Well, that's just good domestic habits."

He laughed. "You know what—for Sinful, you might not be wrong."

I smiled. "But I see your point. And yeah, I suppose neither of us will ever completely relax, but then you're not completely relaxed either. As long as we're all involved in chasing criminals, there's always going to be a higher level of care that needs to be taken with regard to safety. But wanting that level of security just in case is completely different from needing it because stuff is happening before you've finished unpacking."

Carter reached over and squeezed my hand. "I know. We're going to make sure they're okay. Cassidy's fall was bad but it also put Harrison on high alert. I don't know who's entering their home or why, but they should have gotten their business done before he moved in. He's not your basic homeowner. If he gets the intruder in his sights, there won't be any hesitation."

"I know. And Cassidy has excellent firearm skills. Harrison trained her himself. But you and I know better than anyone that being a crack shot at the range doesn't always translate to the real thing."

"We'll figure it out. Worst case, they can move out until we get a handle on it. Both of us have spare rooms or you and I can bunk up for a while and give them one of our houses and then we all have our privacy. Hell, Ida Belle and Walter have two houses as well. They're not trapped there unless they want to be."

"I offered to let them stay with me when they were looking for a house but they refused," I reminded him.

"This is different. The safety of the person trumps the perceived inconvenience of the host."

I nodded. He had a point. The options were there. I also knew for certain that all the dynamite in Gertie's purse wouldn't blast Harrison out of that house, but at least he had choices if things got worse, and Cassidy could leave if they thought it made sense for her to do so.

I stared out the window and watched the trees go by, praying that things didn't get worse.

Unfortunately, this was Sinful.

———

THE NEXT MORNING, I TRUDGED INTO MY KITCHEN AND poured a cup of coffee. Carter had made a pot before he left for work, and I said a prayer of thanks that he was both an early riser and a considerate partner as I took my first sip. My sleep had been restless all night. Dreams of floating ladies in white and glowing red eyes had persisted no matter how many times I'd awakened and tried to think about other things to redirect my busy mind.

I'd sent Ida Belle and Gertie a text the night before, letting them know that we hadn't found anything of merit, but I'd fill them in this morning. I figured by the time I'd finished this cup of coffee, they'd appear. Sure enough, when I got up to refill my cup, I heard my front door open. I pulled more cups out of the cabinet and was filling them up when Ida Belle and Gertie came in and took seats.

"You look remarkably alert for this early," I said to Gertie. "And remarkably dressed and groomed. What gives?"

"We have a case!" Gertie said, her eyes shining with excitement. "There's only two things I'll get up early for these days. One is a case and the other is that thing I can't talk about."

Ida Belle sighed. "So fill us in on everything."

"Unfortunately, my text covered everything relevant. Lots of questions. No answers."

I gave them the details of our search and the lack of evidence along with an update on the security system situation and our official standing to investigate.

Gertie shook her head when I'd finished. "We've started with little to go on before, but this one feels skinny, even for the stuff we take on."

"I know," I said. "I'm hoping we'll at least be able to form some theories if we learn more about the house and the previous owners. I don't believe this has anything to do with Harrison or Cassidy. I think they're just in the way."

"Did you get the Realtor information?" Ida Belle asked.

I nodded. "A guy named Travis Toups. Sounds like either a stripper or a stand-up comedian."

"That's Mavis Toups's grandson," Gertie said. "And I'm pretty sure he's tried his hand at both. Without success, I might add. The boy has the personality of a rock and the belly of a fifty-year-old fisherman. I don't know what he was thinking."

"I'm pretty sure he's splitting that one brain the family had left with his sister," Ida Belle said. "But it answers my question about what Realtor would take on that house."

I felt a twinge of disappointment. "Crap. If this guy is useless then we're not likely to get anything out of him."

"He's no genius, that's for sure," Gertie said. "But on the plus side, that also means he has no filter."

Ida Belle nodded. "If he knows something or has heard something, it's coming out of his mouth without a thought."

"Well, I guess there's something to be said for fools," I said, then frowned. "But if he's a blabbermouth, we can't approach him the direct route or he'll be telling everyone we're investigating."

"You're right," Ida Belle said. "It's better to pretend we're interested in buying something. It will be easy enough to get him talking about the Leroux estate that way."

"Who's buying?" Gertie asked.

Ida Belle shrugged. "Could be any of us. Walter and I might be looking to combine households. Fortune and Carter might be looking to get married and do the same. You and Jeb might be looking to open a chain of hip replacement businesses."

"Let's go with you and Walter," I said. "The last thing I need is this idiot blasting around town that Carter and I are buying a house together. Emmaline is pretty contemporary in her thinking, but I'm pretty sure she'd like to be the first to know if her son and I decide to make that kind of move."

"Good thinking," Gertie said.

"It's still too early to call," I said, "but I'm going to go ahead and send him an email. Did you guys figure out anything on Scary Mary?"

"She's still in Mudbug," Ida Belle said.

"And still shooting at people," Gertie said. "She's conveniently leaving that part out. Apparently, she took a shot at the meter reader a couple weeks ago. Said he was there to steal her family fortune. Mind you, she has no family and no fortune, so there's no telling what we're walking into on that one."

"We're definitely wearing the vests," I said. "Does she know you two at all?"

Ida Belle shrugged. "She'd probably know our names—assuming she knows people at all anymore. There were some rumblings about dementia years ago, so it's hard to say. But it doesn't hurt that we're in her age group and local to the area."

"The Old Testament is in her age group," Gertie said. "Not me."

"Well, as long as she doesn't go Old Testament on us, we're good," I said. "Did you get a last name?"

"Joseph," Ida Belle said.

"Her name is Mary Joseph?" I asked. "I know religion is big here but isn't that taking things to a whole other level?"

"Well, to be fair, she married a Joseph, so that wasn't her given name," Ida Belle said. "But the universal 'they' say that Mary was big on church before she locked herself in her house and started shooting at people."

I nodded. "So I figure we head to the café for some breakfast, because I need some protein if I'm going to have to run from bullets, and we see if this stripping-comic-Realtor gets in touch. If so, we'll see if we can meet up with him this morning. After that, we'll don our vests and head to Mudbug."

"Is your will up to date?" Gertie asked Ida Belle.

"I got married. I don't need one anymore."

———

TRAVIS GAVE ME A CALL IN THE MIDDLE OF OUR BREAKFAST, and after Ida Belle gave him her song and dance about considering a new house, he offered to meet us at a new listing. He said we could combine getting a feel for what Ida Belle was looking for while also showing us something that was new on the market and, according to him, was going to fly off the shelf. The analogy didn't work at all, but I just told him that sounded great, and we'd meet him there in an hour.

Gertie was already laughing when we pulled up to the house. For starters, it was falling apart—I mean, so dilapidated that it needed a bulldozer, not a new owner. Even worse, someone had decided that rather than replace the rotten siding, painting it all fluorescent pink was a better plan. I was almost blinded when we rounded a corner on the dirt road and came face-to-face with that monstrosity.

"He cannot be serious," Ida Belle said.

"I'm pretty sure he's not capable of being our level of serious," Gertie said. "Not even when he needs to be. Trust me, I had that boy in my classroom when I filled in for a teacher on maternity leave, and he gives a whole new meaning to the words *class clown*. But if he had us drive out here, I guarantee you, it's because he thinks you might buy this mess."

A fluorescent-lime-green pickup truck with huge tires and super high suspension pulled up behind us and I laughed.

"He's serious," I said.

Ida Belle took a look in her rearview mirror and groaned.

"The sooner we get what we need out of him, the sooner we can rinse our eyeballs," Gertie said

We climbed out of the SUV and I watched as Travis stepped out of his truck. Or maybe *jumped* was a more appropriate word. I lost sight of him until he walked around the front of the vehicle and then got my first look at the guy responsible for selling Harrison and Cassidy a haunted house.

Six feet tall even with the cowboy hat. Five foot six without it. Stocky build with decent muscle tone but the gut Gertie had mentioned was firmly in place. Most of his lifting was restricted to a beer bottle. Slightly bowlegged and the buckle he wore was almost as big as his hat. Zero threat unless he managed to clock me with the buckle and smother me with the hat.

"You didn't tell me he was a cowboy," I said.

"Because that would have been lying," Ida Belle said.

"He just likes the look—probably because he thinks he looks taller," Gertie said. "He's actually allergic to horses."

I sighed. There was absolutely no one normal in this town.

"Ladies," he said as he approached, tipping his hat. "You must be Fortune."

"That's me," I said, and shook his extended hand.

"I voted for you for New Year's queen. You looked hot, and not just when you put out that fire. I was thinking when you rode by that if Carter hadn't gotten to you first, I'd have totally made a move."

I felt my trigger finger twitch and Ida Belle leaned over and whispered, "No filter."

"Thanks," I said to him. "I think."

"Hey, just telling it like it is," he said. "So you and Walter are looking for a new house, Ms. Ida Belle?"

"We're thinking about it," Ida Belle said. "I wanted to get an idea about what's available. I have to say, though, that this doesn't do it for me."

"No, ma'am," he said. "Except for that spiffy paint job, this place is awful. It's the land I wanted you to take a look at. I was figuring that given how old you are, you guys should build a house. I mean, you don't have much more time to get exactly what you want and you could do a one-story. I know your joints start to go after thirty, so I figure you don't have any left by this point."

I leaned toward Ida Belle and whispered, "No filter."

Ida Belle unclenched her hands and scanned the land. I had to admit, he had a point about the property. The pink nightmare sat in a nice flat clearing about two acres in size, and huge old oak trees lined both sides, creating a nice border for the property. It backed up to a good-sized bayou with plenty of room to put a pier.

"This *is* a nice lot," Ida Belle acknowledged. "I don't know that I want the hassle of building, but it's definitely something to think about. Fortunately, we don't have to be in a hurry."

"If you say so," he said, looking at Ida Belle as if he was

afraid she was going to keel over right there in the driveway. "But building would probably take six months or better. Don't wait too long."

Gertie started coughing, clearly to cover her laugh, and I was struggling myself to hold one in. I didn't dare look at Ida Belle, because I was certain the expression she must be wearing would send me right over the edge. How on earth had this guy convinced Harrison and Cassidy to buy that house? I would have thought he'd 'tell it like it is' until they were no longer interested.

Or wanted to shoot him, which seemed equally viable.

"I think you were the Realtor who helped my friends out," I said, turning the conversation to the real point of this somewhat amusing exchange. "Ben and Cassidy?"

"Oh yeah!" Travis gave me an energetic nod. "Nice couple. Bought that huge haunted house. I never thought I'd sell the thing."

"Haunted?" I asked.

"Oh yeah!" he said again. "That place is practically crawling with ghosts. I don't know why anyone would want to live in it, but I guess if you only look at the cost per square foot, it was a great deal."

"Not if you're sharing it with people who aren't paying rent," Gertie said.

He laughed. "You always were funny, Ms. Gertie."

"How long did you have it listed?" I asked.

"Not long at all," he said. "Maybe a month or so. No one else in our area would take the listing of course. We all know the stories. Some outfit in New Orleans had it before me. They didn't even bother to put it online, but the agent with the listing got testy with me when I told them the estate had signed me on to take over."

"She's probably even madder now that you got the commission on the sale," Ida Belle said. "What agency was that? I'll make sure I avoid them."

He nodded. "Good idea. It was Duval Real Estate—they're a pretty big outfit—the agent's name was Karmin Blay. I got the impression she was kinda new. Probably got in trouble over not putting up the listing and losing it. She sounded hot, though. Shame she had that attitude. We could have had some beers."

"Ben said it had been sitting empty for some time," I said, turning the conversation back to the house. "Did you have problems with vandals or squatters? I noticed it didn't have a security system."

"None of those kind of problems that I ever saw," he said. "But then, unless you're local, you wouldn't even know the place was out there, so it's not like it's going to get random passersby. And if you know it exists, then you know it's haunted. People don't want that stuff following them home— ghosts or squatters, really."

"You've really thought this out," I said. "But you had no problem being in the house."

He shrugged. "I think it might be kinda neat to have a ghost. Especially if you could teach them things. I mean, think about all the time you could spend fishing or drinking if you had a ghost doing your laundry."

I glanced over at Ida Belle, who was staring at Travis as if sizing up a target. I couldn't really blame her. I could feel my IQ dropping with every minute of our exchange.

"So did you ever see a ghost?" I asked.

"Oh yeah!" he said. Apparently, it was his favorite phrase. "I saw this woman wearing a white dress several times. But I never could catch up to her."

Gertie stared. "You chased the ghost?"

"Well, sure," he said. "How else was I going to swing that

laundry thing? Anyway, the first time I saw her was when I was pulling up to the house, and she was looking out at me from one of the bedrooms upstairs."

"Which one?" I asked.

"The one at the end of the hall on the north side. But when I got up there, she was gone. Then I saw her walking into a room on the opposite side of the second floor one day when I was taking measurements, but she disappeared again before I could catch her."

"Did you hear her?" I asked.

He wrinkled his brow. "You can't hear ghosts. I mean, unless they're playing a piano or something—hey, I have an old guitar—"

"So you only saw her," I interrupted. "You never heard any noise like footsteps or a door opening?"

"She wouldn't need to open doors," he said, looking confused. "She'd walk through them."

"Right," I said. "Did you see her any other times?"

"Oh yeah! I saw her outside the house walking in the woods one night when I went to put my listing sign in the yard."

"And did you follow her then?"

"Nah, I was late for a poker game, and I was the one bringing the beer."

Of course he was. "Did you ever notice things moved around in the house?"

He shook his head. "Don't see why a ghost would move things around."

"Well, it might be that she can't," I said. "Which means she couldn't do laundry either."

He frowned, giving that thought far too much consideration.

"I guess you're right," he said finally. "I suppose it's just as well I sold the place. I can use the commission to have my clothes laundered."

"Did you take a lot of pictures for the listing?" I asked. "I noticed there were only five online when I checked after Harrison told me he was considering it."

"Oh yeah! I took a bunch, but my broker told me to only put up a couple and maybe that would get people curious. I think it was really because he just didn't like all the clutter in the place. He's one of those guys who prefers his house to look like no one lives there except for the furniture. I suppose it's easier to clean, though." He brightened. "*Or*, I could clean off those family pictures on my living room shelves and use them to store chips and ammo."

Since it was the first thing he'd said that made sense, I nodded.

"Would you mind sending me those extra photos?" I asked. "I have someone who might be interested in cataloging the antiques for Ben and Cassidy, and that way I could give him an idea without having to spend half a day taking my own pictures."

"Oh yeah! I can do that. No problem."

I handed him my business card and pointed out my email.

"Despite the ghost thing, I'm surprised no one else was interested in the house," I said. "I mean, it is rather impressive in a Stephen King sort of way."

"Oh yeah! There was this one dude who looked at it before your friends, but I don't think he had the money for it. We get that sometimes—people just wanting to see the inside of something. He asked a lot of questions too about the previous owners and the guy who built it. Not sure why he thought I'd know anything about all that. Dude built that house like a thousand years ago."

"I don't suppose you remember that guy's name? Maybe you have it on your calendar?"

"Matthew? Mark? Mac? Something like that. I dropped my phone in a beer stein last week and lost everything on it. Did you know you could do this thing called 'backup' and then if your phone dies, those smart guys can just put it all back on a new phone?"

I held in a sigh. "You don't say. Can you describe him?"

He shrugged. "Tall."

Given Travis's height, 'tall' might be anywhere from five foot eight to seven foot even.

"Age?" I asked.

"Heck, I don't know. I mean, I don't spend time scoping out dudes, you know? Older than me, maybe? Why do you want to know so much about him?"

"Just wondered if anyone might have been disappointed that my friends bought the house first. It's a lot of house, so if they ever wanted to sell, then he might be a good place to start since he's already shown interest."

"Oh, I get it. But they could just list it with me again. I mean, I sold it to them. I can sell it to someone else. Sure would be nice to make a big commission on the same place twice. I'd get my truck repainted."

"Something less apparent—maybe a nice navy blue?" I asked.

"Heck no! That green's awesome but it's starting to fade. It used to really pop."

"Well, Travis," Ida Belle said, "you've given me something to think about with this lot. I'm going to talk to Walter about building versus buying an existing structure. That might be a better direction for us."

He nodded. "You let me know. I have a couple other lots, but this is the best one. Honestly, I don't have any houses nicer than what you guys already have, so there's not much point in showing you any."

"I appreciate your time," Ida Belle said. "Say hello to your grandmother when you see her."

"I will." He headed off to his truck, and we climbed in Ida Belle's SUV and all sat silently for a couple seconds.

"Someone pull up a Stephen Hawking workshop on their phone," Gertie said. "We need a palate cleanse."

"I know you warned me," I said, "but can I just say, 'wow.'"

"Oh yeah!" Gertie said and Ida Belle and I groaned.

"Well, the one interesting thing is that Travis saw the same ghost that Cassidy did," I said. "So we have some corroboration. And he saw her more than once and one of those times was in the same room Cassidy saw her in."

Ida Belle nodded. "It is rather interesting. I mean, I certainly didn't think Cassidy was seeing things or being overly dramatic, but when someone with no filter and a lack of creative thought says the same thing, it adds another layer of credibility."

"I don't know...that whole ghost-doing-the-laundry thing was fairly creative," I said.

Ida Belle waved a hand in dismissal. "That was just extreme laziness pushing through."

"What about the agency who had the listing before Travis?" I asked. "You ever heard of them?"

"I've seen the name online when I'm looking at listings in New Orleans," Ida Belle said. "But I've never talked to anyone there."

"I wonder how willing this Karmin would be to talk to us," I said.

"If she's mad, that could go either way," Gertie said.

"True," I agreed. "So what do you think about this guy who asked to tour the property? Lookie-loo?"

"Quite possible," Gertie said. "But I wish Travis could have remembered the name."

"Yeah," Ida Belle agreed. "Unfortunately, I think the Travis avenue of inquiry is tapped out."

"Maybe the additional pictures will tell us something," I said. "I want to compare them to the items in the house, and maybe we can pinpoint if anything is missing."

"That would be a big break," Ida Belle said. "All it takes is finding one stolen item that's been hocked and we might be able to track it back to the thief."

I nodded. "Well, now that our patience has been tried and our trigger fingers are itchy, let's go see Scary Mary."

CHAPTER NINE

MARY LIVED IN ONE OF THE ORIGINAL NEIGHBORHOODS close to downtown Mudbug. It looked a lot like our neighborhood except the houses were older. It had large lots with huge oak trees that were probably a hundred years old. The houses were set farther back on the lots than mine was, and giant azalea bushes created borders on the sides of most properties. The bushes were beautiful when blooming, and they provided some privacy, although anyone could just step right through them. Until Godzilla had chased him up a tree, Ronald had made a habit of doing it. Now he made a habit of using the front door.

Mary's house had the old white clapboard siding and could have used a good power wash. The front porch was sagging a bit but overall, the place looked structurally safe, which surprised me a bit. Usually, contractors weren't all that happy to work places where they might get shot, and I couldn't imagine someone Mary's assumed age climbing onto her roof to make repairs. But then a flash of Gertie and the stripper pole went through my mind, and I switched my thought process to 'anything's possible.'

Ida Belle backed into the driveway so that we were getaway ready and left the keys in the ignition. We'd donned our vests back at my house, so we were as good as we were getting. We climbed out of the SUV and headed onto the porch, Gertie clutching a casserole at almost neck level so that Mary could see we came observing Southern rules for visiting without calling.

We stood on the sides of the door, just in case Mary answered by firing first and asking 'who's there' later, then I reached over and knocked. Almost immediately, I heard someone ranting inside. So on the plus side, she was still alive and verbal. On the negative side, her mood didn't seem all that grand. A couple seconds later, the door flew open and a shotgun barrel came out.

I could have easily grabbed it and disarmed her, but I didn't figure that was a good way to get her to talk. So instead, I grabbed the casserole and held it in the doorway.

"Mary?" Ida Belle called out. "This is Ida Belle and Gertie from over in Sinful."

"Sinful?" Mary asked. "This ain't Sinful."

"I know," Ida Belle said. "We came to visit you. Gertie brought you one of her famous chicken casseroles."

"Hmmmph," Mary said. "Might have heard something about those. You going to show your faces or just stand there lurking like those religious men I sent packing last week?"

Ida Belle and Gertie poked their heads around. Ida Belle's eyes widened, and Gertie started shaking as though she was trying not to laugh out loud.

"We brought a friend with us," Gertie said, sounding somewhat strangled. "Her name is Fortune."

"Good morning, Mrs. Joseph," I said, still holding my position. "It's a pleasure to meet you."

"I don't like strangers in my house," Mary said.

"She's dating Deputy LeBlanc," Ida Belle said. "That's Emmaline's son. You remember Emmaline LeBlanc, right?"

"'Course I do," Mary said. "She's a God-fearing woman of class and high moral standards. Don't have too many of those among the young these days."

As Emmaline was well into her fifties, I had to smile at the 'young' comment. It really was all relative.

"Well, seeing as she's stepping out with Emmaline's boy, I guess she's okay," Mary said. "But she better not try any funny stuff. I won't have no one pilfering my silver."

"No ma'am," Ida Belle said. "She's actually the one holding the casserole, so her hands aren't available to pilfer."

"Then you best come in," Mary said. "Can't have you standing around on my porch or those religious men will get the idea I'm open to such things. I was in the first pew Sunday morning and night and every Wednesday evening for over seventy years, like any good Baptist. Just cause my back gives me problems and I don't go to the Lord's house anymore don't mean I need strangers on my porch telling me about Jesus. I know all I need to know."

"That's because she used to babysit him," Gertie whispered to me as Ida Belle stepped inside.

I rounded the corner, still clutching the casserole, figuring it could be used as a weapon if things went south, and got my first look at Mary. I blinked. It was like watching a historical film.

Old as Sheriff Lee or better. Five foot five. A hundred pounds and at least ten of that was her outfit. Muscle had probably fled along with Moses and his people when they left Egypt. The rifle was good quality, but there was no way she could aim to shoot me before I got away. Threat level low but still somewhat questionable. She did have a purse looped over her elbow.

But the outfit was the real kicker. It was one of those long gowns with big ruffles and sheer fabrics, and the entire thing was canary yellow. Her hat was an enormous wide-brimmed straw one and had more flowers on it than my bushes produced in a year. I was surprised her neck was supporting both the hat and her head.

She gave me a long stare, then hitched the rifle up on her shoulder like a soldier and headed down the hallway. Since she didn't fire or slam the door in our faces, I assumed that was our cue to follow her. Ida Belle looked over at me and shrugged as we headed after her. The hallway opened into a kitchen at the rear of the house with big windows on the back wall that looked out over a large yard.

"I'll bet your bushes are beautiful when they're blooming," Gertie said.

Mary sat in a chair at the kitchen table, one hand still clutching the rifle. "Of course they are. Any Southern woman worth her salt has mature azalea bushes and some roses. Planted those roses myself—won at the state fair five years running. Will you all sit down? It's hurting my neck staring up at you. And don't be thinking I'll be serving you anything. Didn't ask for visitors, and I'm not inclined to act like the hired help in my own home."

"Of course not," Ida Belle assured her, but she didn't look remotely mollified.

"Do you still maintain everything yourself?" Gertie asked, obviously trying to get Mary to relax and talk about basic things. "Looks like you'd need a ladder to trim some of them."

"Of course I maintain them," Mary said, sounding indignant. "Takes a while with my knees and my back but I don't want fools traipsing around my yard, butchering my bushes. Young people can't be depended on for anything these days. The whole world is going to hell in a handbasket."

She shot me a dirty look, which I assumed implied I was carrying said basket.

"Yes, young people can do some odd things," Ida Belle said. "In fact, that's why we wanted to talk to you."

Mary looked at me and frowned. "This one in the family way?"

"What?" I said. "No! It's not me that's done something odd. It's friends of mine."

Mary rolled her eyes. "It's always a friend."

"This time, that's actually true," Ida Belle said. "A young couple who are friends of Fortune's bought the Leroux estate."

Mary stared at me as if I'd broken wind at her kitchen table, her expression a mixture of shock and disbelief.

"Why on earth would they want to do that?" Mary asked. "See, this is exactly what I was talking about. Young people don't have the sense God gave a goose."

"Is there something wrong with the house?" I asked. "I heard it was haunted."

Mary looked up at the ceiling. "Lord, give me strength. If He wanted us to stick around after we died, then He wouldn't have gone to the trouble of making us a place in Heaven. That place isn't haunted, and I don't know how a good Christian could believe such nonsense. Maybe I should send those Jesus men your friends' way."

"Oh, I don't believe the house is haunted and neither do my friends," I said. "But I do think someone is trying to scare them. One of my friends saw a woman wearing a white dress in the house, but when she went to look, the woman was gone and there was no other way out of the room. The Realtor saw the woman several times as well."

Mary frowned, seeming to consider this. "Why would someone want to scare your friends?"

"The only thing we can figure is that someone isn't happy they moved into the house," Ida Belle said.

Mary nodded. "That makes a lot more sense than ghosts. Unless this woman friend and the Realtor are the foolish sort."

"The Realtor is questionable on intelligence but appears honest to a fault," I said. "And I assure you, the woman who saw the ghost is not silly even though she's young. She's a medical doctor and works in the ER at the hospital."

"A doctor, you say?" Mary considered this. "It amazes me the things women get up to these days. Well, I certainly hope she's not crazy given that she's got to save people's lives. I guess you might be right. Maybe someone *is* trying to scare her."

"But what we don't know is why someone would want to do that," Ida Belle said. "Her friends just moved to town, so they don't have any enemies here. Because of that, we assumed it had something to do with the house, and you were the only person we could think of who might remember things about the house and the Leroux."

Mary nodded. "I suppose I might be one of the only ones left in the area that was around back then and still has my right mind. But you two are no spring chickens. Don't you remember anything?"

Ida Belle and Gertie both shook their heads.

"The house was built before we were born," Gertie said. "We were still kids when all the other stuff happened. And back then, there weren't cell phones and the internet, so you didn't find out things instantly like you do now with everyone telling you what they had for breakfast and the like."

"People kept their business to themselves," Mary agreed. "The way it should be. That internet is the gateway to hell. All day long, I see young people walking down the street, staring at those little phones. People don't produce anymore."

"So true," Gertie agreed. "Ida Belle and I were just kids when Celine disappeared. Our mothers probably heard some talk, but they wouldn't have repeated gossip about adults to Ida Belle and me because they were proper. And by the time we were old enough to take notice of such things, it was old news, and Ida Belle, Marge, and I left for Vietnam after that."

Mary shook her head. "I remember when you three set out to do men's work. Didn't understand it then or now, but that's on your mothers. Anyway, I don't see how I can help your friends. Could have told them not to buy the place, but it's too late for that."

"Why don't you think they should have bought the house?" I asked. "I mean, you don't believe in ghosts, and it's a really beautiful house."

"Maybe it's cursed," Gertie said.

Mary snorted. "Don't hold no beliefs in all that voodoo nonsense either, but what I do believe in is good and evil and I think some places are just bad. Maybe it's because bad people lived there and did bad things. I don't believe in all that paranormal stuff, but I *do* believe in evil."

"And you think the house is evil?" I asked. This was a new angle.

"I think if a place has had too many bad things happen, it holds that bad energy," Mary said. "That house...there wasn't happiness there." She leaned forward and looked at me. "Take a look around this kitchen—out those windows—and tell me what you feel."

What I felt was like I was sitting in judgment from a woman who was still holding a rifle and might be sitting on a lot more firepower in that huge purse. But I figured I'd better come up with something that mollified Mary and kept her talking.

"Content, secure," I said.

Mary nodded. "My daddy built this house and I was raised here. They passed it to me on my marriage and moved back to north Louisiana where their people were from. They were devout Christians with strong values and work ethic. They made a good life here and so did I. My daddy met a strong young man when I was of age to be considered and after courting for the proper time, we were married. I was widowed early because of the war but I had my go at it, which is all a woman can ask for. Didn't have children before he went off, though, which was a shame."

"You could have remarried," Gertie said.

"I did my duty," Mary said. "I made a good marriage to a decent man like you're supposed to. Never found another after him who suited. The war changed men, for the worse if you ask me. After my husband passed, I had my volunteer work at the church and started my roses. Was fortunate enough to have parents who provided a trust, so I didn't need to earn a living. This house represents over a hundred years of good living and you can feel it."

"I suppose the Leroux house represents sadness and tragedy," Gertie said. "Have you ever been in it?"

"When Lovelie passed, some of the women went to bring food, as we are called to do in those circumstances," she said. "But the butler wouldn't even let us in the door. Fine by me, I said. It is not a place for godly people."

"So what's the real story of Lucien and Lovelie?" I asked. "Did you ever meet them?"

"I saw Lucien some in town," she said. "The wives and mothers were sewing for the military men, and when we were done doing our chores and that of our absent husbands, we spent any spare minute at the church sewing. Oh, he was a handsome devil, I'll give him that, and had more charm than any Hollywood man I've seen on television. He'd come to the church and talk and smile and disrupt things, getting silly women all giddy."

"But not you?" I asked, unable to help myself.

Mary glared at me. "I took my vows before God. Oh, he made his pass at me, all right, but I wasn't having any of it. At first, I thought he'd come for the baked goods—the man loved homemade sweets—but he had his sights set on far more than dessert and I wasn't looking to be his next prize."

I was having a really hard time imagining a young, attractive Mary, so I just nodded. It was probably better not to try to come up with words.

"But there was something wrong about him," Mary continued. "I didn't feel he was trustworthy. And I was right on that one. He took up with ladies in town after his wife drowned herself—*married* ladies."

"Did any husbands ever find out?" I asked.

"Never heard that they did, but then able-bodied American men were off to war," Mary said. "The US government wasn't knocking on the door of some Frenchman asking him to take up arms."

"So he had a big playing field," Gertie said. "What about Lovelie? Did you ever meet her?"

"As far as I know, Lovelie never left the estate, but then, she didn't have anywhere to go," Mary said. "She wouldn't have fit in with the locals with that voodoo nonsense, and her people in New Orleans had shunned her for taking up with Lucien."

"What about Celine?" Ida Belle asked.

"Never once saw the girl," Mary said. "Not sure anyone around here did unless they worked on the estate."

"So what happened to her?" I asked. "Surely there was talk."

"Of course there was talk," Mary said. "But all people had were questions. Far as I know, no one ever found an answer."

"What do you think?" Gertie asked.

"I think she followed her mother into that bayou," Mary said.

It was a grim thought but held a certain logic.

"How did Lucien die?" Gertie asked.

"They said it was a heart attack," Mary said.

"But you don't believe them?" I asked.

Mary shrugged. "If that's what the doctors want to call a man's choices catching up with him, then who am I to say differently? Doesn't change the fact that the whole family is long dead and gone."

"I don't suppose you know anyone who worked at the estate?" I asked. "Maybe someone's still alive?"

"I heard a rumor that Clotilde Bassett was at an assisted living place in New Orleans," Mary said. "She was a maid at the estate when she was no more than a kid herself. She was about the same age as Celine if I'm remembering correctly."

"Do you know which assisted living center?" I asked, my excitement growing. Finding a person who'd worked at the estate would be like hitting the lottery.

"Can't recall, but I think it was Verna Warner's great-aunt —God rest her soul—who was there." Mary clutched the rifle and rose from her chair. "If you ladies will excuse me."

She headed out of the kitchen and I looked over at Ida Belle and Gertie. "Is she going to the bathroom or to bed?"

"Who knows?" Gertie said.

"Should we leave?" I asked.

"No!"

They both replied at once.

"If we leave without the proper salutations, she'll consider it a slight," Ida Belle said. "And there's always a chance we'll need her another time."

Gertie nodded. "Don't want to burn bridges."

"Then I hope it's the bathroom," I said. "I don't want to wait here while she takes a nap."

"At her age, there's always the possibility of falling asleep in the bathroom," Gertie said.

"Things to look forward to," I muttered.

"What the heck are you doing in my house?"

Mary yelled and we all whirled around to see her standing there, pointing the rifle at us.

"You run around quoting the Bible, but you're just wolves in sheep's clothing," Mary said. "Well, you're not stealing from this old lady."

"Mary, it's Ida Belle and Gertie," Ida Belle said. "Remember? We came to ask you about the Leroux estate."

"We brought you a casserole," Gertie added and picked up the dish.

"Get out!" Mary yelled as she lifted the rifle and fired.

CHAPTER TEN

Thank God she wasn't a good shot, but she wouldn't be returning the casserole dish.

Gertie was already dropping it when the bullet split it in two. We all dived away from the table and scrambled for something to hide behind as she continued to unload on her kitchen. I would have taken a chance rushing her, but I'd ducked into a dining room a good twenty-five feet away. She could definitely fire before I reached her and sooner or later, she'd hit something. My luck, it wouldn't be the vest I was wearing.

Gertie was wedged between the refrigerator and the wall, and Ida Belle had dived into the utility room. Neither was in a better position than me, especially Gertie, who was a sitting duck if Mary changed angles. She took another shot and a pane in the back window exploded, then she moved forward, and I knew in another two steps, she'd have a clear shot at Gertie. I had to do something now.

But just as I started to leap around the door, I heard a sizzling sound and saw something fly from the refrigerator toward Mary. I barely got my head back around the corner before the firecrackers started zipping everywhere and exploding all over the kitchen. One of them landed on the curtains and they went up in flames.

"My bad!" Gertie yelled. "That was supposed to be a smoke bomb."

Mary screamed and started firing toward the refrigerator. Gertie pulled the door open just in time for one of the shots to catch a gallon of milk. It blew up along with another container that looked like potato salad, most of which went over the door and landed on Gertie's head.

Mary, who was still trying to make her way across the kitchen, hit a patch of milk and her feet flew out from under her. She fired again, taking out her kitchen lights as she went down, and I was pretty sure that was all the firing power she had left.

"Last round!" I yelled.

Gertie bolted from behind the refrigerator, potato salad streaming down her face, and yelled at Mary as she passed.

"Needs more salt!"

"Get out of there before she reloads!" I yelled.

I bolted into the kitchen, grabbed a pitcher of tea, and flung it onto the flaming curtains before darting back into the dining room. Another bullet blasted through the doorway and took out the chandelier in the dining room. Holy crap! Mary had a modified rifle.

"Bail!" I shoved open the window in the dining room, grabbed Gertie's arm, pulled her across the room, and practically tossed her out the window. Another shot hit the window-pane above me and glass shattered everywhere. I dived out and landed in a huge azalea bush, right on top of Gertie. I scrambled off her and rolled underneath the house and Gertie half crawled, half slid under as well.

"It's too quiet," Gertie whispered.

"She's probably reloading," I said. "Start crawling for the front of the house. Maybe we can make a dash for the SUV from the corner."

"Where's Ida Belle?"

"Probably out a window on the other side as soon as you were clear."

We started crawling for the front of the house, and I tensed every time I heard footsteps overhead. We were almost to the front of the house when I heard sirens. Thank God, someone had called the cops. I heard car doors slamming and running feet. I stuck my head out from under the house and through the bushes and looked down the barrel of a nine-millimeter.

"This is all a mistake," I said to the deputy holding the gun on me.

"Bet your butt it is," he said. "We don't take kindly to crimes against the elderly in this town. I want you to keep your hands on the ground and crawl out of there and bring your buddy with you."

I sighed and started crawling through the bush. I could have easily disarmed him, but I suspected that wouldn't help my case any. And if he had a partner, things could go downhill really fast. When I got out of the bush, I heard footsteps approaching from the side of the house and then someone laughing. I knew that laugh.

Harrison put his hand on the deputy's arm and told him to lower his weapon. I yanked leaves out of my hair and glared at him as I rose.

"You know this woman?" the other deputy asked Harrison.

He nodded. "She was my partner at the CIA. She's a PI now—lives in Sinful."

"Then why was she trying to rob an old lady?"

"I wasn't robbing anyone," I said.

I heard grunting behind me and turned around to help Gertie out of the bush. At the same time, Ida Belle crawled out from under the porch. The deputy looked from Ida Belle to Gertie to me, then back to Harrison, and I could see his level of confusion was off the charts.

"Would someone tell me what's going on here?" the deputy asked.

"Not until I know you've taken Mary's rifle away," I said. "If she still has that rifle, then you can haul me to jail and I'll talk to you there."

"I've got the rifle." A voice sounded behind us and I looked up to see yet another deputy walking out of the house, a very irritated Mary stomping behind him.

"You can't take my gun," Mary said. "I have rights. I can defend myself and my property."

"That's correct, ma'am," the deputy holding the rifle said. "But since we're here, you don't need to anymore. So are these the women who broke into your home and attacked you?"

"Broke in?" I stared. "Are you kidding me?"

"Why don't you tell us what happened?" Harrison said, still grinning.

"It's your fault," I said.

"My fault?" The grin slipped just a bit.

"Yeah," I said. "Mary is probably the only person in the parish who was alive when your house was built. We were here for information."

"We even brought a casserole," Gertie said.

"I didn't see any casserole," the deputy said.

"That's because the anti-Annie Oakley blasted it," Gertie grumbled. "And that was a really good dish."

"Be glad she *wasn't* a sure shot," Ida Belle said, "or they'd be calling the coroner."

"Anyway," I said, "we were talking to Mary about the

Leroux estate because my friend Harrison and his fiancée Cassidy just bought it and he wanted to know about the history. Things were going fine until Mary went to the bathroom, then she came back and didn't remember who we were or that she'd invited us into her house."

"I would never invite burglars into my house," Mary said.

"You don't have anything worth stealing, you old coot," Gertie said.

"That modified rifle is nice," Ida Belle said.

"Not when it's being fired at you," I said.

The two Mudbug deputies glanced at Harrison, looking worried. At first, I figured it was because they were afraid they were going to have to arrest the new guy's buddy—aka me—and they didn't like the CIA connection involved.

Then one of them asked, "You bought the Leroux estate?"

Clearly, their discomfort had nothing to do with Mary, the missing casserole, the gunfire, or arresting me. They were nervous because Harrison had moved into the local haunted house.

"Yes," Harrison said. "And I did ask my friends if they could find out some history on it, so I suppose I am somewhat to blame for this."

"Wait!" Mary leaned over and studied us. "Is that you, Ida Belle? You wouldn't believe it but some of those idiots selling Jesus door-to-door just tried to rob me."

I looked at the deputies and waved my hands in Mary's direction.

One of them sighed and motioned to his buddy. "Another false alarm," he said.

"False alarm?" I asked. "She tried to shoot us after inviting us in. There *was* a crime committed here. It just wasn't by us."

"Ma'am, we're not arresting a crazy old lady and putting her in a jail cell. First off, no one wants to listen to her, and we don't want the medical liability. Second, the ADA is not going to press charges so it would be a waste of time all around."

"At least keep the rifle, or you might need body bags the next time," Gertie said as Mary walked back inside the house.

"That I can do," the deputy said.

Mary ran back out the door and yelled. "I've been vandalized. Someone call the cops."

"Can we go?" I asked. "Before she locates another weapon and decides we're all serial killers."

They waved us off and Harrison followed us to Ida Belle's SUV.

"I'm sorry you ran into problems on my account," he said. "You sure you guys are all right?"

"I'll be better once I get this potato salad out of my hair," Gertie said. "And this vest off. I haven't had a deep breath since I put the darned thing on."

Harrison blinked. "You're wearing vests?"

"Well, since Mary has a reputation for shooting at people, I figured it was the smart move," I said.

His eyebrows went up. "A reputation for shoot— You know what? I'm invoking that Sinful policy thing, and I don't want to know."

"You'll want to know about Mary," Ida Belle said. "This won't be the last call you take here."

"Did you learn anything, at least?" he asked.

"We might have a lead on someone who used to work in the house," I said. "I'll let you know if anything pans out."

He nodded.

"Oh, and Harrison," I said, "it's probably best to keep this sort of thing—meaning the gunplay—between us."

"You mean don't tell Carter." He frowned.

"*Or* tell Carter that you're the reason some crazy lady shot at his girlfriend," Ida Belle said.

"No problem keeping it quiet," he said quickly then headed off.

"I hope we don't ever need anything from Mary again," Gertie said. "And if we do, I'm bringing food in disposable trays. I don't care whether it's appropriate or not. That woman is a menace."

"Let's hope that tip on Clotilde Bassett is good," I said. "Because I'd hate to think we did all that for nothing."

———

WE WERE ON OUR WAY BACK TO SINFUL WHEN CARTER called. I was afraid the cop grapevine had already filled him in on our afternoon activities, but he actually had information for us for a change.

"I'm putting you on speaker," I said.

"In trying to find reasons for the haunting problem, I pulled a police log on the house," he said. "There are reports of random intruders as far back as the records go, which is only about ten years."

"Was an intruder ever caught?" I asked.

"A couple times some of those ghost hunter people were picked up by Mudbug deputies, but most of the sightings were of the lady in white, and they were made by new owners shortly after they moved in. Mudbug is closer for response, so that explains why I've never gotten the call-outs, but they never found anything. Just took a report and filed it."

"Well, at least that explains why none of the owners hung around for long," Gertie said.

"Probably, but that's not the interesting thing," he said.

"If ten years' worth of ghost sightings isn't interesting, then I can't wait to hear what is," Ida Belle said.

"Lucien's death was ruled suspicious," Carter said. "And do you know who was wanted for questioning?"

"Celine," I guessed.

"Yep," Carter confirmed.

"Well, now we know why she disappeared," Gertie said. "And I'll bet it wasn't into the bayou like people speculated."

"Unless she felt guilty," Carter said.

"That whole guilt thing is very Catholic," Gertie said. "I'm not sure the Catholics are claiming voodoo under their umbrella just yet."

"The voodoo thing is rumor too," I said. "For all we know, she popped dear old dad, cleared out the bank accounts, and moved to New York to become Priscilla, the eccentric art critic with six Pomeranians."

"If the cause was suspicious, then it wasn't a gunshot wound," Ida Belle said. "So what was it listed as?"

"A heart attack was cause," Carter said. "Manner is what's up for speculation. Forensics back then was nothing like today."

"Could have been poisoned," I said.

"And reading between the lines on the very few notes we have, I get the feeling that's where the sheriff back then was going with it," he said. "But without knowing the man, I can't say if it was fanciful thinking or he was onto something."

"It wasn't Sheriff Lee?" I asked.

"He was probably fighting," Ida Belle said.

"I thought the Civil War was earlier," I said.

"Ha," Carter said. "But Ida Belle's right. The guy who filed this report was Sheriff Michael Pratt. You guys ever heard of him? Or know him?"

Since my parents weren't even alive then, I assumed he was talking to Ida Belle and Gertie.

"I have a vague recollection," Ida Belle said and Gertie

nodded. "But we were just kids then and didn't have much cause to cross paths with the cops."

"Unlike today," Carter said.

"Different times," Ida Belle said. "He wasn't a local. I want to think they brought him in from Baton Rouge to fill the position. There was a shortage of men at the time."

"He walked with a limp," Gertie said. "I remember because I would always ask Mama why and she said it wasn't polite to ask about other people's ailments unless they wanted your help."

"She's right," Ida Belle said. "I remember that as well. Probably why he wasn't at war with the others. But I don't recall anything else."

He nodded. "Did you guys have any luck with the Realtor or Mary?"

"We're not sure yet," I said. "Mostly more rabbit holes at this point. We'll let you know if we come up with anything solid."

"Okay. I've got to run help Deputy Breaux. Maisey Jackson's out boating."

As Maisey's preference was boating sans clothes, we all cringed.

"It's barely 50 degrees outside," Gertie said.

"Apparently, she's wearing boots, a scarf, and gloves," Carter said. "But nothing else."

"Good luck with that," I said and hung up. "Things like that remind me why I didn't go the official law enforcement route."

"Yeah, but for someone who's not forced to apprehend naked people, you do run into them a lot," Gertie pointed out.

"I don't need any reminders," I said. "I'm still trying to bleach my mind of our last case. So do you guys know this Verna Warner that Mary mentioned?"

"Not well," Ida Belle said. "She was a Sinful resident but some years younger than us. She married and moved off right after high school, but I think one of the Sinful Ladies is a distant relation. She can probably get us a way to get in touch."

"Good," I said. "Work that angle then."

"What are we doing next?" Gertie said. "Besides taking off these vests and me getting a shower?"

My cell phone rang and I checked the display. Harrison.

"Did Mary call to complain about another break-in?" I asked when I answered.

"Not yet, and I'm hoping she saves that for when I'm working in another town," he said. "Listen, I have a situation —there's an issue with the closing of my condo sale, something to do with a mistake they made recording documents. Nothing that can't be fixed by a visit to the courthouse, but I have to do it myself and in person. I can catch a flight this afternoon and be back late tomorrow night—next morning at the worst—but I don't want to leave Cassidy alone."

"Of course not," I said. "She can stay with me."

"Actually, I was kind of hoping the three of you would come stay with her," he said. "I don't want Cassidy to be alone, but the thought of clearing out and letting this a-hole have full run over my house makes my blood boil."

I completely understood his sentiment, but he wasn't the only one involved.

"And what does Cassidy think?" I asked.

"She's all for it," he said. "Look, I know it's a big ask, but I'm afraid she's never going to feel comfortable in that house until we catch this guy and figure out what the heck is going on. And I really want things to work here."

"I do too," I said. "If she's game, we'll pack up some stuff and head over in a couple hours."

"You don't need to check with your partners in crime?" he asked.

I laughed. "No. Even a real ghost wouldn't keep them away from a mystery."

"Okay, I'll let Cassidy know. And Fortune...thanks."

I disconnected and filled Ida Belle and Gertie in.

"We need to bring equipment," Gertie said.

"Do they have internet yet?" Ida Belle asked.

I shook my head. "I was thinking about getting a couple of portable security cameras. There's some battery-operated models with an SD card. No guarantees we'll get anything on them, of course..."

"But it's worth a shot," Ida Belle said. "And it would probably be good to have some anyway. You never know when they'll come in handy."

"I have another idea," Gertie said.

"If it involves costumes of any sort, I'm out," I said.

"Or dancing poles," Ida Belle said.

Gertie sighed. "You two are hopelessly boring. But I think we should bring Rambo."

I looked at Ida Belle. "That's actually not a bad idea. That dog could smell a breath mint in Florida. If another ghost pulls a disappearing act while we're there, Rambo might be able to show us how."

"I'm game," Ida Belle said. "But we should check with Cassidy first. Not everyone wants a puppy loose in their house. And we have to keep him in our sights at all time. If humans are getting in and out of the place undetected, I don't want to think of the options for losing a puppy in that mess."

I gave Cassidy a call and got enthusiastic approval. "Our packing list just got a little bigger, but she thinks it's a great idea. Let's go pick up some cameras, pack our bags, and head out to track a ghost."

CHAPTER ELEVEN

WITH THE PUPPY ALONG, PACKING TOOK SOME EXTRA TIME and planning, and it was getting dark by the time we arrived. Harrison had left for the airport hours before, and Cassidy looked relieved to see us at the door. She also looked determined. I didn't blame her. We all were.

"Oh my God!" she said, and reached for the puppy as soon as we stepped inside. "I've never seen a bloodhound puppy in person. He is the cutest thing ever."

Ida Belle beamed like any proud parent and Gertie and I nodded in agreement.

"His name is Rambo," Ida Belle said.

Cassidy smiled. "Very appropriate. What's all this? Are you guys moving in?"

She waved her free hand at the bags and boxes.

"We picked up some portable security cameras and brought some other supplies," I said. "If anyone comes in this house tonight, we want to catch them."

"Hopefully you won't have to shoot anyone," Cassidy said. "Blood is hard to get out of some things."

Gertie laughed. "I really like you."

Cassidy shrugged. "ER doctor engaged to former CIA agent—getting blood out of things is part of the job description."

"It's nice to have another professional on tap," Ida Belle said.

"But we're definitely not looking to shoot anyone," I said.

"It still happens sometimes," Gertie said.

"Not this time," I said. "If we shoot people, they usually die. Then they can't tell us why they're sneaking around."

Cassidy nodded. "If there's something in here that somebody wants, I want to know what it is and get it out. Harrison told me about your run-in with Scary Mary. I don't want you guys taking those kinds of chances again."

"Get in line," Ida Belle said. "I believe the expression you used was 'part of the job description.'"

She sighed. "Okay, but at least be careful. I don't want our situation to get any of you injured or worse. Or to put it another way, I don't want to see any of you in a professional capacity."

"Bound to happen sooner or later," I said. "Especially if Gertie insists on keeping that stripper pole."

Cassidy shot me a look that was a combination of nervous and slightly appalled, but she was smart enough not to ask.

"Well, you have a choice of bedrooms," she said. "They're all upstairs—I hope that's all right. And, if you recall, some don't have en suites, but you can still all have a room and bathroom to yourself."

"Lead the way," I said. "I want to dump off my things and get these cameras in place. Then we can let the puppy roam and see if anything triggers him."

"You really think the intruder will try again with all of us in the house?" Cassidy asked.

"You mean all of us *women* in the house?" I asked.

Cassidy laughed. "If he only knew. But I see your point."

"Short of the house being empty or you being here alone, a houseful of women and a puppy is probably the least threatening scenario the intruder can get," I said.

"So he thinks," Gertie said.

"And we want him to keep thinking that until he's caught," Ida Belle said. "Fortune's right. Harrison leaving town might be just the opportunity we needed to end this nonsense."

It only took thirty minutes to get the cameras tested and then I selected some strategic locations around the house to place them, starting with the room that Cassidy had seen the ghost in. None of us were staying in that bedroom or the one where she'd seen the red eyes. Ida Belle and I, because we wanted to give the intruder good passage to enter and get caught. Gertie, because she said there wasn't enough glitter and sexy time in the world for her to do it.

We'd split the rooms up with me in the one nearest the ghost room and Ida Belle nearest the red eye room. We'd put Gertie in between the main stairwell and the attic entrance. We had cameras in both the end rooms as well as one in the attic facing the entry. Then I'd put a couple downstairs that covered a broad range of rooms and hallways. If the intruder showed, we'd get him.

We spent another hour walking the house with the puppy, allowing him to check out everything that caught his nose. The exposure to everything now meant only something different was likely to garner his attention later on. After his big adventure, Ida Belle gave him dinner and a potty break, then Cassidy tossed a giant throw pillow on the floor for him to nap on while we unpacked the stuff Gertie had put together for dinner.

"The cameras were surprisingly easy," Cassidy said as we took a seat in the living room with our dinner.

I nodded and picked up a huge roast beef sandwich. "And all the random stuff sitting around definitely made them easier to hide."

"So do you guys have any theories about what someone could be after?" Cassidy asked.

"No clue," I said. "All we know is it doesn't have anything to do with you, so that makes it about the house. I suppose it could be something to do with a previous owner, but I doubt it. I think whatever is going on goes back to the beginning."

"Why do you think that?" she asked.

I shrugged. "A hunch."

She nodded. "Ben said you were like a human radar. That you picked up things that no one else did. He said it saved his life far more than once. If he's never told you how much he admires and appreciates you—and I assume that's the case because, you know, tough guy—I want you to know that he does."

I felt a blush creep up my neck. "The feeling is mutual. I'm pretty sure us being paired up is the only reason we're still around today, so our debts sort of cancel each other out."

Cassidy smiled. "And now you have these ladies working with you. How did that happen?"

"That's a long story," I said.

"But we take down the bad guy in the end," Gertie said.

"Tell me," Cassidy said. "We've got nothing but time."

————

AFTER WE'D EATEN, WE SAT IN THE LIVING ROOM, DRAPES open and in full view of anyone spying, and thoroughly entertained Cassidy with our story of my arrival in Sinful and my first unofficial case. We left out Ida Belle and Gertie's real military background, but Cassidy didn't need to know it in order to believe what we were telling her. Harrison had already told her enough stories about the things the three of us had done. Then we talked about some of our misadventures with Gertie's purse and a couple of other things that she was sworn to secrecy on, and finally, everyone was yawning.

It was around 11:00 p.m. when we all decided to call it a night. Ida Belle took Rambo out for one last potty break and then we headed upstairs. Cassidy left the lights on in the hallways downstairs and upstairs, and we made sure all the interior doors were open. If anyone appeared in a room, hopefully the light from the hallway would be enough to capture them on camera.

I checked the windows in my room to ensure they were properly latched, then closed my door and locked it. It hindered my ability to hear and move around somewhat, but Cassidy hadn't been comfortable with us leaving our doors open and unlocked. She wanted answers, but not at anyone else's expense. I had a feeling she'd prefer to capture the intruder on camera, take it to the police the next day, and let them deal with arresting him. And that would be an awesome and peaceful end to all the trouble, but things were never that simple. I knew the chances of her coming upstairs to check the doors was slim to none, but I would have felt guilty ignoring her request in her own house, so I'd complied.

My room was a good size and had a door that connected to a bathroom that also had an entry from the hallway. The exterior wall had two huge windows that looked out over the backyard. The wall with the bed on it was shared with the ghost room. Both the red eye and the ghost bedrooms spanned all the way across the home from east to west, making them far bigger than the rooms located off each side of the hallway, and each contained an en suite with no hallway access.

The en suites in each bedroom were located on the front

side of the house with the bedroom area at the rear. There were windows on all three exterior walls in both of the rooms, including in the bathrooms, but I'd checked them all thoroughly. No one was going to enter the house through one of those windows.

It had been a long day and I was tired, but I knew I wouldn't be able to sleep. Not immediately. If we edged toward morning with no alerts, then I might drift off. But since morning was several hours away and the only chair in the room was horribly uncomfortable, I grabbed my iPad, propped up the pillows against the headboard, and reclined on the bed, still fully dressed.

I had queued up a couple books before I left my house because you never knew how good a signal you could get out in the middle of nowhere. And this house definitely fell under that description. I deliberated between the forensics textbook, a book of interviews with serial killers, and a fiction book that Ida Belle said had women riding dragons and sword fighting and opened up the fiction book. I'd never read anything like that and was curious what Ida Belle deemed worthy of her reading time.

I was five chapters in and ready to proclaim Ida Belle a genius when I heard a noise in the next room. It wasn't loud but it didn't feel like old house creaking stuff to me. I swiped over to text messages.

Me: Noise in ghost room. Anywhere else?

Ida Belle: Nothing on my end.

Gertie: Only what came out of my end.

Me: Hold position.

Gertie: Can I get off the john?

Ida Belle: Get off or I'll come in there and shoot you.

I stepped out of bed and crept toward the door, grateful for the large rug that covered most of the hardwood floor.

When I reached the door, I put my ear to it and listened but didn't hear anything. I was just about to ease the door open when Rambo started going off at the other end of the house.

I bolted out the door just as someone in a white gown ran out of a room at the front of the hallway and down the stairs. As I sprinted toward the retreating figure in white, all the lights in the house went off. Moonlight streamed in from the floor-to-ceiling windows on the back of the house, casting a dim light over the stairwell and into the hallway. Ida Belle and Gertie both came out of their rooms, and I yelled at them to check the room at the other end, before dashing down the stairs. I slid to a stop at the bottom and scanned the area, trying to figure out where the intruder had gone. But as far as the light carried, the rooms and the hallway were all empty.

The light on my pistol wasn't nearly as good as my flashlight, but I didn't want to give up a hand to use both, so I decided the pistol light would have to do. I headed for the back living room and kitchen area and did a fast check. The exterior door was still locked, as were all the windows, and no one was hiding in a cabinet or the pantry. When I headed into the hallway on the other side, the door to the master suite opened and Cassidy stuck her head out, one hand clutching a flashlight and the other her pistol. When she saw me, she lowered her weapon.

"Oh, I thought—" she began. "And then the lights went out."

"You thought right," I said, my voice low. "I chased someone down the stairs."

Her eyes widened. "Where did they go?"

"Had to be this hallway," I said. "I've already checked the kitchen area, and obviously they didn't run into your room."

She shook her head. "I haven't even gone to sleep yet."

I nodded. "Cover me and let me know if anyone comes up

behind us, but stay back. And if any shooting starts, get the hell out of here and call the police."

"What about Ida Belle and Gertie?"

"They can take care of themselves. Just make sure you're out of cross fire."

Her eyes widened a little, and I didn't blame her. The thought of a gunfight being played out in your home was one that all normal people found frightening. And it wasn't that Ida Belle, Gertie, and I enjoyed them. It was more that we were trained to handle certain situations regardless of location.

I started down the hallway, entering one room at a time for a quick scan, but everything was clear. Finally, I got to the end of the hall and entered the library. My senses were already on high alert, but they went into overdrive. Something about this room was different. The large sitting area was dimly lit by the moonlight streaming through the back windows, but all the other areas were blocked from illumination. I crept around all the cubbies and crannies that had been built into the room, peering under tables and behind chairs and recliners, but there was no one there. I checked all the windows at the front of the house, and they were locked, and I was about to head to the back and take a look at those as well when Ida Belle and Gertie burst into the room.

"Anything upstairs?" I asked.

They both shook their heads.

"Everything was clean," Ida Belle said. "No windows unlocked and the tape across the attic entry hasn't been disturbed. What did you see?"

"A woman wearing a white gown going down the stairs. The lights went out when I took off after her. But so far, nothing down here is out of place. All I have left to check is the windows at the back."

"Cassidy said no one has come in or out of any of the

downstairs rooms, and her flashlight illuminates up to the entry where the moonlight takes over some," Ida Belle said.

"I'll check the windows," Gertie said and headed across the sitting area to the back of the room.

As she walked, I glanced over at the windows and thought I saw one of the drapes move, but in the dim light, I couldn't be sure. Then as Gertie approached, the intruder in white flung the drapes into Gertie and knocked her over, ripping the drapes completely off the wall. In her drape-wrapped fall, she discharged her weapon and blew the head off a stuffed duck hanging on the wall.

The intruder dashed into the library cubbies and I ran after her. I could hear Gertie yelling behind me and hoped she'd taken her finger off the trigger. The intruder had a good lead on me but with the three of us in the library and Cassidy manning the hallway, she was trapped. I yelled to Cassidy that the intruder was coming her way but when I got through the cubbies and into the doorway to the hall, the only person there was a very confused Cassidy.

"Where did she go?" I asked.

"No one came out the door," she said. Then her eyes widened, and she lifted her gun. "Behind you!"

I whirled around and saw a giant wall of white rushing toward me.

CHAPTER TWELVE

"Don't shoot!" I yelled as Gertie, still wrapped up in the drapes, hit me and sent us both down onto a table, then crashing onto the floor. I heard a pop as we hit the ground and felt something tingling on my skin, but it wasn't loud enough or painful enough to have been gunfire. Something hard and heavy fell onto my arm and I yanked it away. I'd dropped my gun when we fell and couldn't see anything covered up by the thick drapes and Gertie. Then light from flashlights penetrated the drapes, bouncing toward us, and I heard Cassidy yelling for Ida Belle. But with Gertie still thrashing around, I was just getting more tangled.

"Help!" Gertie yelled. "He's got me! The ghost has got me!"

"You're the ghost, you old fool!" Ida Belle yelled. "Stop moving."

Gertie went still and I dug my way out from under her and the drapes and over the huge brass vase, which was apparently what had fallen on my arm. I checked for injury and frowned when I saw sparkly pink stuff all over my arm. I brushed it with my other hand and groaned. The pop I'd heard must have been a plastic bag of glitter exploding.

Ida Belle finally got Gertie unraveled and she sat up, glitter shining all in her hair. I could only imagine I looked the same.

"Why did you have glitter on you?" I asked, since it had to have been on her body as she wasn't carrying her purse.

"I sprinkled it around objects in my room to see if ghosts moved them," she said. "I must have forgotten it in my bra."

"You're supposed to sprinkle *salt* around objects to see if they moved," Ida Belle said.

"I was out of salt," Gertie said. "I had plenty of glitter."

"Of course you did," Ida Belle said. "And now so does Cassidy. She'll be vacuuming it up from this rug for the next forty years."

"I'm more worried about how long it will take me to get it out of my hair," I said. "It's already starting to itch."

"Are you guys all right?" Cassidy called from the doorway, where she was still standing guard with her flashlight and her gun.

"We're fine," I said and leaned over to shake out my hair. "The intruder didn't leave the room?"

She shook her head. "I've been standing right here. No one came out this door."

"And the back windows are all locked down," Ida Belle said.

"Then she has to still be in the library," I said.

Cassidy's eyes widened. "No way!"

"There's no other way out," I said. "Ida Belle, go get Rambo. Gertie, take the open area and go through it again, looking under tables and behind chairs. I'll take the cubbies. Cassidy, stay here at the door and keep your eyes and ears tuned."

I started systematically checking the cubbies, working my way toward the back of the library. But when I got to the end of the room, I hadn't found the intruder tucked away behind a recliner or crouched under a desk. Gertie was double-checking the back windows when I got to the end of the cubbies and she shook her head. As we were about to head back to the doorway, Ida Belle came in with the wriggling Rambo, Cassidy close behind.

"No sign of the intruder, I guess?" Ida Belle asked.

I shook my head. "I checked all the cubbies and Gertie checked the main sitting area. It's all locked up and there's no one lurking anywhere."

"Well, she can't walk through walls!" Cassidy said.

"Maybe that's exactly what she did."

"You don't believe she's an actual ghost," Gertie said.

"No," I said. "But I was thinking about how this room is designed. With all the storage spaces, nooks, and cubbies, there's so many different angles to the room that I think there could be a secret door in here."

"Like the attic entry," Cassidy said. "But where would it lead to? It can't be exterior because the house is solid stone around this room. And if it was interior, then it could only lead to one of the two rooms that share walls with the library."

"I checked both of them," Ida Belle said. "They're empty and the windows are locked down."

"And if anyone had exited one of them into the hallway, I would have seen them," Cassidy said.

"Maybe there's a secret door to a hiding space and she's still inside," I said. "When Gertie tackled me with the drapes, I smelled perfume and I got a whiff of it again when I was searching the cubbies. None of us is wearing any, so it must be the intruder. Let Rambo have a sniff of the drapes and turn him loose in here. Maybe he'll be able to tell us where our ghost went."

The hours of training Ida Belle had spent with the puppy, on top of the excellent breeding, paid off. I smelled the drapes and found a spot where the perfume was detectable and Ida

Belle let Rambo sniff it. Then she put him down and gave him the order to find it. The puppy stuck his nose in the air first and sniffed, then set out for the cubbies, pausing periodically to sniff again. Finally, he came to a stop at the cubby with two chairs, which by my best estimation was on the back side of the huge fireplace.

He ran inside the cubby, right up to the wall behind the chairs, which were facing the walkway, plopped down, and started baying. I headed in and ran my fingers down the wall, scanning every inch for an indication the wood and the trim weren't connected. When I got to the bottom, I pushed on one of the squares outlined with molding and thought I felt it give. I gave it a good shove, and the entire thing opened inward.

It wasn't a huge opening, but an adult with a decent amount of flexibility and good knees could definitely duck into it. I scooped up the puppy before he could run inside and handed him to Gertie, then motioned to Cassidy for her flashlight. Finally, I waved Ida Belle over to cover me because whoever was inside probably wasn't going down without a fight.

I squatted down in front of the opening, my pistol ready to fire, and pushed it open as far as it would go. I couldn't hear anyone moving inside, so I stuck the flashlight in first, then poked my head in for a look.

And blinked.

I wasn't surprised often but this one I hadn't seen coming. There was a small ledge just inside the secret door—one that would allow a single adult to stand—and beyond that and stretching straight up and down was a wood ladder bolted into the stone wall.

"Is she in there?" Cassidy asked.

"No," I said. "Well, at least not right here. There's a

ladder leading down and up. My guess is up leads to the bedroom above us or the attic and down leads outside the house. I'll bet that's where she went. I'm going to check it out."

Cassidy crouched and looked inside. "Wait! What if she went upstairs and is still in the house?"

"Given that Gertie fired a gun in here, I'm going with not likely," Ida Belle said. "Especially if down leads to an exit."

"But she could be down there with a weapon," Cassidy said. "You'll have no coverage, and retreat is iffy back up that ladder."

"I agree with Ida Belle," I said. "She didn't hang around. She underestimated us and barely got away. She's not sticking around for more gunfire. And given that she didn't return fire, she might not even be armed."

"I'm going with you," Ida Belle said.

"Me too," Gertie said.

"No," I said. "Gertie, stay here with Cassidy just in case she was stupid enough to stick around or even more stupid and comes back. Plus, we need you guys up here in case we get trapped and need a rescue. The sides are solid stone, so my guess is phones aren't going to work. If we aren't back or you haven't heard from us in twenty minutes, then send out the cavalry."

"Do you want me to call Carter now, just to be safe?" Cassidy asked.

I thought for a couple seconds, then nodded. "Yeah. It will take him at least thirty minutes to get here and that's assuming he's dressed and not asleep. I figure this comes out somewhere in the woods nearby, so we should be back by then. He needs to know what we've found, and then we can look at the camera footage as well."

"What about the power?" Gertie asked. "I have trouble

believing it conveniently went out when you went after the intruder."

Cassidy sucked in a breath. "You think there's two of them?"

I nodded. "That would explain how you could see a ghost disappear in one room, then red eyes in another on the opposite side of the house."

"I think the breaker box is on the back outside wall of the house," Cassidy said. "Do you want me to check it?"

"No," I said. "Just stay put in the library until we get back. I don't think they stuck around, but I'd prefer you stay inside in an easily defended position."

"And where we're ready to fire if the wrong person comes out of that wall," Gertie said.

"Or tries to go in it," I said. "I don't want someone outflanking us."

"What if it branches off down there?" Cassidy asked. "Do you want me to find you some string or chalk or something else you could use to mark your way?"

I shook my head and a flurry of pink glitter dropped onto the floor. "I'm good."

I crawled into the wall and worked my way onto the ladder, then started down, praying it was in good shape. The wood looked old but as I progressed down, it appeared to be solid. It was only about twelve feet down and when I reached the bottom, I called up for Ida Belle to follow. A narrow tunnel ran south directly under the library and toward the woods. I was willing to bet anything there was an exit some distance from the house and this was how the intruders had been accessing it.

As soon as Ida Belle got down, we set off down the tunnel, me leading with my pistol and Ida Belle pointing her flashlight ahead of us to illuminate the path. The tunnel was so narrow that my shoulders sometimes rubbed against it as I went, and at times, I had to crouch a little or my head would have scraped across the top of it.

"No one sprinted down this, that's for sure," Ida Belle said.

"She didn't have to," I said. "She had a big head start."

"Why do you think she was hiding in the drapes?" Ida Belle asked. "You think she figured we'd clear out of the house instead of looking for her? Because she could have just popped into the panel and disappeared straight off."

"She might have been hoping we'd leave the house but the panel was a little stuck when I tried it. Maybe she couldn't get it open right away and ran to hide when she heard us coming. It's not like you can just jump in that access, either, unless you're a circus performer."

"You're probably right—she ran out of time and panicked."

I touched the walls as I walked, still marveling that all of this was even here.

"Lucien had to have built this and erected the house over it," I said. "That's why it's so narrow. It had to support the weight of the house above it and is on somewhat unstable ground. You can't go too deep here, or you'll be into the water table, especially this close to the bayou."

"Probably why it's solid stone."

"Yeah, and I'm guessing the layer we see isn't the only one."

"I think I see another ladder ahead."

We inched forward and sure enough, the tunnel stopped at another ladder, leading straight upward.

"Here goes," I said and started up.

When I got to the top, I positioned my pistol in my right hand and pushed on the trapdoor with my left. It was so heavy it barely budged with my first attempt, so I doubled up on my shove and it fell back, making a soft thud as it hit the ground.

I poked my head out and stared at a giant cypress tree. I was right. The tunnel emerged in the woods.

I climbed out and called for Ida Belle to come up, then scanned the area surrounding the exit. Ida Belle stepped out, lifted the trapdoor, and dropped it back in place. It was covered with fake turf and blended right in with the dense terrain. Ida Belle stepped on it and shook her head.

"Not a hint of echo or movement," she said. "No one could accidentally find this. Not from this end."

"I don't think anyone would accidentally find it from the other end either, unless crawling on the floor behind chairs and tackling walls like a linebacker is a favorite pastime. Someone knew the tunnel was there and has been using it to access the house."

I pulled out my cell phone and dialed, happy when the call went through and Gertie answered.

"It's me. The tunnel comes out in the woods south of the house. I can't see the house from here, but with the thick woods and no lights on, that doesn't surprise me. We're going to look around here and see if we can find her trail. She had to have a getaway vehicle tucked somewhere."

"Okay. Carter is on his way and he said for all of us to stay put. I just laughed. Do you want us to look into the power situation now?"

"Yeah, go ahead. I think you're clear, but if I see anything that changes my mind on that, I'll call."

Ida Belle leaned over. "Keep Rambo with you. He'll hear someone coming long before you do and won't hesitate to let you know."

"Got it," Gertie said and disconnected.

"I think I found something over here," Ida Belle said and pointed. "There's a path just on the other side of this dirt area beneath that grove of cypress trees."

I followed her across a dirt clearing and saw the narrow path leading through the brush.

"It's too narrow to have been used for very long," she said. "But it has been used recently."

We slowly made our way down the path, scanning the area for any sign of human interaction. We'd probably gone a quarter mile or better when the path came out at the end of a dirt road. It had obvious signs of recent use but was still mostly overgrown on the sides and down the middle of the roadway. The remnants of a long-deteriorated house stood off a bit from the road.

"The roads here kind of weave, and we've taken a straight diagonal walk through the woods," Ida Belle said and shone her light off to one side. "But I think this connects back to the first unpaved road you turn onto to get to the house."

I nodded. When it came to navigation, no one beat Ida Belle's sense of direction.

"I'll bet she stashed her car here," I said. "Let's follow the road out to put it all together."

The road was easier to traverse than the path, but we still went slowly, not wanting to miss anything along the way. Finally, the small dirt road connected to a bigger dirt road that I recognized. Ida Belle had called it correctly.

"You think we should request a pickup?" Ida Belle asked.

Given that we'd traversed the woods diagonally, then walked the lesser dirt road to the main dirt road, I estimated we were a good two miles from the house if we took the main road back. Through the woods was shorter but a harder trek. I was just about to pull out my phone and call for a ride when I saw headlights approaching.

"That's Carter," Ida Belle said.

"How do you know?"

"The headlights indicate the make, model, and year of the truck, and I recognize the sound."

I shook my head. The things people committed to memory were sometimes odd but often came in handy. Like now. I stood in the middle of the road, ready to wave him to stop. He looked somewhat confused when he saw me standing there, but I figured we'd fill him in on the way.

"Is that glitter in your hair?" he asked.

"It's a long story," I said.

"Gertie?" he asked.

"Okay, so maybe not that long," I said.

It really needed no further explanation, so Ida Belle and I launched into the details of what had led us to hitching a ride with him.

"Well, at least we know how someone was getting in and out of the house without a trace," he said. "But why would they continue to enter when there are people living there? What can be so important they can't wait for Harrison and Cassidy to be out of the house?"

"They're not exactly nine-to-fivers," I pointed out. "With both of them working different shifts, there might be someone at home the majority of the time."

Ida Belle nodded. "And it wouldn't take much asking to get the skinny on the new owners. A new cop and a new ER doctor—especially a woman—are beyond gossip-worthy around here. I doubt there's anyone who doesn't know at this point."

"Add to that the intruders might have day jobs or other responsibilities themselves, so they probably can't sit in the woods all day waiting for the driveway to empty out," I said.

"I get it, but still, it's a huge risk," he said. "Like tonight—we have to assume she was watching the house before entering since she waited until after you went to bed. And since you deliberately sat in the living room with all those huge windows opened, all it took was a glance inside and she would have known how many of you there were. Why try that with four people inside?"

"Four *women*," I said.

He looked momentarily surprised, then chuckled. "Yeah, guess I didn't think about that one. Still, since the intruder is a woman, you'd think she wouldn't be mired in gender roles."

I shrugged. "If she did her homework, then she knows Harrison is the cop and the biggest threat. Cassidy is a doctor and Gertie's purse weighs more than she does."

"And is more lethal," Ida Belle said.

"True, but the intruder doesn't know that," I said and Carter frowned.

"So add silver-haired ladies, a young, thin blonde, and a puppy, and she probably thought it was relatives visiting and we were all no more dangerous than we look," Ida Belle said.

"I'm going to guess she's no longer under that assumption given all the hardware you guys were flashing around," he said as he pulled into the entry for the house.

"And Gertie might have fired off a round in the library," I said.

CHAPTER THIRTEEN

CARTER GRIMACED BUT WASN'T EVEN GOING TO ASK ABOUT Gertie's misfire. Still, I saw his hands tighten on the steering wheel as he pulled through the gate.

"The lights are back on," Ida Belle said.

"That's a plus," I said.

Gertie and Cassidy were out the front door before we even came to a stop and gave us all a questioning look.

"We followed the trail out to a kinda road and followed that road to the main road and caught a ride with Carter, who had good timing," I explained. "What was the deal with the lights?"

"The main breaker was tripped," Gertie said.

"And the box is on the outside, right?" I asked.

"Yes," Cassidy said. "On the back of the house, right off the utility room. The first thing on my list when the sun comes up is getting a lock for it. Then I'm going to ask the contractor about moving it inside when we start renovating."

"Definitely two people then," I said. "The main breaker won't trip without a major event, which we didn't have, or human intervention."

A loud howl reminded us that we were all standing outside and Rambo had been left alone. We hurried inside and Cassidy retrieved him from the packing box she'd put him in when they'd come outside to greet us. The puppy made a beeline for Ida Belle, who scooped him up and gave the wriggly mass kisses and told him what a good boy he was.

"He's definitely got a nose on him," Gertie said to Carter. "He took one sniff and led us straight to that secret panel."

"Show me," he said.

We headed to the library and Rambo started howling the closer we got to the panel. Ida Belle managed to quiet him down with a treat and Carter bent down and stuck his head in the opening.

"You followed this thing down and out of the house?" he asked. "You realize you were completely vulnerable, right?"

"Yes," I agreed. "But I don't think the intruder wants to kill anyone."

"Doesn't mean she wouldn't," Carter said as he rose back up.

"If we'd cornered her, maybe," I said. "But given her head start, I don't think she had to worry about it."

He half grunted but he knew I was right.

"I'm going up that ladder," I said. "I want to see where it comes out. I need someone in the south bedroom. If I can't find an obvious way in, I'll knock and see if you can find it from that side."

"You three go upstairs," Carter said. "I'm going to cover the ladder down on the off chance that anyone comes back."

Ida Belle, Gertie, and Cassidy set off and I ducked into the passage and started up the ladder. Carter leaned in after me, his flashlight pointed up so that I had both hands free. When I got to where I estimated the floor of the bedroom to be, I started looking for a panel. The wall holding the ladder up wasn't made of stone like the tunnel underneath the house. This was standard interior framing, so two-by-six squares of plywood, and what remained of the insulation. Since they all looked the same and there was no indication of a landing anywhere, I assumed the secret door would open up to the ladder space and you'd step out of the room and onto the ladder.

I pushed around on the areas that I thought were aligned with the floor of the room, but nothing budged. I frowned, wondering if my theory had been wrong and the other opening was only in the attic. But then, how had the intruder disappeared from the other bedroom? And how had they created the red eyes in the bedroom I was trying to find access to?

I knocked on the wall, hoping they could hear me on the other side. I heard some movement and several seconds later, a panel popped open just above me. When I moved up and looked closely in the dim light, I could now see the hinges on the back side, hidden by insulation that didn't look quite as old as the rest. I stepped up and crawled out of the tunnel and into the bottom of the linen closet.

I yelled back down at Carter that I was in the bedroom, then headed out of the closet.

"I was a little low," I said. "The gap between the floors must be bigger than I anticipated."

Ida Belle nodded. "That helps explain why you don't hear people walking above you. This house is constructed very solidly."

"Does the ladder keep going up?" Cassidy asked.

"Yes," I replied. "We'll find the access in the attic next."

"Why on earth would Lucien build all this into the house?" Cassidy asked. "It had to be him, right?"

"It was definitely part of the original construction," Ida Belle said. "There's no way to go back and add this sort of thing without tearing up a bunch of stuff. And I'm not sure what it would take to build that tunnel under the house after the fact."

"Looks like our friend Lucien wanted to make sure he could get away if anyone came looking for him," I said.

"Well, given his habit of chasing after the wrong women, I'm sure he pissed off plenty of people," Gertie said.

"And there was the war as well," Ida Belle said. "Lucien had money and wasn't required to go fight. There was likely some resentment along those lines."

I crawled back into the closet and yelled down to Carter that I was going to continue up the ladder. The attic access was easier to find because the ladder ended, so there weren't as many options. With my finger, I easily located the hinges hidden in the insulation and gave the panel a shove. The area it opened into was pitch-black, which I thought was odd since I was sure the others would have turned on the lights when they came up. Even with all the clutter, some light should have filtered into the space.

Figuring it must be another closet and the door was closed, I crawled through the opening, then took out my flashlight. I was surprised to find myself in a narrow corridor that given the length, I estimated ran up to the front wall of the house. I followed the corridor, looking for an exit into the attic along the way, and when I got to the corner, saw that it turned and ran alongside the front of the house as far as my light reached.

What the heck!

I started off again and located hinges when I reached what appeared to be halfway. I pushed on the panel and light from the attic crept in. I poked my head out and came face-to-face with a stack of boxes, but I could hear Rambo going off and Ida Belle trying to console him. I crawled out and wrinkled my nose as I took in a whiff of dust.

"Over here," I called out, and wound my way through the boxes until I found them.

"Rambo, be quiet." Ida Belle stroked the baying puppy, trying to calm him. "He started up as soon as we got into the attic. Probably heard you."

"Where did you come from?" Gertie asked. "We were looking for you to pop out somewhere on the side wall."

"The ladder comes up into a corridor that runs to the front of the house, and it looks like all the way to the other side," I said. "There's an access panel to the attic behind those boxes. I'll bet there's another ladder down on the other end that comes out in the room Cassidy saw the woman in."

"That would explain how she disappeared," Gertie said.

"And how she got into the house and up to the room without anyone seeing her," Ida Belle said, trying to control the wriggling puppy.

I nodded. "I'm going to go back into the corridor and try to find an access to the other room. Gertie, take Rambo and head to the ghost bedroom. Cassidy, go to the library and tell Carter to come upstairs with you and Gertie. Ida Belle, cover me at the midpoint up here and make sure no one comes up behind me."

We all left to carry out our respective orders, and after I ducked into the corridor, Ida Belle crouched and stuck her head in and took a look.

"You know," she said, "this case might be the coolest one we've worked on yet. I mean, not the trying to scare our friends part of it, but this house is something else."

"It's definitely outside the box," I said. "And I appreciate a changeup, but I don't think Cassidy, Harrison, and Carter will be as excited about all this as we are."

"No, but we'll get it handled," Ida Belle said.

I grinned. "We always do."

I set off down the corridor until it ended and easily spotted the hidden panel. I popped it open and as suspected, there was a ladder leading down.

"Found the ladder!" I called to Ida Belle. "Go ahead and head to the bedroom."

I started down and when I was close to what I estimated was the bedroom floor, I started scanning for hinges again. I located them quickly and gave the panel a shove. It popped open and I found myself looking inside the bedroom closet. I crawled out and immediately threw my hands up as all three of them had guns pointed at me. Rambo let me know his displeasure from a baby crib in the corner.

"Sorry," Cassidy said. "We heard a noise in the closet and Rambo went off and...well..."

"So you couldn't hear me coming down the ladder or walking in the corridor upstairs?" I asked.

They all shook their heads.

"Well, this explains how the intruder was getting in the house and moving around without being seen or heard," I said.

"Unless she wanted to be," Carter said. "Most burglars don't wear long white nightgowns to commit their crimes. If anyone caught sight of her, she wanted them to believe that the house is haunted."

"It's clever," Ida Belle said as she came into the room. "People who see her can't find her and if they talk about it, others will think they're crazy."

Carter nodded. "So most people don't talk."

"Until Travis took the listing and Cassidy saw her," Gertie said. "Travis has a reputation for no filter, and Cassidy knew she wasn't imagining things and that we would believe her."

"Definitely not a situation the intruder wants," I said. "She took a big risk coming back into the house, even with the secret passages."

"Surely this is the end of it," Cassidy said. "We'll just close them up so no one can get in and then she has to give up on whatever treasure hunt she's on."

I glanced at Carter and his frown said what I was thinking —he didn't think the intruders were going to give up that easily either.

"Given the amount of risk they've already taken, I think we need to move forward as if we're certain they're not going to give up," I said. "And I do mean *they*. Remember, someone was outside tripping that breaker when she was inside. The fact that it's more than one person bothers me, and there's something else. Come with me and bring Rambo."

I headed downstairs to the library and directed Ida Belle to put Rambo down. He ran immediately to the tunnel access and set up a howl.

"I realize that he can probably still smell the remnants of perfume even though we can't," I said. "But why does he only bay here? He ran right by the pile of drapes on the floor and the smell is probably clinging harder to them than it would be holding in the passage."

I walked closer to him and he stopped howling, sniffed the air, then spun around and rushed over to my feet and started up again. Then he scratched at the side of the shoe. I frowned and lifted up my foot and noticed dark staining on the bottom. I pulled it off for a closer look.

"Does that look like blood?" Gertie asked.

Cassidy leaned over and smelled. "Could be. It's too faint to be sure and the rubber overpowers whatever is there."

"I didn't hit her, did I?" Gertie asked, giving Carter a sideways glance.

"No way," Ida Belle said. "There would be blood on the floor up here and I haven't seen any."

"What about the ladder?" Cassidy asked.

I checked my hands but didn't see any sign of blood on them. "I think it would have had to be pooled somewhere for me to have enough on my shoe for Rambo to zero in on it."

"Could have picked it up in the woods," Ida Belle said.

"Or in the tunnel," I said. "I need to go back down there again."

Ida Belle picked up Rambo and I opened the panel. As soon as the door opened, Rambo started howling like I had never heard him do before. Something was definitely up, and it was bigger than the faint leftovers of perfume. I ducked inside and headed down the ladder, then pulled out my flashlight and shone it around the stone floor at the bottom. To the left of the ladder, right up against the stone wall, was a darker circle and when I crouched down, I could see a sneaker print in it. And there was a slight smell that I hadn't picked up on earlier when Ida Belle and I hurried down the tunnel.

A smell I knew.

CHAPTER FOURTEEN

THIS MUST HAVE BEEN WHERE I PICKED UP THE STAIN ON MY shoe and since it was up against the wall, explained why Ida Belle didn't have it on her shoes. She had probably stepped off the ladder right in the middle of the small space. But what I couldn't figure out was why the blood was right there. It was an odd place, unless...

I felt the bottom of the stone wall and realized that what I'd thought was missing mortar was actually an empty space at the very bottom. I ran my fingers across the empty space until I hit the wall, then took a close look at the wall. In a couple of places, I found gaps in the mortar that looked like indentations. I gave the wall a decent shove and felt it move just enough to let me know that I was right. I leaned into it and gave it a harder shove and a large chunk of wall—maybe three feet square—slid open. I shone my light inside and immediately spotted the source of the stain and the smell.

"Carter, you need to get down here," I called out. "And bring Cassidy with you. We've got a body."

"What?!" Cassidy yelled.

Carter came down the ladder first and Cassidy was right

behind, her expression one of complete disbelief. I pointed to the opening and they both crouched and looked inside. The heap in white was slumped against the rear wall of the nook, which was roughly five feet by five feet and six feet high.

"I thought you said Gertie didn't hit anyone," Cassidy said.

"She didn't," I said. "Whoever this is hasn't run for a day at least."

Cassidy blew out a breath. "I knew that. The smell...I just...I can't seem to think straight."

"If you weren't overwhelmed, I'd be more concerned," Carter said. "This was a lot to absorb before a body got thrown into the mix."

"Why would there even be a secret room down here?" Cassidy asked.

I shrugged. "In case you had to hide out here for days or to store supplies for if you had to make a quick exit. Maybe store ammunition or gold coins. Or there's always the popular choice—maybe store a body?"

Carter frowned and started to move into the room, but Cassidy put a hand on his arm. "Let me."

The body was slumped onto its side, as if she had crawled to the wall and died there, her body slowly crumpling forward and to the side. Cassidy reached to brush back the long red hair that covered the intruder's face and jerked back in surprise when the entire mass of hair slid off the corpse, revealing a bald head.

"That's a guy," I said. "Look at the neck and the hands."

We all took a step closer and peered down at the man, wearing a white dressing gown, as Cassidy touched the body.

"He's cold," she said.

"Any idea on time of death?" Carter asked.

"I'm not an expert on that end of things, but if you take into account the cooler temperatures and humidity, then add some to that given that he's underground and it's even cooler down here, probably forty-eight hours give or take. The ME should be able to pin it down better."

"So the night you fell," Carter said.

"Oh my God," Cassidy said. "This must have been...he must have..."

"Cause of death?" I asked. "There's blood pooled on the floor beneath his stomach. I'm going with a bullet or a stabbing."

"Can we move him?" Cassidy asked.

"Let me take some pictures," Carter said, and pulled out his phone.

"Are you going to be in trouble with the ME if we disturb the body?" I asked.

Carter shook his head. "Since Cassidy is an ER doctor and I'll document the scene, he'll be okay with it. Given that our perp died in the commission of a crime against the homeowner, I need to get an ID and jump on this right away. I'll call him as soon as we're back upstairs. There's no signal down here."

He pulled out his camera and took pictures of the body and the surrounding area, and then he and Cassidy carefully turned the body over. According to his expression, he'd left this world in shock. Wide green eyes stared up at us and his mouth was open as if to scream. It didn't take an ME to spot the bullet hole in the middle of his chest.

"Small caliber," I said.

Carter nodded. "Looks like a nine-millimeter."

"Which means it could be one of ten bazillion people," I said.

"I'd put him at midtwenties," Cassidy said.

I nodded. "Six foot even. About a hundred eighty pounds. Scar on right elbow suggests surgery for compound fracture in the last couple years. That and the fact that he's got two broken fingers that healed incorrectly on his right hand lower the threat level, but I can't give you a completely accurate assessment without seeing his muscle tone."

Cassidy stared at me.

"It's sort of this thing I do—you know, to size up a target," I said.

"That's either impressive or scary. I'll let you know when I figure out which," she said.

"I don't recognize him," Carter said.

"I don't suppose we could get lucky enough to find a wallet in his pajamas," I said.

Carter pulled the gown to the side and a pair of grungy blue jeans and T-shirt emerged from underneath. He checked the pockets then shook his head.

"I need to get the forensics team down here," he said.

"I guess people don't carry ID around when they're committing crimes, right?" Cassidy asked.

"You'd be surprised," Carter said. "But I doubt we'll have to wait long. Given how he died and what he was doing when he died, I'd say there's a way better than average chance that his prints are on file. Let's head upstairs and I'll call this in."

We headed back to the library and filled Ida Belle and Gertie in on the situation below. Carter pulled out his phone and showed them pictures of the intruder.

"I've never seen him before," Ida Belle said.

"Me either," Gertie agreed.

"Time of death is probably the night Cassidy fell, which tracks with what she saw that night," Carter said.

"But it also means there were at least three people working this," I said. "The question is why did this one take a bullet? Was it a fallout between conspirators or were they competitors?"

"Good questions," Carter said and blew out a breath. "I don't like this turn of events. This has gone from a suspected burglary attempt to murder. Cassidy, I think it's time you and Harrison considered moving out for a bit. You have plenty of options for places to stay, and all of us are happy to have you."

Cassidy bit her lower lip and I could tell she was conflicted.

"But if we leave, we're just making it that much easier for these people to find what they want and disappear," she said. "I think if you'd asked me before Fortune found the body, I might have said fine, just let them find whatever and go. But now that I know someone died, it feels like I would be letting them win."

"I'll stay," I said.

Carter shook his head.

"Before you start," I said, "you know she's right. And don't tell me it doesn't irk you as much as it does me to think these people might get away with murdering this guy and causing Cassidy's fall, which could have turned out way worse than it did. If it was your home, we'd have to blast you out of there with Gertie's purse."

Cassidy gave Gertie a nervous glance.

"You know that's the truth," I pressed.

"I could declare the entire house a crime scene and then no one could legally be inside," he said.

Gertie snorted. "Yeah, because the law was a deterrent for whoever these people are. All the law does is keep the honest people from doing illegal things."

We all stared at her.

"I mean the bad kind of illegal things," Gertie said. "Not the kind of illegal things we do. We only break the law to help people. Well, and maybe to have some fun."

"Good luck evicting a former CIA operative from his own

home," I said. "I don't care if you are technically his boss. You know how that would go."

Carter sighed. "Fine. But no one is staying here alone. If there's not at least two loaded guns walking this place, then you all have to leave."

"Surely they won't be coming back after this," Cassidy said. "If they're watching the house—which they have to be, right—then they'll know we found the body."

"Whether they're watching or not, you don't have to worry about that one getting around," Gertie said. "A body in this house will be big news. Before the paramedics get to the ME's office, half the parish will know about it."

"So no way they'd risk it, right?" Cassidy said.

"You wouldn't think so," I said.

But I didn't believe it.

"I need to call the ME and get a team out here," Carter said. "I'm sorry about all this, Cassidy."

She shook her head. "It's necessary. At least now I know I didn't see a ghost walk into the bayou that night. He must have waited until he saw me looking out the window, then walked into the bayou to scare me."

Ida Belle nodded. "I would appreciate the cleverness if not for the purpose."

"I'm going to check the camera footage while we're waiting," I said. "Maybe we'll luck out and have a good image of our visitor tonight. Once the victim is identified, we might be able to match our other ghost as a known associate."

I collected the cards from all the cameras and started queuing them up on my laptop. Carter returned in time to help me scan them, but the one from the bedroom next to mine was the only one that got a somewhat decent capture of the ghostly intruder. Still, with only the light from the hallway coming into the bedroom, the capture was dim and a little blurred.

"There's no point in checking anything after the lights went out," I said. "So this is all we have to work with."

"Can it be cleaned up?" Ida Belle asked.

"Maybe," Carter said. "I'll see what our tech guys can do. Do you think this is a woman or another man with a wig?"

I shook my head. "Hard to say. This one is shorter than the other, but that's no indicator. Could be a smaller man. Could be a woman who doesn't have a chest large enough to push out the nightgown. I didn't catch anything in gait that indicated one way or the other, but then, I didn't get to see a lot before we went dark."

"Does anything about her look familiar to anyone?" Carter asked.

We all shook our heads.

"It would be hard to come up with a particular person from just this," Ida Belle said. "And they're probably wearing a wig, right, since the hair looks a lot like what the dead guy was wearing."

"These people have taken some creative risks to search this house."

"I wish we knew what they were after," Cassidy said.

"Something worth dying for," I said.

———

THE SUN WAS ALREADY UP BY THE TIME THE FORENSICS TEAM finished and headed out. The body had been removed some hours before and Carter had already elicited a promise from the ME to head in early and attempt to identify the man and call Carter immediately if he got a hit. We'd gotten permission from the ME to move the body upstairs after the scene had been documented.

Carter didn't worry about the forensics team gossiping because they knew what that could do to a homicide investigation, but he didn't trust the paramedics to not blab about the tunnels over a beer with friends. The last thing we needed was alerting the world that there were alternate entrances to the house, so they'd moved the body into the house and placed it in the entry for pickup.

They'd had a rough go of it finding evidence in the tunnels but had finally located other blood spatter that they deemed would have been the intruder's and he would have been moving at a rapid pace given the spread. The drops started midway between the tunnel entrance in the woods and the room where he was found, causing us to believe he'd been shot somewhere around the exit in the woods and had retreated back to the house and hidden in the room, maybe hoping the killer would assume he'd gotten away and leave. But he'd died before he could make a run for it.

Cassidy had called Harrison and put him on speaker so we could all fill him in. It was a conversation full of interruptions and the kind of exclamations you'd expect from a former CIA operative, but he finally got it all and promised to be on the first flight out of DC as soon as he wrapped up his business.

He also supported our plan of remaining in the house, as I figured he would, but also voiced his concerns, as Carter had. Carter had promised to hang out there when he wasn't on call, and I had assured him that if the situation changed and warranted more firepower, I had no doubt that Mannie would be willing to help out.

Ida Belle, Gertie, and I were going to go home long enough to pack up some more clothes and other supplies, and for Gertie and me to get the glitter out of our scalps. Then we'd be official residents for as long as necessary. Ida Belle was going to keep Rambo with us since he'd proven to have both a stellar nose and ears, and an uncanny ability to determine what was a smell or sound worth alerting over and what wasn't. I'm sure Walter was as thrilled about our new residency as Carter, but they both knew there was no changing our minds.

Carter stayed with Cassidy while we collected our stuff and picked up some necessary staples at Ally's bakery, the General Store, and the liquor store up the highway. Walter supplied us with the hardware needed to shore up all the entries to the house and a lock for the breaker box, and we headed back to the house with the back of Ida Belle's SUV piled high. Cassidy took one look inside the vehicle and blinked.

"I think there's more in here than Harrison and I brought from DC," she said.

"It's just the necessities," Gertie said.

Carter laughed. "Boxes from Ally's bakery, cases of beer, and at least four bags of chips. What's in the black case?"

I stared at him. "Do you *really* want to know?"

He thought for a second, then shook his head and walked off.

"What's in the black case?" Cassidy asked.

I grinned. "More alcohol and ammunition. There was a sale."

Cassidy laughed. "My favorite word."

We made quick work of the unloading and were having croissants and coffee when the ME called. It was a quick conversation with just a 'great' and a 'thanks' and then Carter disconnected and accessed his email.

"Our perp was in the system," he said.

I leaned over as he opened a file.

"If he's both the burglar and the guy who got shot, is he a perp or a victim?" Gertie asked.

"Technically both, but I'm labeling based on why he's dead," Carter said. "Since he was likely killed during the commission of a crime, then he's the perp. It's not like he got caught in random cross fire while accidentally being in someone else's house, dressed like a ghost."

"Hey, things happen," Gertie said and I had to smile.

"Our perp's name is Elijah Charitte," Carter said. "He's from New Orleans and is a frequent flier with the local PD. Theft, assault, drugs, and the usual assortment of stuff on the more minor side of crime."

"Hence why he has the opportunity to die in my house instead of being in jail," Cassidy said drily.

Carter nodded. "There's nothing here that suggests he's overly violent. The assaults were the bar-fighting type, not part of the theft stuff and never a domestic situation."

"Well, then we'll have to assume that whoever he got mixed up with on this was far more serious about violence," I said. "Any known associates?"

"There's a couple names here," he said. "I'll run them and see what I come up with. If you guys are good, I'm going to head out. I need to figure out next of kin and get access to Mr. Charitte's residence, assuming it's still the one on his license. The three of you are staying put, right? This is an official murder investigation now. I don't want your name showing up in a case file again. The ADA is already tired of seeing it."

"Umm," I said. "Let us know if you find something out."

He headed off and Ida Belle looked over at me. "Are we really going to sit here all day while he checks out the perp?"

"Of course not," I said. "I want to talk to the other real estate agent and see if Elijah ever inquired about the house. And we need to come up with a pic for him. For all we know, he might have been the guy Travis showed around."

"I thought Travis said the name was Matthew or Mark or something along those lines," Gertie said.

Ida Belle shrugged. "We're talking about Travis here, and since the first two names that came to mind were both biblical and Elijah is as well, it could very well be that Elijah is the customer he can't remember."

"In Travis's world, that makes perfect sense," Gertie said.

I nodded. "Don't worry about things here, Cassidy. We're not going to leave you here without coverage. I'm going to call Mannie."

"I don't want to bother him," Cassidy said. "He's already got a job and it's not serving as my bodyguard."

"He's the perfect person to shore up the tunnels and do a sweep of the house to make sure there's nothing we missed," I said. "We'll be here tonight, and Harrison will be back tomorrow probably, so it's not a big deal. Trust me, he'll find the entire thing an interesting break."

I called Mannie and gave him a rundown of the situation. He agreed to head out immediately. Ida Belle, Gertie, and I were just preparing to leave when my phone rang. I checked the display and my eyes widened.

Big Hebert.

I showed the display to Ida Belle and Gertie then answered.

"Mr. Hebert? What can I do for you?"

"No Mr. Hebert stuff. It's Big for family."

"I appreciate that, sir."

"Mannie has filled me in on the situation with your friends. I understand they've purchased the Leroux estate."

"That's correct."

"That's an interesting property with a questionable history. I considered purchasing it a couple times myself but it's too remote. Anyway, he said the dead man was Elijah Charitte. I am acquainted with Mr. Charitte."

"Really? How so?"

"He was asked to exit a couple of my bars for lifting wallets."

I didn't even bother to ask if he'd called the cops because I already knew the answer.

"He's an opportunist rather than a skilled professional criminal," Big continued. "So I was surprised to hear he was involved in something with this type of scope. His reputation is more for being one who follows, not leads, and in my experience, the followers are usually not the ones who get shot. They're too useful to the ones above them because they take orders without question and are expendable when a scapegoat is needed."

"That's a good point."

"I also have a potential avenue of investigation for you. A retail tenant of mine in the French Quarter is Destiny Charitte. She has a voodoo shop called Enlighten that's been in the family for decades—in fact, her great-grandfather was Arcade Charitte, Lovelie Leroux's father. Historically, she's been an excellent tenant, just as her mother and grandfather were, but the last two months, she's been behind on the rent."

"Holy crap! That's a fantastic lead. We were just about to walk out the door and I know exactly where we're going."

"I feel the need to advise you to be careful with this. Many mock the paranormal and presume things like voodoo are all in the minds of others, but there are far more things unexplained on this earth than we have an answer for. Don't underestimate the unknown. And if you need anything, I'm always available."

I thanked him and disconnected, then filled the others in on what he'd said. They were as blown away by the potential connection between the house and the perp as I was.

"Are you going to tell Carter?" Cassidy asked.

"Not until after we talk to Destiny," I said. "We don't know for certain that they're related."

"But in order to find out, you're going to have to tell her..." Cassidy's voice trailed off.

"Yes," I said. "But if Elijah and Destiny are family, she's not likely to talk to the cops, unless she *really* doesn't like him."

Ida Belle nodded. "People are far more forthcoming with us than they are with law enforcement. If Carter gets to her first, she's likely to clam up for good, especially if she has any idea what he was up to."

"But if she knew, then she'd lie about it to you too, right?" Cassidy asked.

"Maybe," Gertie said. "But Fortune can usually tell when people are lying. Only the best get by her."

Cassidy nodded. "Ben is the same way. I guess the CIA trains you guys that way."

"More like the CIA recognizes the inherent ability in some agents and uses it for their own benefit," I said. "But they do help refine it. Anyway, we better take off before Carter runs down Destiny and ruins our investigation."

Cassidy laughed. "I'm sorry, but the irony is just overwhelming. I thought Ben was exaggerating when he talked about your complete disdain for the rules, but he might have actually sold it short."

"That's why I'm a PI and not a cop," I said. "The rules often get in the way of progress."

"The CIA had rules," Cassidy said.

I grinned. "But like me, they preferred results."

CHAPTER FIFTEEN

ENLIGHTEN WAS LOCATED IN A LESS-TRAVELED AREA OF THE French Quarter but then, I supposed the shop wasn't exactly an impulse buy kind of place. I hadn't been able to locate a website for it, so I presumed Destiny was serious about her offerings and not looking to bilk tourists on some trinkets. As soon as I walked in the shop, I could see that was the case.

The shelves all contained clearly labeled bottles of powders and liquids and looked more like an apothecary than a retail shop. There were no T-shirts or shot glasses. Just objects and ingredients that I presumed were used for voodoo practices.

I'd deviated from our norm on this round of questioning because I had no idea if Destiny was related to Elijah, was part of what he was up to, or was the one who shot him. So Ida Belle went in with me, to enforce the 'I'm not a cop' thing. Gertie, who had done more reading on the whole voodoo thing, was going to wait outside and go into the shop right after we left posing as a patron and see if my conversation prompted Destiny to make a phone call or talk to someone else inside about what I'd said. With any luck, she could pick up on something helpful.

A bell above the door rang when we walked in, but no one was in the front of the store. I sent a quick text to Gertie telling her there was a doorbell and to position herself nearby, then stepped closer to a shelf to determine what kind of bones occupied a glass container. I had just decided it was chicken bones when a woman emerged from the back of the shop.

Midthirties. Five foot seven. A hundred forty pounds. Good muscle tone. No obvious injuries. Threat level probably still low unless this voodoo stuff worked or she was the one shooting people.

She gave us a curious look as I imagined we weren't her usual customers. "Can I help you ladies?"

"Maybe," I said. "Are you Destiny Charitte?"

She frowned, obviously picking up on the fact that this wasn't a normal shopping visit.

"What's this about?" she asked.

"Do you know an Elijah Charitte?" I asked.

She glanced at Ida Belle again, then back at me, clearly confused. "You're not cops," she said, making a statement rather than asking a question.

"No," I said.

Her expression flickered with aggravation. "Then what has my worthless cousin done now—scammed this lady out of money?"

"He died in our friend's house," I said.

She stared at me for several seconds, then blinked. "He what?"

"He was found dead in our friend's house," I said.

"But how...was there an accident?"

"No," I said. "I'm sorry to tell you but he was shot."

Her eyes widened. "Did your friend..."

"My friend is not the one who shot him, but Elijah *had* broken in."

She shook her head. "So you're saying my cousin broke into

your friend's home and someone other than your friend killed him and then...left?"

"That's correct. And unfortunately, that's all we know. But I was hoping you could help us figure out why he was there in the first place, which might help with finding who shot him."

"Me? I run a legitimate business. I've never been in trouble with the law and am the last person Elijah would have confided in about committing a crime. We're not close. Haven't been since we were kids when he came to live with my family after his father passed."

"Can I ask why?

She shrugged. "He had issues even then, as one would expect, but no matter what my parents did, he insisted on causing trouble. He carried that into adulthood, never bothering to grow up or take responsibility. The only time I ever heard from him is when he needed money and when I started refusing to help, he stopped calling."

"Then maybe you can help with some background information on the house," I said. "My friends bought the Leroux estate."

She sucked in a breath. "Elijah was killed in the Leroux house? That's bad mojo. Really bad."

"Why is that?" I asked.

"Lovelie was a powerful priestess who was shunned by her father, my great-grandfather. She put a hex on our family, forbidding us to enter her home."

"Or else?" I asked.

"Bad things would happen," she said. "Elijah knew better than to set foot in that house. Lovelie won't tolerate a traitor in her midst."

I stared, starting to wonder about her sanity. "You think Lovelie is still alive and killed Elijah?"

"I think she killed Elijah. She doesn't have to be alive to do it."

"But he was shot," Ida Belle said.

"If Lovelie wanted it, she could make it so, especially in her own domain," Destiny said. "She didn't have to pull the trigger for it to happen."

"Well, there's a new angle on murder," I said. "But I'm not sure how the DA is going to get a conviction on a dead woman."

"Prison time is going to be a bear as well," Ida Belle said.

"You mock what you don't understand," Destiny said. "That house is cursed. The man who built it was evil and he pulled a young, impressionable woman into the mire with him. Her father tried to warn them both that such a pairing could never work and that Lovelie needed to be with her family—people who understood what she was."

"So you're saying Lucien corrupted Lovelie and turned her to the dark side of the arts?" I asked.

"When great power courses through someone, there is always an internal war," Destiny said. "It takes an enormously strong person to fight the constant pull of the other side. Family keeps those specially blessed from lapsing away from sanity. Lucien, being an immoral man, fed that insanity until Lovelie paid the ultimate price. When morals are compromised while the evil self has control, the good self can't live afterward with the things that were done."

"And that's why she killed herself?" I asked.

"Yes. The power requires us to be always vigilant, always respectful. Deviating from the path is dangerous. It takes only a small amount of evil in your midst to infect the whole."

"What about Celine?" I asked. "Was she powerful like her mother?"

"My guess is yes, but no one knows for certain," Destiny said. "She was only seen once outside of the estate before she vanished. There were rumors, of course, but nothing was documented that I'm aware of."

"What do you think happened to her?" I asked.

"I think the evil that now dwells in that house took her away like it did her mother. Like it did Elijah."

"You said Elijah came to live with you after his father passed. What about his mother?"

"His mother was never part of his life. My uncle was a university teacher and was indiscreet with a foreign exchange student. She hid the pregnancy from her parents and returned to Europe shortly after giving birth. As far as I know, my uncle never heard from her again."

"Assuming Elijah grew up with the same teachings about the house and its history that you did, why would he risk going in there?"

She frowned. "I don't know."

"Did Elijah have power?"

"Of course, he was family, although his power was limited by the circumstances of his birth. But Elijah was lazy and never practiced improvement or control. He thought our beliefs outdated and fanciful—the kind of thing Hollywood loves for a movie twist. He had no respect."

"So he didn't believe in all this," I said. "That would explain why he wasn't scared of the house."

She sighed. "Even knowing how Elijah was, it's still hard to accept that he could deviate so far from his upbringing. I don't doubt your words. I simply don't understand. Why that risk? That house?"

"I have to assume he was trying to steal something," I said. "Someone has been accessing their home for some time now—

even before they bought it—as there have been multiple sight-ings of intruders. But the thing is, the contents were included in the sale and there are antiques all over the house. Nothing of significant value that we're aware of, but those things don't appear to go missing. Is anything of great value contained there?"

"I don't see how. Lucien was obviously a rich man when he came here, but according to my grandfather, when Celine disappeared, a huge tax bill was owed on the estate. Even if they'd had any desire, none of my family could have covered the debt. Given that this country was already in a conflict and moving toward another war when Celine disappeared, money was scarce and the sale of the property didn't even bring enough to cover what was owed. There was one bank account in Lucien's and Celine's names, but it held less than a hundred dollars."

"Maybe all his money went into the house, the upkeep, and the servants," Ida Belle said. "I've never heard that Lucien held a job."

Destiny gave her a curious look.

"I'm from Sinful," Ida Belle explained. "My mother talked about the Leroux estate some, but I was too young to be part of the gossip when it was actually happening. So anything I heard was second- and thirdhand and a lot of years later."

Destiny nodded. "Yes. All that I've heard about Lucien, Lovelie, and Celine has been passed down through stories, but most lacked substance. The truth is, no one knows what happened to Lovelie after she left New Orleans. All we have to fill in the blanks is speculation. But really, what does it matter all these years later?"

"It didn't matter, until Elijah turned up dead in the house," I said. "And given his relationship to the original owners, I can't believe that his presence there was random."

She frowned. "No. I agree that it would be too much of a coincidence. At one time, I would have said it impossible that Elijah would have lapsed so far as to enter that evil place. Ultimately, his disrespect was his end. Can you tell me what will be done with his body?"

"The ME has it now," I said. "Since it's a murder investigation, the cops will decide when it's okay to release it. You should contact Deputy Carter LeBlanc at the Sheriff's Department in Sinful. He's handling the case. Do your parents and your grandfather still live here?"

She shook her head. "My grandfather passed about ten years ago, and my parents located family in Haiti several years ago and after visiting, decided to move back to their roots. They love the simpler life they have there, where our beliefs are a daily way of life and properly respected. This will hurt them even though Elijah's choices were not their fault. I expect they'll have some harsh words for me as well."

"Why is that?" Ida Belle asked.

"As the eldest, it's my responsibility to be the spiritual guide for the family here."

"Do you know where Elijah lived?" I asked. "Or know any of his friends? Maybe someone who was around him more recently would have an idea what he was doing."

"My cousin moved around a lot because he had a problem keeping up with rent. I know because I bailed him out a few times before I realized it would never end. I don't know where he was living now. As for friends, he didn't have what I would call real friends. He had people rotating in and out of his life who were like him—trying to see what they could get for the least amount of effort. But if it's as you think, and Elijah thought there was money to be had, he would never have told the kind of people he hung out with."

"Is there any place he frequented?" I asked.

"He used to spend too much time in a dive bar in the Ninth Ward—Ruby's...Rudy's...something like that. But it's not the sort of place I'd recommend you enter. If you'll excuse me, I need to contact the deputy, then break this news to my sister and my parents. Thank you for coming to tell me."

"We're sorry for your loss," I said.

She gave me a nod and headed toward the door at the back of the store. Ida Belle and I exited the shop, and Gertie slipped inside while we had the door open so the chime wouldn't go off again. Ida Belle and I headed for her SUV to wait on Gertie.

"What do you think?" Ida Belle asked. "She seemed surprised—granted more about the location than that Elijah was dead. But then, given his criminal history, that makes sense. Sooner or later, things go south for repeat offenders."

"I don't know what to think. She claims no knowledge of what happened to Lovelie after she left New Orleans, but if that's true, then how does she know Lovelie put a curse on the family to keep them from setting foot in the house?"

"Probably stories told around the campfire—so to speak—and usually told by parents to scare kids into not doing foolish things."

"Maybe. But she's holding something back."

"I'm guessing a lot of something given Elijah's rap sheet. That's just the times he got caught. Doesn't mean she knew what he was up to this time, although she could probably make a better guess than we could. The bottom line is he had to be there looking for something, and he wasn't alone. You think they're looking for Lucien's missing fortune, figuring he hid it somewhere in the house?"

"It doesn't sound like he had a fortune to hide," I said. "I mean, why not pay the tax bills? He had to know he was at risk of losing the house, and his daughter still lived there with him. Surely he wouldn't want them homeless."

"Maybe his riches were exaggerated. Maybe he spent it all on trying to make Lovelie happy. That house had to have cost a fortune, and while hired help was cheap back then, comparatively, a whole staff wouldn't have been. But unless Elijah and the person who broke in last night are looking to tap into that evil Destiny thinks is there and summon a demon or something along those lines, they're looking for something. And it has to be big if things have gotten around to murder."

"I agree. I just wish we had a clue as to what it is."

"When you're talking about mostly recluses from so long ago that most everyone who associated with them is dead now, it definitely ups the difficulty level. We need to keep looking for Clotilde Bassett. Verna Warner is off with some senior adult tour group traipsing across Scotland. I left a message asking what facility her aunt was in, but who knows when I'll hear back, and that's assuming Mary isn't confused or just outright wrong."

"That's definitely a possibility." I motioned toward the shop. "Here she comes."

"Good God, she's got a bag. I'm not allowing her in my truck with some hex potion or whatever else she's decided to carry out of there."

As soon as Gertie opened the door, Ida Belle turned around. "Identify the contents of that bag before getting into my vehicle."

"I thought you didn't believe in this stuff," Gertie taunted as she climbed inside.

"I believe in the smell," Ida Belle said.

"Relax, it's just some bath salts for sleeping."

"You almost drowned last week when you fell asleep in your bath," Ida Belle said.

"That was a fluke," Gertie said. "I'd had pasta, wine, and extra sexy dessert with Jeb. I was wiped out. Anyway, I could hardly go into the shop for no reason and since old people are always complaining about how they can't sleep, it seemed as good an excuse as any."

"I'm surprised she didn't tell you to head down the road to the drugstore and get something commercial," I said.

"She gave me kind of a curious look, but I insisted that my rich friend's maid had sworn by salts she'd gotten at Destiny's store. She must have bought it because I got a bag. I have to say though, it does smell kinda odd. I have no idea why it would be considered soothing."

"I knew it," Ida Belle said. "As soon as we get around the corner, you're throwing that away."

"It cost me twenty bucks," Gertie said.

"It's a business expense," I said. "I'll reimburse you. So did you get anything worth buying stinky bath salts?"

"She called someone right after you left. I could only hear one side of the conversation, of course, but she told the person that Elijah was dead and where he'd died. She said it better not be about the jewels. Then she said something about needing to purify the body before burial, otherwise the family wouldn't be protected from the evil his body had brought away from the house. Then she turned around and caught sight of me and hung up."

"Jewels?" Ida Belle said. "That's one that hadn't come to mind. I don't recall anyone ever mentioning jewelry in relation to the family."

"Me either," Gertie agreed. "But if Lucien was catering to Lovelie and was rich at the time they ran off together, then he might have bought her some pretty pieces as gifts."

"But surely they would be long gone by now," Ida Belle said.

I nodded. "One would think he would have sold them to

pay bills. But still, it must be something the family was told, or she wouldn't have mentioned it to whoever she called."

"You were right about her holding something back," Ida Belle said and sighed. "I really wish we could find Clotilde. She might be able to explain some of this."

"Assuming she's still alive and has her right mind," Gertie said. "She and Mary would have to be about the same age, and you saw how that one went."

"Well, if she's in a senior facility, at least she won't be armed," I said.

"You say that, but have you ever been hit by one of those toilet seat risers?" Gertie asked.

I stared. "Of course not."

Gertie waved a hand in dismissal and I wasn't even going to ask.

"That Destiny is a strange one though," Gertie said. "You should have heard her tone when she was talking about purification and evil. She really believes all that."

"I agree," I said. "She was clearly upset that Elijah was in the house."

I told Gertie about our conversation with her.

"Sounds like Elijah went the opposite direction of the way he was brought up," Gertie said. "But he wouldn't be the first to lose his raising over money."

"I think it's time to tackle the attic," Ida Belle said. "Or maybe the library. If there are written records anywhere about the Leroux and this jewelry, they might be in one of those places."

I nodded. "We'll formulate a plan with Cassidy as soon as we get back to the house. In the meantime, let's go see if we can find that Realtor."

"Do you want to call ahead for an appointment?" Ida Belle asked.

"No. I don't want her to waste time pulling listings before we get there, and I don't want to tip her off to our real reason for being there. Let's just head over and hope we catch her in the office. If not, we'll make an appointment while we're there."

"On it."

CHAPTER SIXTEEN

DUVAL REAL ESTATE WAS IN THE FRENCH QUARTER, NOT too far from the voodoo shop. It was a short drive over and there was a handy parking lot just a couple buildings down from the office. Ida Belle told Gertie to toss the stinky bath salts in the trash bin, but I saw her slip them into her purse while pretending to throw them away. As long as they weren't flammable, they probably weren't going to hurt anything, so I let it slide. We headed inside and a perky young woman greeted us with an enormous fake smile.

"Do you have an appointment?" she asked.

"No," I said. "We just happened to be in town for another issue and wondered if by chance Karmin Blay is available to chat with us for a few minutes."

The receptionist checked her computer screen and nodded. "Ms. Blay isn't due to leave for another twenty minutes or so. May I get your name and your area of interest?"

"My name is Fortune Redding, and I'm interested in a house listing of hers."

I could tell she was somewhat irritated at my vague

response on the house but I didn't care. The statement I'd made was true and covered everything she needed to know.

"Ms. Blay can speak with you," she said when she hung up the phone. "Down the hall, second office on the left."

The office door was open, and a woman behind the desk rose as she saw us and waved us in before extending her hand across the desk toward me.

Midtwenties. Five foot seven. A hundred twenty-five pounds. Really nice muscle tone—some was genetics, but the rest was a stellar gym commitment. A curious smile and shrewd eyes. Threat level low unless I wanted her to sell my house and really needed the money.

"I'm Karmin," she said as we shook. "It's nice to meet you. Please sit."

We all sat in front of her desk and she gave us that big, fake Realtor smile. "So you're interested in one of my listings?"

"Not exactly," I said. "I'm hoping to get some information on one of your former listings."

"Oh, well, I can still represent you as the buyer as long as the home is still for sale," she said.

"Friends of mine just bought the house—the Leroux estate."

"I don't understand," she said. "If your friends just bought the house, how can I help you?"

"There's been some issues at the property and since you had the listing before my friends purchased the home, I wanted to see if you had any history on it."

She frowned. "What kind of issues?"

"Intruders," I said. "And then last night, we found a body."

"Oh my God!" She sat straight up, her eyes wide. "You're not...you're serious?"

"I'm afraid so, and my friends are rightfully concerned."

"Of course! That's horrible."

"We have reason to believe the man was a burglar. When

you had the listing, did you ever notice things missing from the home? Or see anyone on the grounds?"

She glanced around, clearly nervous, then shook her head. "I never noticed anything missing, but then, I probably wouldn't have. I only went in twice—once to take measurements and pictures and then another time to put my lockbox on the front door."

"And you never saw anything strange?"

She hesitated, seeming to be contemplating her next words, then sighed. "Look, I dropped the ball on the listing. I never got it online and my boss is super mad at me over losing the sale. But the truth is the place gave me the creeps. I didn't want to show it, so I just kept putting things off. Then the estate fired us for nonperformance and the property sold right after, so I've been in the doghouse ever since."

"Why did it give you the creeps?"

"You'll think I'm crazy."

"Try me."

"I saw a...well, a ghost. It was when I was taking pictures. She went across the walkway upstairs."

"Did you call the cops?"

"No. I was afraid they wouldn't believe me, and if I'd gotten the cops involved with a listing, I'd probably have been fired. We have to disclose things like police investigations, especially if they're currently taking place."

"Did you try to find the ghost?"

"No way! I grabbed my purse and hauled butt out of there. I had already started my car when I realized I hadn't locked the front door. I dropped the keys twice trying to get it done."

"But if you didn't go look, how do you know it was a ghost and not a burglar?"

"First off, there was no sound. Who walks with no sound? And she was wearing this long white gown. I've been in New

Orleans all my life, and I've heard some weird things, but I've never heard of a burglar wearing a gown."

"The upstairs landing is carpeted," I said. "And the dead guy was wearing a gown and a wig."

"Oh my God," she whispered. "What if he'd come after me? I thought... Well, you know the rumors. And then there was the fact that it was so dark inside because the power wasn't on and it's in the middle of nowhere."

"Do you carry a gun?"

"What? No. I carry Mace. I guess I *should* carry one, and after this, I'll be looking into it. Why do you ask?"

"Because the man was shot at close range."

Her eyes widened. "He was murdered? I didn't think... when you said there was a body, I thought it was a fall or an OD by a squatter or something."

"The man's name was Elijah Charitte. Does that name sound familiar?"

"No. Should it?"

"I thought he might have been hired to make repairs or something else along those lines. Something that would explain why he had access to the house."

"The house was being sold as is, so any repairs would have been on the new owner. The estate had a company that went through it periodically and made critical repairs, but I don't know who those people were. I don't understand any of this."

"I don't either and neither do my friends, which is why I'm trying to run down information on the house, because while the squatter theory is nice, the house is really too remote to tempt them."

"Right. That makes sense. I wish I could tell you something to help, but I don't know anything else. The most recent owners died years ago, and the estate is who hired us. But I don't think anyone from the law office handling the estate has ever been there. They're in New Jersey."

"And you never showed the house?"

She shook her head. "But then, it's hard to get interest in a place you don't even have listed for sale. And with that location, the house isn't going to pull drive-by traffic."

I rose from my chair. "Thank you for your time."

"No problem," she said. "I wish I could have helped."

We headed out and climbed into Ida Belle's SUV.

"Wait here for a minute," I said. "The receptionist said Karmin had to leave for an appointment in twenty minutes."

"You picked up on something," Ida Belle said.

"Let's just say I find her story somewhat odd," I said. "She sees a woman upstairs and flees. I get that much, but why not call the cops and report an intruder?"

"Sounds like she was more afraid of her boss than the ghost," Gertie said.

"But she didn't put up the listing and lost the sale," Ida Belle said. "If she was that afraid of her boss, she would have gotten it done."

"Those two things seem to oppose each other," Gertie said.

"Exactly," I said. "I mean, maybe she was looking for another job and hoping to avoid the house until she bounced. Or maybe she kept making excuses in order to avoid doing it and her boss bought them until they lost the listing. Or maybe she's just incompetent and silly and I'm reaching."

"She did seem genuinely shocked when you told her about the body," Ida Belle said.

"And even more when you said it was murder," Gertie said.

I sighed. "Maybe I'm losing my touch."

"Why would you say that?" Gertie asked.

"Because we've questioned two people today and I couldn't tell if either was outright lying."

"I think some people are just far better at it than others," Ida Belle said. "And then some are so invested in dishonesty that the lies become their truth."

Gertie nodded. "I'm afraid the ability for people to lie without indication is becoming more common as conscience seems to be on the decline."

"Here she comes," Ida Belle said and pointed.

Karmin exited the building and headed our direction. We all ducked down and I peered over the dash as she got into a sleek Mercedes convertible with the top down and drove off. Ida Belle immediately set off after her.

"Good Lord, she drives faster than me," Ida Belle said as we squealed around a corner, trying to keep up with the speeding Mercedes.

Gertie rolled across the back seat and wound up upside down with her feet up on the window.

"Seat belt!" Ida Belle yelled as we made another hard turn in the other direction.

I heard bumping in the back seat again and a couple seconds later, Gertie said, "Well, at least I'm back in my seat."

"Where is she?" Ida Belle said.

I scanned the street, but there was no sign of the Mercedes. Then as we passed a delivery van, I saw it tucked behind in a parking space on the street.

"There!" I said.

Ida Belle whipped into a space a couple cars down and we watched as Karmin finished applying her lipstick, then jumped out and hurried into an expensive-looking restaurant.

"Looks ritzy," Gertie said.

Ida Belle nodded. "I don't think the odds are good on us getting in there. Not dressed like this."

"It wouldn't be smart to try," I said. "It looks like a small place. She'd see us."

"Jackpot!" Gertie yelled, and Ida Belle and I both glared.

"Look!" Gertie pointed to a terrace on the second floor where Karmin had just walked out and was approaching a table where an elegant-looking woman sat.

Karmin gave the woman a big fake smile as she approached and I saw the woman's lips start to turn down before she caught herself and forced the same big smile.

"Looks like they're related," Ida Belle said. "I'm going with her mother based on the similarities."

"And the fake smiles," I said. "Doesn't look like either of them is thrilled to be eating lunch together."

"Can you see what they're saying?" Gertie asked.

I pulled my small binoculars from the glove box and trained them on the two women. It was a sideways view and looking up, so not the best angle, but I could still make out some of what they were saying.

"The mother said something about expectations and charity," I said. "And something about embarrassing her and her familial responsibilities. Then she said Mercedes."

"And there she goes," Ida Belle said as the woman rose from the chair, cast a stern look at Karmin, then left without another word.

The server returned with a glass of wine and Karmin downed it and put the glass back on his tray along with some bills. Then she left.

"That went well," I said.

"That looked like every conversation I had with my mother," Gertie said. "Except she wasn't snooty. But that exasperated and disappointed expression is one I know well."

Ida Belle nodded. "Looks like Karmin is not living up to family standard, and that standard appears to be high. I'm no diva but the Mercedes, haircut, manicure, clothes, jewelry...it all looks well beyond middle class."

"Maybe Karmin's not so great at working because she's never had to," Gertie said.

"Sounds about right," Ida Belle said. "Do you want me to try to follow her again?"

I shook my head. "Karmin's problems with her mother don't forward our case any, and I don't think there's anything else to get from her. Let's try that bar that Elijah used to frequent."

"The one Destiny said we shouldn't go to?" Ida Belle asked, one eyebrow raised.

I laughed. "If Destiny knew us, she'd be calling to warn the bar."

———

DESTINY HADN'T UNDERSOLD THE SHADINESS OF THE BAR. I'd witnessed four crimes in process on the street before we'd even parked. I really hoped no one attempted to mess with Ida Belle's vehicle while we were inside because it wouldn't end well for the other guy. When we climbed out of the SUV, everyone nearby stopped what they were doing and stared. I'd seen people eyeing the vehicle and figured with the dark tint on the windows, they thought it was cops, but then when they got eyes on us, it was apparent that no one knew what to think.

The low talking started as we made our way to the bar. I could hear the music cranked up inside but the people were even louder. Given that it was early afternoon on a weekday, I wasn't sure what to extrapolate from that. I said a silent prayer that no one started trouble with us and opened the door. As we stepped inside, the voices faded away and we were left with music blaring from a set of crappy speakers.

I ignored everyone and headed for the counter. The bartender eyed us suspiciously as he made his way over.

Fortyish. Six foot two. Two hundred sixty pounds—a lot of it in his gut. This man had been drinking too much of the profits. No threat given that his pistol was currently wedged between his waistband and a fat roll, but the fact that he was open carrying let me know that my alert level needed to be on high.

He had just stepped in front of us when I felt an arm slide around my shoulder and one hand drop down onto my breast. I heard a sharp intake of breath, but before Gertie had even finished sucking it in, I grabbed the hand, twisted it around using only his thumb, and dropped the offender to the ground.

"You ever touch me again, and you'll have to have this arm surgically removed," I said. "Are we clear?"

He just nodded, and I pushed him over and turned back to the bar.

"Dude, you got off easy," Gertie said. "I'd take that butthurt look back to your table before you really hack her off."

A woman sitting at the bar next to Gertie lifted her bottle at me, and I thought she was going to fall off her stool with the gesture. Obviously, she'd been there a while.

"Nice," she said.

The bartender gave me the side-eye. "You a cop?"

"No."

"You just took down a guy twice your size."

"I like those Jackie Chan movies."

"Uh-huh. What do you want? Because you're not here for the booze or the company."

"Do you know Elijah Charitte?"

He frowned and appeared to be considering how to answer, which answered my question, but that didn't seem to occur to him.

"Yeah," he said finally. "Why? He owe you money?"

"Do a lot of people come in here looking to collect from him?"

"No, but then a lot of the people he owes know better than to come in here."

"Ah. They need to watch more Jackie Chan. When was the last time you saw him?"

"About a week ago, maybe. What did he do?"

"Got shot and died."

The bartender shook his head but didn't seem remotely surprised. "You shoot him?"

"I don't know who shot him, but I'd like to find out. You see, someone shot him while he was inside my friend's house—uninvited, of course—and I'd like to know what he and the person who shot him were doing there. My friends don't like finding dead people in their home."

"It's a real hassle," the woman next to me said.

I shot her a glance—probably similar to the one I used for Gertie a lot—but wasn't about to ask.

"How was Elijah paying for drinks?" I asked.

The bartender shrugged. "Don't know and I don't ask those kind of questions—especially in here." He waved a hand. "If I knew about these people's lives, the cops would have me in court 24-7 testifying."

It was a valid, albeit frustrating, point.

"Did he have any friends in here—people who might not be afraid to listen to his personal problems?"

"People in here don't have those kind of friends," the bartender said. "If Elijah was working a burglary thing with someone, I doubt it was anyone here. The people here would knife him and cut him out of the job, especially if it was remotely lucrative. These people are hard-core and only work solo. Elijah wanted everyone to think he was the same, but he was weak."

"So you're saying if he was going to partner up with someone, it would have been another amateur."

He nodded. "That would be the smart move. Not that Elijah was all that sharp, but I think he knew better than to put any job he had in mind on blast in here."

"And yet he's still dead."

"Well, there is that, but he's had the cash for drinks for a month or better, so he was working something and I can guarantee you it wasn't on the books."

"You have any idea where he lived? Maybe he had a roommate or a neighbor who could tell us something."

"I think he was renting a room at the motel down the street back several weeks ago. No idea if he was still there. But it's one of those you can do by the hour up to a month, so not the sort of place ladies want to go roaming around. Although, with your Jackie Chan thing, you might be all right."

He turned around and headed to the other side of the bar where some men were yelling for more beer, and I assumed our conversation was over.

"Had a hot one on the line," the woman next to me said.

"Excuse me?" I said.

"Elijah," she said. "He said he had a hot one on the line. Said he was going to cash out and live like a rapper."

"Did he say where this cash was coming from or who he was working with?"

She shook her head. "Nah. People don't tell Ole Brenda anything important. Can't keep a secret when the booze is doing the talking."

She started laughing.

"Well, thanks, Brenda," I said. "Let's get out of here."

"I think you should stay," a man's voice sounded behind me.

I turned around and saw the chest-grabber standing there with two other men of equal size and I was guessing equal IQ. Ida Belle leaned back against the bar and pulled a protein bar out of her pocket.

The bartender hurried over and she said, "You might want to call 911."

"Cops or ambulance?" he asked.

Ida Belle shrugged. "Depends on if they're slow learners or not."

He grabbed the phone and started dialing.

"We don't like your kind in this bar," Chest-Grabber said.

"You mean people with good hygiene and basic manners?" I asked.

Brenda started laughing and he shoved her off her stool.

"Make that the coroner," Ida Belle said to the bartender as she reached down to help Brenda back up.

I stared at him, my blood boiling. "You have a real problem touching women when you're not welcome to. Maybe someone should fix that problem."

"You think you're going to do that, little girl? You got lucky once because I wasn't ready."

"Are you ready now? I can give you a minute, but not much more because I've got things to do."

"You talk too much," he said.

Then lunged.

CHAPTER SEVENTEEN

THERE WOULD BE NO NICE GIRL THIS TIME. I GRABBED HIS outstretched arm and twisted it up behind his back, breaking his wrist and dislocating his shoulder as I went. He howled in pain and his buddies started to rush me. Gertie reached into her purse, and I prayed she didn't pull out lit dynamite or worse—pink glitter. Her hand emerged with the bag from the voodoo shop and she flung the contents in the air, where it landed right in the faces of the approaching bad guys.

They all yelled as though they'd been doused with acid, and let's face it, for people who obviously hadn't seen a bar of soap in a while, bath salts probably felt like it. They stumbled backward, clutching their faces and screaming while everyone else in the bar stood unmoving, shocked expressions on their faces.

Then all of a sudden, the crowd came out of their stupor and the entire bar emptied as if Moses had directed his people out of Egypt.

I turned Chest-Grabber loose and stepped away and he turned around, clutching his injured arm next to his stomach, his hand dangling. "You broke my arm!" he yelled as he sank into a chair.

I shrugged. "Guess you'll have to stop touching women. If you're still not clear on that, I can break the other."

I looked over at Brenda. "You good?"

"Stellar," she said. "And thank you."

I gave her a nod and turned around to face the bartender, who was still standing there, holding the phone.

"What's up with your customers?" I asked.

"Warrants," he said and put the phone down. "No big deal. I needed to restock the coolers up here anyway and I can't so much as go to pee or they steal me blind. They'll all be back tonight."

"Then I guess my work here is done," I said.

His eyes widened and he opened his mouth but before he could get a word out, Ida Belle, who was finishing up her protein bar, used her free hand to slide a beer pitcher over to me. I glanced in the mirror behind the bar and without even turning around, clocked Chest-Grabber's buddy right in the face as he ran up behind me, looking as if he was going to try a choke hold. His nose exploded and I sighed, as I really liked this T-shirt and now it was ruined. It had worn to that soft feel like you were walking around clothed in Charmin Ultra Soft.

He dropped onto the floor and didn't move. I was pretty sure he wouldn't for a while. The bartender recovered from his shock and glared at the last one standing.

"I've had about enough from you three. Get out."

"But he's out cold," the last idiot argued.

"Then drag him," the bartender said.

"I ain't got but one good arm," Chest-Grabber said.

"You got three between you and that's more than your brain cells," Ida Belle said. "I suggest you figure it out."

"What about Brenda?" I asked, as the woman was the only person left in the bar.

"She can sleep it off in one of the booths," the bartender said. "Wouldn't be the first time."

I handed him a couple hundreds. "For the mess and maybe Brenda can have a couple drinks on me."

He nodded. "Appreciate it. And what you did for Brenda. She's a nice lady...she's just lost her way. Good luck with your search, but be careful. If Elijah was tangled up in something that got him killed, he was in way over his head. It's a different sort of criminal that resorts to murder. I've seen them all in here and it's the ones without a conscience who scare the hell out of me."

I nodded and turned to leave. "Let's get out of here."

Ida Belle and I started walking off.

"I can't see the door!" Gertie yelled.

I looked back to see her stumble toward us, arms outstretched as if she were an extra in a zombie movie, and shook my head. Ida Belle grabbed one of her arms and led her out.

"You've got that stuff all over you," Ida Belle said as we hit the sidewalk. "This is why I put pet protectors on my back seat."

"I'm not your pet," Gertie groused as Ida Belle tried dusting the bath salts off her clothes.

"Heck no, you're not. Rambo is a lot better behaved."

"I have a bottle of water in my purse," Gertie said.

I dug it out, not even commenting on the fact that the stinky bag that held the bath salts was tucked in the corner. I handed it to Gertie and she poured water in her eyes and then wiped her face with her shirt, the water activating the smell of the salts.

"I kept those guys from attacking Fortune," Gertie declared as we climbed into the SUV.

"You kept those guys from a compound fracture, which I

was kind of looking forward to," Ida Belle said as she pulled away. "Now you smell like cheap perfume and dirty feet. You can't do any undercover work. People will know you're coming a mile away. And why do you always do this crap when we can't roll down the windows? Areas like this are the reason I got bulletproof glass."

"You got bulletproof glass because we get shot at a lot and because it's cool," Gertie said.

"That's not the point at the moment," Ida Belle said. "Don't you have something in that purse of yours to cover the smell?"

Gertie dug around and pulled out a roast beef sandwich and waved it in the middle of the front seats.

"Great," I said. "Now I'm hungry."

Ida Belle sighed. "*Now* my SUV smells like a Victorian hooker was feeding a men's basketball team roast beef in the locker room *after* the game. And I'm going to hard pass on anything that Gertie's been carrying in her purse."

"Then let's plan to grab something to eat after we check out the motel," I said. "Some of us were taking out the chest grabbers while others were eating protein bars."

"I prefer to stay out of the expert's way," Ida Belle said. "Unlike *some* people who have to be in the middle of everything."

Ida Belle pulled to a stop at the end of the street and I pointed across the street to a dilapidated U-shaped structure with a Vacancy sign.

"Is that it?" I asked.

"Must be," Ida Belle said. "It's the only one in the direction that bartender pointed."

"Good Lord," Gertie said. "If it wasn't for the drug dealers near the vending machine, I'd think it was abandoned."

About the time I checked out the suspected drug dealers,

one of them pulled out a gun and shot the vending machine, then reached in and pulled out a bag of chips and started eating them right there in the middle of the broken glass.

"That's an extreme case of the munchies," Gertie said as Ida Belle pulled over at the curb across the street and stopped.

"And a complete lack of concern for law enforcement," I said. "Which tells me people around here don't call the cops."

"Or they don't make much of an effort to come when called," Gertie said.

"You still want to check it out?" Ida Belle asked, giving the drug dealers the side-eye.

"Of course," I said. "But I think you two should stay in the vehicle and cover me. That looks like the office on the right side of the building. Pull up in front of it and I'll go see if Elijah had a room here."

Ida Belle pulled across the street and I could see the drug dealers checking out her vehicle as we parked. I hoped to God they didn't try anything because there was more firepower in that SUV than small countries had accumulated, and that wasn't even including what was in the purse of the loose cannon in the back seat eating a sandwich. I checked my weapon to make sure I was ready to go, told Ida Belle to leave the car running, and headed inside.

I didn't think it was possible, but the inside of the office looked even more run-down than the outside and smelled like Bourbon Street on the Wednesday after Mardi Gras. I rang the bell at the front desk and heard some movement in a back room. Finally, a woman with arms the size of an oak tree and more tattoos than I've ever seen on one person's body came out and glared at me.

Five foot eleven. Two hundred eighty pounds and a lot of muscle. Also a lot of fat, which meant she probably wasn't quick. But if she managed to get her hands on me, I had no doubt she could tear me into pieces like a grizzly bear. Threat level medium in enclosed spaces. Low as long as I had room to flee.

"You ain't looking for a room," she said.

"How do you know that?"

"Because your tennis shoes cost more than I rent here for a month. What do you want?"

"I want to know if Elijah Charitte has a room here."

"I don't talk about the people who stay here. It's better that way."

"It's also better if people don't die in my friend's house while trying to steal something, but here we are."

She raised one eyebrow. "He's dead? Robbery, huh? Your friend pop him or did he jump out a window or something?"

"Someone popped him, but it wasn't my friend. In fact, we don't know who it was or what he was stealing, but we'd like to. My friends are concerned someone else—someone more competent and who has no problem shooting people—might take up the torch."

"Sounds like your friends' problem to me."

"Going to be your problem as well if the cops find stolen property in his room, because that wasn't the first time he'd been in their house. But since my friends would prefer their items not sit in an evidence room for who knows how long, I'd like to do us both a favor and collect them before the police show up."

She studied me for several long seconds then shrugged. "Fine by me. But I doubt you'll find anything in there. If Charitte had anything of value, he'd have ditched it as soon as it hit his hands. You said the cops are coming?"

"As soon as they figure out where he was staying."

"How did you figure it out?"

"I know people. Your vending machine needs repair, by the way."

"Not my machine. Not my problem. Charitte was staying in room 124, but I ain't seen him in a while—several days at least."

"Did he have a car?"

She shook her head. "Never saw one. Had an old bicycle he rode around some. Looked like it was going to break in two it was so rusted out."

"What about friends? Anyone staying in the motel know him?"

"This isn't a friendly sort of place."

"I can see that. Do you mind giving me a key to the room?"

"Don't have a spare. Just give the door a good shove and it will come open."

"Alrighty then. Thanks for your help."

"Wasn't trying to help."

She turned around and went back into the office. I headed out and climbed back into the SUV.

"Back up in front of the room," I said and gave her the number. "I want to be able to make a quick getaway if needed."

"I'm going to be more surprised if we don't have to make a quick getaway," Ida Belle said.

She drove across the parking lot and was inching closer to where the drug dealers were when I spotted the room. I missed it at first because the door was open and someone was walking out.

Someone I recognized.

"That's Destiny!" I said.

Ida Belle sped up and pulled past the room, then whipped into the first parking space a couple cars down. We watched as Destiny climbed into an old sedan and drove off.

"What was she holding?" Gertie asked.

"Looked like a book," Ida Belle said.

I nodded. "An old leather book."

Ida Belle looked over at me. "You thinking what I'm thinking?"

"Yeah," I said. "Someone in the Charitte family *did* document things—like maybe the jewelry—and Elijah found out and decided to try to cash in."

"So Destiny lied," Gertie said. "She knew what Elijah was after."

"At least had a good idea," Ida Belle said. "She also knew where he was living."

"Or figured it out before we did," I said. "She had time to run it down while we were questioning the Realtor, and probably knew better people to ask than going to the bar."

"And she didn't think we'd go there when she tossed out the name and location," Gertie said.

"I wonder what else she knows," Ida Belle said. "I wish we could get a hold of that book."

Gertie shook her head. "Even I'm not crazy enough to try to steal what looks like an heirloom from a voodoo family."

"I wonder if she's planning on purifying it or destroying it," I said.

"Either or both," Ida Belle said. "She seemed pretty stringent about their practices."

"And more aggrieved than sad that Elijah had gotten himself killed," I said.

"Maybe not so much that as where it happened," Ida Belle said.

"Well, she beat us to the punch here," Gertie said. "You still want to look in his room?"

"Yeah. Might be something else worthwhile. Same plan—park in front of the room and you two stay put and cover me. If those two drug dealers make a move in this direction, honk and I'll get out of there."

Ida Belle pulled down the parking lot, putting some

distance between us and the drug dealers, and backed into a parking space in front of the room. There were no cars close by, so they had a good view of the dealers and would be able to see them move in enough time to get me out of there. I pulled on gloves, grabbed a screwdriver, and headed to the room door.

Sure enough, all it took was a good bump for it to pop open, which made me wonder why the person who killed Elijah hadn't done it here. I seriously doubted a murder at this motel would draw much police interest. Finding a body here was likely no big surprise and given Elijah's record and the overall sketchiness of the area, there would probably be more time spent making assumptions than actually investigating.

The room was tiny and sparse and the furniture was held together with duct tape. I'd expected run-down, but this was barely better than a cardboard box. I wondered why they were even allowed to remain open. Both the closet and the dresser were empty, and the few clothes that Elijah had were scattered on the unmade bed. Although I was loath to get down on the floor, I checked under the bed and in between the mattresses. The bathroom held only a bar of soap so I headed back into the living room and used my screwdriver to remove the return vent from the wall.

Jackpot!

There was a duffel bag stuffed in the space. So either the book Destiny left with hadn't been in the bag or she didn't care about the rest of the contents. I pulled the bag out and unzipped it, not remotely surprised by what was inside. Silver candlesticks and a couple of picture frames and several crystal globes. I had no doubt they'd come from the Leroux house.

I searched every corner of the bag and found a key in a side pocket. I pulled it out and checked the paper tag on the end. It was a Duval Real Estate tag and the address to the Leroux house was written on it. It certainly provided a much easier way into the house before Harrison changed the locks. Elijah had probably lifted the key when Karmin was there doing her measurements, which would explain her ghostly sighting and feeling creeped out. And given her fear of losing her job, I'm sure she never admitted to losing the key. Probably just had another made and moved on.

I took a couple pics of the items, then zipped the bag up and tucked it back into the vent. Finally, I screwed the cover back on. Hopefully, when the cops got around to searching the room, the bag would still be there. I was just tightening the last screw when I heard a single honk.

Not good.

Then Gertie yelled, "I got this!"

Even worse.

CHAPTER EIGHTEEN

I RAN OUT THE DOOR JUST IN TIME TO SEE GERTIE POP UP through the sunroof of the SUV and sit on the edge. Then she lifted up an AK-47 and yelled for the drug dealers coming toward us to stop where they were.

Apparently, bravery was high and IQ low in these parts. Instead of retreating, they both went for their weapons, and Gertie fired off a round right in front of them to stop their progress. Unfortunately, the recoil on the gun was too much for her precarious perch on the edge of the SUV roof, and she went tumbling backward, sending another spray of bullets into the air.

The drug dealers wised up and took off running. I ran for Gertie, who'd rolled under the SUV to avoid the bullets—because what goes up must come down—and pulled her up with one arm while grabbing the gun with the other. I shoved both into the back seat and barely got in behind her before Ida Belle tore out of the parking lot.

"Have you lost your mind?" Ida Belle swore as she blew through a stop sign at double the speed limit.

"I told them to stop before I fired," Gertie said, as if that explained everything.

"I told you to bring fireworks," I said.

"Like that's any better," Ida Belle said.

"She's never killed anyone with fireworks," I said. "It's the lesser of two evils."

"I've never killed anyone with a gun either," Gertie said. "I mean, not recently."

"It's not from lack of opportunity," I said. "Where did you get that thing? Because it does not fit in your purse."

"It was under the seat," Gertie said. "I found it when I dropped an egg roll."

"There's an egg roll under my seat?" Ida Belle asked.

"It's still winter," I said. "Worry about the egg roll later. You had an AK-47 under your back seat?"

"Yes," Ida Belle said. "And it was supposed to stay there unless *I* decided to shoot it."

"The cops are definitely coming for this one," I said. "I don't care where the hotel is located."

"Did you tell the manager your name?" Gertie asked.

"No way," I said.

"Then we're fine," Gertie said. "It's not like she's going to randomly identify you at Ally's bakery or the General Store."

Ida Belle shot her an incredulous glance before cruising through another stop sign. "I'm pretty sure her description is all Carter would need, especially when coupled with a spray of bullets by an old lady with a semiautomatic weapon, and who both fled in a black SUV with a getaway driver."

"You've got your fake plates on, right?" Gertie asked.

"I always have them on if you're going to be in my vehicle," Ida Belle said. "What does that tell you?"

"It could still be someone else," Gertie argued.

"Who?" Ida Belle asked. "Who else could it be?"

"Well, he can't prove it," Gertie said.

"He doesn't have to prove it!" Ida Belle said. "He's not trying to arrest us, but this could cause serious trouble between Carter and Fortune. You know how he feels about you carrying a weapon. If Carter had his way, you'd never leave your house."

"Until she removes that stripper pole, I don't think he wants her there, either," I said.

Ida Belle pulled onto the on-ramp for I-10 and sped up even more. "I assume our business in New Orleans is done, right?"

"Definitely," I said.

Ida Belle drove like a madwoman until we left the city limits, then she slowed to just under warp speed and looked over at me.

"After all that, did you get anything?" she asked.

I told them about the duffel bag with the key and the silver.

"He must have been stealing some easy-to-fence items while he was looking for the jewels," Ida Belle said.

"That's what I figure," I said. "And I figure he lifted the key from Karmin at some point while she was inside."

"Which also explains her seeing a ghost," Ida Belle said.

"Yeah, but it doesn't get us any closer to identifying the other two intruders," I said. "If he was working with someone, then why didn't they collect that silver and sell it?"

My phone rang and Mannie's number came up.

"Is everything all right?" I asked.

"Yeah, I'm here with Cassidy now, and we've got some information for you," he said.

"Okay, you're on speaker. Go for it."

"Cassidy showed me the tunnel system and we went out to the exit in the woods for me to assess closing it up. I told her to bring the puppy since he seems to have a real knack for picking up on scents that don't belong, and it paid off bigtime."

"That's my Rambo," Ida Belle said proudly.

"He set off into the woods so fast I was glad we had him on a long lead," Mannie said. "He picked his way through the brush and led us right to the bank where a small flat-bottom boat with a trolling motor was tied off behind some cypress tree branches."

"Anything to indicate the owner?" I asked.

"It had been stripped of anything pertinent, but I called Carter to fill him in and he found a report of a stolen boat, matching this one's description, filed in Mudbug two days ago. And there's more. There was a complaint this morning of a break-in at a camp about a half mile up the bayou from the house. The owner showed up and found a broken window and food wrappers and empty soda cans inside, along with a cell phone. It was a burner, but Carter's betting they lift Elijah's fingerprints off it."

"Elijah didn't have a car that we're aware of," I said. "I bet he was staying in that camp and using the boat to get to the tunnel access. Two people in NOLA who saw him regularly said they hadn't seen him in several days, so it tracks."

"And that would explain the creeper that Harrison saw and the one you and Carter chased," Ida Belle said.

"I agree," Mannie said. "I also got some more background on Elijah from one of the Heberts' contacts. His father didn't die from natural causes. It was suicide. He'd taken up with another student, and this one admitted to it and her parents got involved. The university fired him, and he took himself out shortly after. Doesn't really help solve our current mystery but it gives us more perspective into the things that shaped Elijah into the adult he became."

"That's a lot for a teen to cope with, that's for sure," I said. "Unfortunately, he didn't appear to be a good judge of character because this went as badly as things can go."

"Agreed. Did you find out anything useful in NOLA?"

"A few things, but nothing that helps identify the other two intruders."

"I had a thought on that one. The only information released to the public is that a body was found in the house—no indication of where he died, right?"

"Nope. Carter wanted that information withheld."

"I figured as much. So what if we don't close up the tunnels?"

"You're thinking since Elijah wasn't shot in the room where he died, the killer might not *know* where he died, therefore he doesn't know we discovered the tunnels."

"Exactly. I think we should set a trap."

"I'd love to, but I'm sure his partners, or competitors as the case may be, know we found the body. Even if they'd risk coming back, I doubt it would be so soon."

"Not with everyone in the house. But if they think we're all gone... Whatever this is about was worth coming in again last night while it was occupied. If the house is supposed to be empty..."

"Cassidy? How do you feel about that?" I asked, because after all, it was her house.

"I think we should go for it," she said. "I want this over with, and I mean completely. I don't want to be wondering who's trying to get into my house every second of the day."

"Okay. Let's wait until Harrison gets back and then come up with a plan to make it look like the house is empty."

"It shouldn't be hard to spread that around," Ida Belle said.

"A couple of well-placed comments and things circle around quickly."

"Sounds good," Mannie said. "Then I'll hold off on shoring up the accesses.

And I'm available to stand guard and help with the trap. The Heberts have cleared me for anything you need."

"I appreciate it," I said. "I think we're good for tonight. Harrison should be back, and Ida Belle, Gertie, and I will stay —assuming Cassidy is good with that—and maybe we'll be able to get everything set for an exit tomorrow."

"Got it."

He disconnected and I looked over at Ida Belle and Gertie, about to talk when my phone rang again. I looked at the display and frowned.

"Hello, Travis," I said and put him on speaker. "What can I do for you?"

"You remember I said I gave that Mac, Mark, Mike guy a tour of the Leroux house? Well, I just saw him at a strip bar in the French Quarter. I was putting a twenty right up a—"

"I get it," I interrupted.

No filter, Ida Belle mouthed.

"So I was busy with the twenty and looked across the stage, and there he was."

"Seriously?" I had to admit, I was surprised. I'd figured Elijah was the one who'd gotten the tour from Travis, so this was a detour I hadn't seen coming.

"Oh yeah! Carter already talked to me this morning about the house, so I know all about the body, and he asked about tours and stuff just like you did and showed me a pic of the dead guy to see if he was the one I showed the house to. I mean, not when he was actually dead but from before, you know, when he wasn't dead?"

"I get it."

"Man, I can't believe you found another body. You know, you're really hot, but I'm thinking maybe you wouldn't be a good person for me to hook up with. I don't want all that negativity in my life, and finding dead people is pretty darn negative."

"That's too bad," I said and rolled my eyes. "I'll take you off my list of potential replacements for Carter."

Gertie collapsed on the back seat, holding her hand over her mouth, but I could see her entire body shaking. Even Ida Belle didn't bother to control her grin.

"Oh yeah! So since I been watching all those detective shows, I figured this guy I took on the tour might be in cahoots with the dead guy. And since I ain't interested in being the next body you find, I ducked out of there quick-like. Didn't even get my private dance."

"I'm sorry for your loss."

"Me too. But I got a picture of that dude before I jetted... and the dancer. I already sent it to Carter—the dude, not the girl—but I figured I should send it to you too, since you asked and because it's your friends and all. I feel really bad about the house situation. I don't want my clients moving into murder homes. It's bad for my reputation."

"I'm sure that was my friends' first concern as well. Thanks for the information, Travis, and I'll be looking for the picture. You might want to stay out of the bars for a couple days—see if Carter can wrap this one up."

"I'm out of fives anyway. Just got twenties left, and that girl was the only one I'd spend a twenty on. Except you...before the dead guy thing, of course. Fact is, I'd probably drop a fifty on you if it wasn't for all the corpses and stuff."

"Goodbye, Travis," I said and hung up.

Ida Belle and Gertie started laughing out loud now, and I couldn't help but join them.

"I keep thinking I've heard it all," I said, "then this town throws me another curve ball."

Gertie nodded. "His parents were bald by the time he hit junior high—father *and* mother."

My phone signaled an incoming text and I opened it to see the photo Travis had sent. The light was surprisingly good, but then it was the middle of the day and the club was one of those open-wall type on Bourbon Street.

Yellow shirt, the message read.

I enlarged the photo on the guy wearing the yellow shirt. "I've never seen him before."

Ida Belle glanced over and shook her head. "Me either."

Gertie looked at the phone and frowned, then drew my hand closer. "I've seen him somewhere...and recently."

She flopped back on the seat, staring up at the roof of the SUV. Then after a couple seconds, she bolted upright and yelled.

"Got it! He was in a photo in Destiny's shop. There were some pictures of what I assumed was family on the back wall where I was looking at a voodoo doll, and he was in one of them with Destiny, an older couple, and another woman maybe a couple years younger than Destiny. There was a caption that said it was taken in Haiti."

"Her sister and parents, maybe," Ida Belle said.

"Interesting," I said. "If it was a family picture taken in Haiti, then he's probably related."

"They did all favor each other," Gertie said.

"So that makes another family member who wasn't afraid to go into the Leroux house," Ida Belle said.

"That has to be who Elijah was working with, right?" Gertie said.

"It certainly seems that way, but then why did he shoot Elijah?" I asked.

"He got greedy?" Gertie suggested. "Wanted it all for himself, or maybe he was afraid Elijah would blow it and the police would catch on?"

"The odd thing to me is the timing and the location," Ida Belle said. "Why kill Elijah before they found the jewels? And why do it at the house, which was bound to bring police interest?"

I nodded. "You're right. If they'd found the jewels the night Elijah was shot, then he would have been long gone. So something happened that made him kill Elijah on the spot. Which makes the entire thing even more interesting."

"You going to tell Carter about all of this now?" Gertie asked.

"Yeah," I said. "We've gotten all we can out of Destiny. I doubt she'd give up another family member, even if she knew he'd been in the house. She held back on the jewels and the motel where Elijah was living, even though it was clear that she was angry about what Elijah was doing when he died."

"Mostly where," Ida Belle said.

My cell rang again and I glanced at the display.

Carter.

"Speak of the devil," I said and answered.

"I have a cop buddy in NOLA I was running a couple things by when a call came in about an old lady spraying a parking lot with an AK-47."

"Wow," I said. "The seniors are really going the extra mile with this 'take back your neighborhood' thing."

"Elijah Charitte was staying at that motel, wasn't he?"

"I couldn't say."

"Couldn't or won't?"

"Which one is better for you?"

"Jesus. Neither."

"Has Destiny Charitte called you yet?"

He sighed. "About ten minutes ago. How is it I have every database known to man at my disposal, and you still get the jump on me?"

"You had paperwork so I had a head start. And I have one database you don't have access to."

"I kinda figured that after I got a call from Mannie. Is there anything in this state the Heberts don't have their fingers in?"

"Doubt it. So do you want me to fill you in or what?"

He sighed again and I took that as my cue and covered everything we'd found out.

"Sounds like I need to press Destiny about the guy in the photo."

"And I'd push her on why two people in her family are so interested in the Leroux estate. Why now? Tell her someone ID'd her coming out of Elijah's room carrying a book. Her family's had a shop in the French Quarter for generations, so it's plausible that someone would recognize her. At the very least, she suspects what they're after, or she wouldn't have gone to the motel."

"That could work. You didn't take anything?"

"Nope. Wore gloves and put everything back where I found it. I just took some pics of the silver to compare it to the pictures Travis sent me, but I'm guessing the items came from the Leroux estate and probably weren't the first he fenced from there."

"Have you talked to Mannie this afternoon?"

"Right before you called. He told me about the boat and the camp."

"Forensics already lifted Elijah's prints off the boat and cell phone but unfortunately, it was a burner phone and the only number called was another burner. There's a second set of prints in the camp that don't match the owner, but there's no match in the system."

"Get some off this guy from the strip club and you might have your match. Harrison will be back this evening but we're sticking around another night. We want to see if we can find any old household records. Maybe get an idea of where this jewels theory came from. And Mannie suggested we leave the tunnels open and fake everyone leaving the house. Put out word that it's empty..."

He was quiet for several seconds. "What did Cassidy say?"

"She's all for it and Harrison will be too. She's never going to feel safe in that house unless we figure all this out and put an end to it."

"I know. I'll head over there tonight after I get off work, and we can sort out the details. I want this over with for them as much as they do."

"You just want Gertie to put down her gun and get back on the pole."

He hung up.

When we pulled into my driveway, Ronald burst out of his house and ran across the lawn. We all stopped to watch, mainly because he was doing it in stilettos that kept hanging in the thick grass.

"You could have used the sidewalk," Gertie said.

"Or not worn those shoes," I said. "They look a little fancy for around the house."

"I'm breaking them in," he said as he clomped up the stairs onto my porch.

He dropped onto the bench next to my front door and sighed. "I don't know why I bother. Anywhere I would wear these shoes has valet. It's not like I'd be walking farther than the door to a chair."

"Well, if you elected to run across the lawn in a brand-new pair of..." I looked at the shoes but came up with nothing.

"Louboutins," he said. "You can tell by the red bottom."

"Awesome," I said. "So what's so important that you're risking Louboutins and an ankle? You could have called or gone barefoot."

He stared at me, clearly horrified by the barefoot comment.

"I heard you found a body. Why do you keep doing that?" He waved a hand in dismissal. "Stupid question. So is it true? The Leroux home is infested with criminals and not ghosts?"

"'Infested' is a strong word but perhaps accurate in this case, as we're certain there was more than one—intruder, not body. But they were dressed like ghosts, probably to scare people away."

"Fascinating," he said. "So you've seen no sign of anything paranormal."

"Not even a shadow."

He thought about this then nodded. "Okay then. If you'd still like my help, I'm willing to go through the house and give you some pointers on the art and furniture and such."

"So you're okay with a dead guy in the house, but Casper's a hard pass," I said.

"Exactly. Unless the dead guy comes back. Then I'm out of there like last year's Versace."

"Well, we're staying there again tonight," I said. "We're going to try to find records from when Lucien lived there."

"Why?"

"Because we think the intruders are looking for something valuable from his time there—jewels, to be exact."

Ronald popped up and grabbed a porch post to steady himself. "Jewels! That's the ultimate. I want to come. I can help. I know historical architecture and art. If anything is still hidden in that house, I might be able to find it."

"I'll have to clear another guest with Harrison and Cassidy," I said. "And you have to wear flats."

He squealed and clapped his hands, and promptly fell off the porch into my bushes.

CHAPTER NINETEEN

With Ida Belle, Gertie, Ronald, Carter, Mannie, Rambo, and me all in residence, it was a full house at the Leroux estate. Harrison had arrived home just before we all descended, and Mannie had brought him up to speed on everything that had been discovered that day.

"It's a good thing you have all those bathrooms," Gertie said when we were all collected in the living room.

I stared. "There's no intermission. We're not all going to have to go at the same time."

"But we could if we wanted to," Gertie said. "Maybe I should add another bathroom to my house."

"You live alone and have two already," Ida Belle said. "If you need more than that, then there's something wrong."

"I had to run upstairs every time I had to go when Godzilla was there," Gertie said.

"Since you're not supposed to have an alligator in your bathtub, that doesn't count as a shortage," Ida Belle said.

"You kept an alligator in your bathtub?" Cassidy asked.

Gertie waved a hand in dismissal. "Everyone makes a big deal out of things."

"Was this a baby alligator?" Cassidy asked.

"He's fairly young for an alligator," Ida Belle said, "but if you're asking in terms of size, he's big enough to eat a human."

Cassidy's eyes widened. "And has he?"

"Only once," Gertie said. "But he was a bad guy, so that was okay."

"Only once that we know of," Ida Belle said.

Cassidy glanced over at Harrison, and I could tell she was starting to question moving here. I had to admit that she'd gotten the bonus introduction as far as southern Louisiana went. We needed to get things to reasonably normal or I was afraid we were going to lose them.

Ronald, who had bolted off as soon as he'd entered the house, ran into the living room, his excitement obvious.

"This place is just fabulous—*fabulous*, I tell you," he said. "You can just feel the history, the romance, the mystery, in every inch of wood and marble. If I'd seen it before I bought my house—although I don't know, my Saks personal shopper probably wouldn't deliver all the way out here—but it's just fabulous!"

Cassidy gave him an incredulous look. "You have a Saks personal shopper who delivers?"

"Honey, with all the money I spend there, I should have my own dressing room," he said.

"So did you see anything valuable?" I asked.

"Nothing of independent merit," he said, "but if you sold off a group of items I identified as collector-worthy, you could probably get twenty or thirty thousand. That's just based on a quick look, and I didn't even look in the second-floor rooms except from the doorway, so first-floor items only. I have an estate sales friend in New Orleans who could give you a detailed list. He puts the most valuable items in his shop in the French Quarter to get top dollar."

Harrison and Cassidy stared.

"Twenty or thirty thousand?" Harrison repeated. "And that's just at a glance?"

"That's a dent in remodeling," Ida Belle said. "And between the second floor and the attic, you might be able to double or triple that amount."

"But why would anyone leave valuable things behind?" Harrison asked. "Why not sell them individually instead of lumping them in with the house?"

Ronald shrugged. "People do it all the time. Sometimes kids inherit and live far away or don't care. But my guess in this case is that the house passed through so many hands, that most don't even know what they had. After all, a guy picked up a Warhol at a flea market for a dollar. It would probably go for one to two million. You really have to be an expert to recognize something of value, especially in art. The things that are pleasing to the eye are not often worth more than the canvas and paint that went into them, but those that aren't as pretty..."

He pointed to a small painting of misshapen fruit and a cracked bowl that hung in a corner of the kitchen. "Take that for example. It's no Warhol but would probably fetch five grand in my friend's store. But here it is, hanging in the kitchen where it can be damaged by grease and heat."

"Five grand!" I stared at the picture. "That thing is hideous and the proportions are all wrong."

"Yes, but the technique is wonderful and the artist has a colorful history that adds to the value of the work," Ronald explained.

"I wonder how much money has been left on the table over the years of turnover here," Ida Belle said.

"Clearly a lot given that thieves have already made off with some of it," Harrison said. "It's kind of overwhelming to think about. I mean, we thought we could pick up a few thousand, but wow, this house is looking like an even better deal now."

"Except for the dead guy," Cassidy said.

Gertie waved a hand in dismissal. "That's just a pest problem. We can fix it."

Cassidy stared at her, then at all of us nodding, and burst out laughing. "You're all crazy. God help me, I've moved out into a bayou of crazy people."

"You're starting to catch on," I said. "But she's right. We can fix this, and then you can sell off all the ugly paintings, remodel your house, get comfortable here, and start planning your live-in therapy retreat."

Ida Belle nodded. "We're going to make this happen for you. It's important to all of us that it does."

Cassidy misted up a bit and smiled at me. "I see why you stayed."

"Hey, what about me?" Carter asked and everyone laughed.

"You'd think that first Realtor would have known better and taken advantage of the contents to sell the house," Gertie said. "She looked like someone who had experience with expensive things."

"A Realtor who knows antiques?" Ronald asked. "I thought that blabbermouth Travis had the listing."

"Hence, the 'first' part of her comment," I said. "The first Realtor never put up the listing—claimed the house creeped her out so she avoided it. The broker lost the listing and then Travis sold it quickly, so now she's in hot water. But she didn't look like she needed the money—expensive haircut, jewelry, car..."

"Who was she?" he asked.

"Karmin Blay."

He gave me a knowing nod. "Serafina Blay's only child and, if you listen to her tell it, her personal cross to bear."

"You know her?"

"Karmin? No. But I know her mother from various charity events. She's...a lot."

"So what's wrong with Karmin?"

"Other than not wanting to be her mother's clone, not much that I'm aware of. She's your typical spoiled, young, rich person, but I've never heard of any malice in her actions. More just a desire to separate herself from her parents and be her own person. I've lived that story."

"That must have been her mother we saw her with—looked like she'd been varnished."

"That's Serafina. The society gossip is that Serafina is threatening to cut Karmin off if she doesn't do her bidding."

"What does her 'bidding' require?" Gertie asked.

"Marriage to an insufferable old toad of her mother's selection and chairing at least ten charity events a year. Definitely producing an heir."

"Gross," I said.

"Agreed," Ronald said. "And it explains why the poor girl's taken a job as a Realtor. Lots of money in it if you can do it well, and she has the upbringing and connections to work with high-end clientele."

"Wouldn't people avoid using her because of her mother?" Ida Belle asked.

"Exactly the opposite," Ronald said. "Serafina is well positioned but not well liked. Basically, people only tolerate her for her money, and her pockets are deep."

"We tolerate Celia and she doesn't even have money," Gertie said.

"That's just because of God, honey," Ronald said. "The crowd Serafina runs in worships other things."

"Speaking of worship," Carter said, "I have a hungry dog, a beer, and a recliner waiting for me at home. Let's get the plan to catch this guy laid out so some of us can get out of here."

"And the rest of us can go treasure hunting!" Gertie said and clapped her hands.

So we got down to business and laid out a plan.

Tomorrow night, we'd catch a ghost.

———

ONCE MANNIE AND CARTER CLEARED OUT, WE SHOWED Ronald the rest of the house. He was wowed by the tunnel system and admired the access points.

"This is all part of the original construction," he said. "You can tell by the wood grain on the access points. It's all from the same lot as the surrounding panels. People don't worry about that sort of thing these days—unless it's a Rolls-Royce interior. They just load up a stack of whatever's at the lumberyard and nail it up. But this is all craftsmanship. Lucien must have paid a fortune for it."

"But that also makes it harder to spot," I said.

He frowned. "Very true. If there are jewels still hidden in this house, they might very well remain that way. Unless you're right on top of this and know what you're looking for, you'd never notice a seam. The matching lot of wood, the choice of stain color and placement in the rooms in relation to how light would hit, are all so well thought out."

"Makes you wonder how Elijah, or whoever, found them," Harrison said.

"Maybe from that book that Destiny took from his room," Ida Belle said.

"But then that would mean someone in their family had been in the house," Cassidy said. "I thought they all believed it was cursed."

"Could be Lovelie told them," I said. "Or one of the men who built it talked and someone else made a note of it. The reality is, we don't know what happened back then. We only know the stories that were handed down, and you know how retelling goes. Combine that with everyone hiding things, and you get only slivers of fact."

Cassidy nodded. "So, the attic or the library? There's all those boxes in the attic."

"If you're looking for personal records, like journals, I'd expect they were hidden as well as the jewels," Ronald said.

"That's a good point," Cassidy said. "But that means *anywhere* in the house. We have to start somewhere."

Then something occurred to me.

"The intruder was in the hallway upstairs when I came out of my bedroom," I said. "I'm guessing they ran downstairs to get away from me because if they'd wanted to search down there, they could have entered the house through the library in the first place."

"And if they wanted to search the attic, they could have exited the tunnels there," Ida Belle said. "And given how well this place is constructed, we wouldn't have heard them."

"So we assume they were going to search a room on the second floor," Harrison said, "but not the bedroom they entered the house in because they left it. And not the bedroom on the opposite side because they could have entered that room from the tunnel as well."

"All the rooms personal to Lucien and Lovelie would have been on the first floor," Ronald said.

"Maybe it was Celine's room they were looking for," I said. "Which one do you think that was?"

"The one with the balcony."

Gertie, Cassidy, and Ronald all answered at once.

I raised one eyebrow.

"It's the most romantic," Ronald said.

"It's the only one with an easy way to sneak out of the house," Cassidy said, and Gertie gave her a thumbs-up.

"That's assuming Lucien didn't fill his daughter in on the tunnel situation, of course," Cassidy said.

"Which any smart parent would have left out," Gertie said.

I had to laugh. It made perfect sense. Celine was home-schooled and hidden away from the world, but that didn't mean she wasn't a normal kid, especially when she hit the teen years. The room nearest the stairs overlooked the rear of the home, was huge, and had a connected bath. It was a perfect teen haven. And with the trellises on both sides of the balcony, it was the easiest way to get out of the house without being noticed.

She wouldn't have been sneaking out to visit among the townspeople or there would have been talk, but I could see her wanting to get out and just 'be' somewhere that her father couldn't control. Maybe she'd met some local kids on the bayou—kids who would have kept her secret because they were sneaking out as well. I imagined her life was very lonely, living out here with only servants and her father to interact with.

We all tromped upstairs to the room that was likely Celine's and started poking and prodding every inch of the walls. At the back of the bottom storage cabinet, Ronald hit pay dirt.

"Ha!" he yelled, raising up so quickly he slammed his head into the top of the cabinet.

He crawled out backward and sat, rubbing his head.

"There's a panel on the back that I think slides to the side," he said. "But it's been painted over, so I can't budge it."

Harrison dug through the toolbox he'd brought up with him and grabbed a screwdriver.

"Let's take the doors off first to make it easier," he said.

He made quick work of the doors, and we all squatted down and looked at the back wall. The cabinet was a couple feet deep and about three feet tall, so we all had a decent view when he reached in and pressed on the back panel. It definitely flexed.

"I think Ronald's right," he said. "I have a utility knife in my box."

I handed him the knife and he muscled through the layers of paint around the edges of the back panel. Then he glanced back at us and pushed the panel from one side then the other. The second push moved it a half inch, and he worked his fingers in and managed to slide the entire panel, exposing a good two-foot section of secret storage.

We all leaned forward to get a good look. There were books and a stuffed bear, a voodoo doll, Mardi Gras beads, and other trinkets that a girl might save. I stared at the collection, thinking about the fact that this represented Celine's life as a child and young woman, and the things that were important to her, and felt a little sad. This wasn't the way life was supposed to be—hiding away the things you loved in secret cubbies, restricted to a house with only your father and people he paid to care for you surrounding you.

"You want me to haul it all out?" Harrison asked. "Maybe there's something inside."

Ronald looked at him and laughed. "You guys really don't see it? Good Lord, I've got my work cut out for me bringing some culture into your lives."

He pointed to the books. "Do you really think a teen girl cares about reading poetry by a dead Frenchman?"

Harrison plucked the old leather book from the middle of the others, and as he pulled it out, the journal that the leather cover had been stripped to hide fell out.

CHAPTER TWENTY

Ronald gave us a triumphant look.

"I might have to hire you as a consultant," I told him as I picked up the journal.

The inside was a girl's handwriting, and when I checked the date, I realized Celine would have been a teen when she started it.

"Pull out everything," I said. "Let's make sure there are no others. And let's go over everything and make sure nothing is hiding inside things."

Harrison started passing the items to the others and they piled them up on the bed. I took a seat at a desk chair and flipped through the journal, scanning the entries. The first several were mostly about her schooling and her extreme dislike of the new tutor. Then I found one more interesting.

I'm worried about Father. After Mother's death, he spent so much time closed up in his room, not talking, not eating. He'd wasted away to almost nothing before he seemed to snap back to normal. Except he wasn't really. He started eating again but he leaves the house all the time to chat with the townspeople he disdained before. I, of course, am not allowed to go. I don't understand why as due to the war, the majority of the people left are women, children, or the elderly. He claims he's protecting me, but I don't see how or from what.

I think he's hiding something.

I NODDED. YEAH, LIKE RUNNING AROUND WITH A BUNCH OF married women. That's definitely not the sort of thing you want your teen daughter to clue in on. The next entry was months later.

NOW I'VE SEEN IT ALL. HE'S HAD CALLERS AT THE HOUSE. A group of silly women, all talking in high-pitched voices and giggling like schoolgirls. My tutor was instructed to keep me to my studies and not allow me downstairs, but I gave her a hunk of chocolate and she fell asleep in her chair after eating it, like she always does. I sneaked out to the landing and peeked into the parlor. They were dressed like they were going to a party. Some even had hats. The butler was racing around, trying to collect all the baked goods they'd brought and provide refreshments for everyone. Clearly, they weren't expected or the butler would have been prepared. He's very rigid and doesn't look happy with their invasion. We've never had visitors for social reasons, and my guess is he was happy with that.

I sneaked down late that night and ate some of the baked goods. One of them made fig cookies, which Father loves but everyone else in the house hates. On a good day, Mother used to make fig cookies for him and my favorite, sugar cookies. I miss her. Not the bad days, but the good ones.

I FELT MY HEART CLENCH FOR THE GIRL WHO'D LOST HER mother too soon. I knew that girl. I *was* that girl. But at least my mother had been healthy and the good times with her totally eclipsed any that weren't so great. I couldn't even think of one, really. It seemed like I didn't really understand disappointment, loss, and grief until she died.

I dragged myself out of my memories and continued to scan the pages as the months ticked by. Cassidy and Gertie had been right—Celine had used the balcony to exit the house. I grew excited when I saw that she wasn't alone—her friend, the young maid Clotilde, went with her. They met some local kids fishing on the bayou late one night. All of them were breaking the rules and had found a kinship. And Celine had found friends. The journaling stopped for a long time and then picked up again when her father died.

HE'S GONE. I DIDN'T THINK I'D FEEL SUCH A LOSS, GIVEN HOW little he took part in my life in the last years. He saw that I was properly cared for and educated, of course, but he didn't spend time with me. I think I reminded him too much of Mother. I could see the hurt in his eyes when he looked at me. The doctor said it was a heart attack. I thought him too young for that sort of thing, but he'd been under a lot of stress lately. He never spoke of things, but I could see it in his face. He lost weight again and started roaming the house all hours of the night, pacing and mumbling, but never performing a specific task.

I know some of the worry is over money. I've heard the whispers among the staff and watched as their numbers dwindled. Father said it was because I was no longer a child and we didn't require as much help, but I don't think he was telling me the truth. By the time he died, only Clotilde remained, but then, she had nowhere else to go. The silly women who flocked to the house to beg favor with Father have all stopped coming. They each took their turn with duty, dropping off food after he passed, but no one has inquired if I needed anything since then.

If not for Clotilde, I would be alone.

· · ·

"You find anything?" Ida Belle asked, breaking into my thoughts.

I nodded and told them the gist of the two entries, trying to keep my voice level so that no one would catch on to my personal reaction to them.

"What about you guys?" I asked.

They all shook their heads.

"It's the sort of stuff you'd expect a teen girl to have—trinkets and baubles and other things that were important to her," Ida Belle said.

"The only item that might be of any value is this bracelet," Cassidy said. "It was inside the stuffed bear."

She handed me a silver bracelet with intricately carved leaves and flowers. In the center of each flower was a different color gemstone.

"This is gorgeous," I said.

Gertie nodded. "I'm guessing it belonged to her mother. It's not the sort of piece one would give to a young girl. And that would also explain why she hid it away."

"Is there anything about what happened after her father's death?" Ida Belle asked.

I flipped to the end of the journal but the last twenty percent or so held blank pages. I paged back to the last entry and read out loud.

THE TAXES ARE PAST DUE ON THE HOUSE. REPAIRS ARE NEEDED and there's no money in the accounts to pay them. But that's not the worst part. The worst thing is that awful man—the sheriff. He came here and questioned me like I was a common criminal. Clotilde says he's just doing his job, but I can tell she's worried. I think something happened to Father. Something other than a heart attack. And this sheriff believes I had something to do with it.

Clotilde says there are rumors in town about me. Stories about the power I have that came from my mother. That I can cast a spell that will kill a man. My mother taught me the rituals and respect of her ways, but I have no ability like the locals suggest. If I had, I might consider turning it on the sheriff although Clotilde says I must keep those thoughts to myself. Clotilde says we have to find a way to leave here. I might know of one. It depends on whether or not there was any truth to the seemingly insane things my father said toward the end.

"THAT'S THE LAST ENTRY," I SAID.

"Do you think she was looking for the jewels?" Cassidy asked. "But what about the bracelet? Surely it's worth something."

"If it was her mother's then she might not have wanted to part with it," Gertie said.

"But then why not take it with her when she left?" Cassidy asked.

"Maybe she didn't leave," I said. "It sounds like both Lucien and Lovelie struggled with mental issues. If Celine inherited them..."

"Oh!" Cassidy blew out a breath. "Wow. I guess I hadn't thought that far, and I'm the doctor. Well, this sucks."

I nodded. I didn't want to consider that end to Celine's story, but I couldn't exactly ignore it.

Ronald, who had taken the bracelet from Cassidy to inspect it, frowned. "I don't think these stones are real."

"No?" Ida Belle asked.

"I can't make a good call without a loupe," he said, "and honestly, we need a jeweler to be certain. The craftsmanship is definitely there but the silver also appears to be a lower grade than what should be used on a piece like this."

"Do you have someone who can give us an assessment?" I asked.

"Of course!" Ronald said. "He's in New Orleans. Do you want his name, or I can go with you and make introductions."

"That would be great," I said. "Maybe we can talk to him tomorrow morning and get at least one question resolved."

Ida Belle sighed. "It looks like if we want more answers, we're going to have to find Clotilde Bassett. I'm going to leave another message for Verna."

I nodded but I wasn't feeling optimistic. Who knows if Mary had gotten things right, and even if she had, Clotilde would be approaching a hundred years old. The chances of her being alive and having a clear memory of things that had happened when she was no more than a girl herself were the biggest long shots ever.

———

IT WAS AN UNEVENTFUL NIGHT BUT BASED ON THE WEARY eyes and slow movements in the kitchen the next morning, I doubted any of us had gotten much sleep. I was on my second cup of coffee and trying to make Ronald understand that there was no way in hell I was ever going to do weekly pedicures with him when Ida Belle ran into the room, waving her phone.

"I got it!" she yelled. "Verna finally called and I got the information about the nursing home. And she verified what Mary said."

I perked up. This might be the big break we were waiting on, at least on the historical perspective side.

"Here it is," she said. "You think it's too early to call?"

I shrugged. "They have people working round the clock, right? All we're doing is seeing if she lives there and if she can have visitors."

I dialed the facility and explained that I was a resident of Sinful and doing some historical research on a house my friends had purchased. A woman named Clotilde Bassett had worked there when she was a young woman and I'd been told she was a resident. If so, I wanted to see if I could schedule an appointment to speak with her.

The nurse who answered was very nice and told me that Clotilde was their oldest resident and was much beloved. She was still able to advocate for herself and there were no limitations placed on who could visit her. Most residents preferred visitors after lunch as they had exercises in the morning, so I made an appointment for one that afternoon and rang off with a smile.

"This could be it!" I said. "This woman could hold the answer to so many questions."

Harrison gave me a big smile. "I have a good feeling about this. Between this woman and what we have planned for tonight, I think we're going to wrap up this entire mess."

Cassidy held up both hands with her fingers crossed.

Ronald's phone signaled an incoming text and he clapped his hand. "My jeweler friend can see us this morning at ten. That gives us time to talk to him, then do some shopping and have lunch before we see Clotilde."

He looked at me. "I am invited to see Clotilde, right?"

I nodded. "Of course."

"You know, we'll have a couple hours to kill," he said, looking down at my bare feet.

"Absolutely not," I said.

He sighed. "Can't blame a guy for trying."

After coffee, Ida Belle took us all to our respective homes so we could shower and change for our day's adventure. I was just on my way upstairs when Carter came in. I'd filled him in on our discovery the night before and had called on the way back to Sinful and told him about the appointments with Clotilde and Ronald's jeweler friend. Since neither of them were going to directly relate to the intruder-murder case, he was happy to leave those to us.

"What's up?" I asked, because he had that look.

"I got an ID on the guy Travis took on the house tour. Gertie was right. His name is Abel Charitte and he's a third cousin to Elijah. Also has a rap sheet longer than Godzilla's tail, but with more edge than Elijah's—more violence and bigger scores. And that's just the things they could make stick."

"If he has a record, then obviously that wasn't his prints in the camp."

Carter shook his head. "But those prints could belong to a friend or relative of the owner. He's lent it out a couple times in the last several months. We're trying to get prints from everyone he could think of to eliminate them, but it's looking more and more like it won't amount to anything."

"So since Elijah didn't own a vehicle for the back and forth, he was using the proximity of the camp to keep him available and was probably the lookout for occupancy. Maybe Abel met him there at night to do their searching. People tended to label Elijah as a follower rather than a leader so this Abel being more accomplished, so to speak, and also family sounds like a good fit for Elijah to partner with."

Carter nodded. "Unfortunately, his last known address was jail and he's been in the wind for two months now. Hasn't checked in with his parole officer either, so there's already a warrant out on him and he's wanted for questioning in two other crimes."

"Sounds like a real peach. You going to question Destiny today?"

"Yes, and both her cousins will be the hot topics. And I'm going to hit her with the motel room sighting."

"That ought to be interesting. She's...different."

"You think she's crazy?"

"No. I think she has deeply rooted beliefs and there's no shaking her from them. That doesn't make her crazy, but it doesn't make her typical either."

"So you're saying she has a different worldview."

"Definitely."

"Okay, well, I better run. I've got a lot of ground to cover before we bait our trap tonight."

I nodded. "Be sure and spread the word everywhere you can that Harrison and Cassidy will be moving out to stay at my place until this is all resolved."

"On it."

I made quick work of the shower and headed downstairs to wait on the others. Ida Belle would be ready in no time, but Gertie and Ronald tended to take longer, especially Ronald. Lord only knew what he was selecting from his wide range of outfits. While I was waiting, I pulled out Celine's journal and read more of the passages. There wasn't anything else that added to the narrative that was important to us, but I liked getting a feel for who Celine was and what it was like living there.

It was clear that Clotilde coming to the estate was a big turning point for her. In Clotilde, she finally had someone her own age to talk to and confide in. Clotilde lived on the estate and based on the later comment that she had nowhere else to go, I assumed that meant she'd been orphaned and that's why she'd taken a live-in position working full time before she was even an adult.

I found it interesting that Celine never mentioned the tunnels, but then she had her balcony escape, and it was easier than crawling on floors, climbing ladders, and traipsing through tunnels to get in and out of the house. Plus, if Lucien was pacing around all the time—which sounded like paranoia to me—there was a good chance he was checking the tunnels.

At one point, Celine developed a crush on a local boy but when he moved away that was the end of her romance. She never talked about anyone else, but I was glad that she'd managed to have this one bit of normal in her otherwise odd and repressive childhood. A knock on my back door interrupted my thoughts and when I opened it, I stared at Ronald in surprise.

His jeans had been ironed, I was certain. But the blue polo shirt and white tennis shoes with a blue stripe were so unassuming that I had to look up and double-check that it was him. I stood back so he could enter and waved at his outfit.

"You're a bit understated," I said.

"I know and you should expect my jeweler friend to give me a rash of crap about it, but we're going to see Clotilde, and she's a Southern woman of a certain generation. I don't want her distracted by my fashion sense when we're there to get the gossip."

"That's sensible. Maybe you could talk to Gertie."

He waved a hand in dismissal. "When you're a woman past a certain age, no one bats an eye. Men still get The Look."

"Sheriff Lee doesn't."

Ronald laughed. "Sheriff Lee is who I aspire to be when I'm old, but with a better wardrobe and in a Rolls-Royce."

I got a text that Ida Belle and Gertie were about to pull in.

"We're up," I said.

CHAPTER TWENTY-ONE

Ronald's jeweler friend was a distinguished-looking gentleman wearing an Armani suit. I know because the first few minutes after our arrival were spent discussing the fabric and stitching, and listening to him chide Ronald—as predicted —for his lack of fashion-forward dress.

Midfifties. Six foot one. A hundred seventy pounds. Decent conditioning but he clearly spent more time doing things you could wear an Armani suit for rather than physically exerting himself. Threat level low, unless he brought up topics like engagement rings.

He gave me a critical eye, as though he was assessing a diamond, then nodded.

"This is the one, right?" he said. "The queen? You were right. Even in all that discount cotton you can't hide that bone structure."

"Ytsken van Gemeren," he said and shook my hand. "Call me Gem. Everyone does."

"Thank God," Ida Belle mumbled.

Then he greeted Ida Belle and Gertie with a bow and kissed their hands. Gertie looked charmed. Ida Belle wiped her hand on her jeans as soon as he looked away.

"Come back to my office," he said. "I want to get a good look at this piece. You said it was found at the Leroux estate?"

"Yes," I said as we walked into his large office and took seats in chairs arranged in front of an enormous fireplace. "Friends of mine bought it recently and there's been some issues with intruders. There were rumors about Lucien having expensive jewels, and we found this in a stuffed animal that we figure belonged to Celine."

He raised one eyebrow. "After all these years? Why would you assume it was Celine's?"

"It was hidden behind a secret panel in her room and there was a journal with it that was clearly Celine's."

His eyes widened. "How incredible! Let me see it."

I handed him the piece that was now enclosed in a jewelry pouch that Ronald had supplied. He pulled it out, gave it a once-over with his naked eye, frowned, then picked up a loupe. It only took him a couple seconds to put down the loupe and shake his head.

"You were right," he said to Ronald. "The stones aren't real. They're decent fakes but nothing that would fool a jeweler for even a half second. And while the silver is real, the quality is below what should have been used for such an ornate piece."

"That's what Ronald said," I said.

Gem looked down at the piece and frowned again. "The thing is, this looks familiar. Give me a second."

He went over to his desk and tapped on his laptop, shaking his head as he clicked. Then he jumped up and shouted. He hurried back over with his laptop and showed us a bracelet that looked just like the one we had except this one had been sold at an auction a few years back for fifty thousand dollars.

"Wow!" I said. "It says here that the piece was part of the Martin T. Aguillard estate and was a custom piece commissioned in 1935 by Aguillard Sr. for his wife to commemorate the birth of their first child. Aguillard Sr. was killed in battle."

"But if this was a custom piece, then why would Celine have a knockoff?" Gertie asked.

"Says here that Aguillard's hometown was Mudbug," I said. "Maybe Lucien saw it and wanted one for Lovelie but couldn't afford the real deal."

"Very possible," Gem agreed. "And it might explain the stories surrounding Celine's one and only entry into society."

I perked up. "You know stories about Celine?"

"If you're a jeweler or NOLA society, you've heard the stories," he said. "It's like campfire tales for rich people. Except they're repeated over martinis and caviar instead of beer and toasted marshmallows."

"Well, don't hold out on us," Ronald urged.

"The stories say that when Celine showed up for that charity ball, she was practically draped with stones. Some of the largest and most exquisitely cut stones that were worn that night and trust me, it would have to have been the mecca of jewels given the event and the era. Celine was said to be as beautiful as the jewels she wore and captured the attention of every male in the room—married and single."

"I'll bet that didn't go over with the women very well," Gertie said.

"Oh, they were more absorbed by the fact that this mere slip of a girl had outsparkled them in a major way," he said. "It's said that one outing kept custom jewelers backlogged for over a year."

Ronald nodded. "Nobody was going to be bested again."

"And then she disappeared," Ida Belle said.

"But apparently, people believe the jewels are still in the house," I said.

"Probably because they think she committed suicide like her mother," Gertie said.

"At least now we know where the rumors about hidden jewels came from," Ida Belle said.

"I wonder if they were even real," Ronald said.

"That's a really good question given the piece we found," I said. "I assume it took a fairly good craftsman to make that."

Gem nodded. "Actually, it took an excellent craftsman to make this. It's handwork, of course, and this sort of thing can only be made by a true artist."

"Would people have been able to tell if the jewels Celine was wearing were fake?" I asked.

Gem shrugged. "If they were as good quality as this piece, not likely. Even if someone had a more intimate knowledge of jewels than the average person, most don't carry a loupe with them and the lighting in large venues is rarely the kind that would disclose the quality of a piece to the naked eye. That's done on purpose, you see, because venues don't want to invest in the highest quality of crystal, but they want to achieve the same look."

"And everyone looks better in softer light," Ronald said.

"Exactly," Gem agreed. "Ronald told me about the trouble your friends have had. I can't even imagine how upsetting it would be. I hope you can make sense of the history and put this all behind them."

"Me too."

"And if by chance you locate some of those rumored jewels, I'd kill for the chance to get my hands on them." He instantly looked chagrined. "I guess that was a wholly inappropriate statement, given the situation."

I shrugged. "But an accurate one."

THE ASSISTED LIVING FACILITY THAT CLOTILDE RESIDED IN was one of those with different sections, depending on the level of care needed. I was glad, and a bit surprised, to hear that Clotilde had an apartment in the section with the lowest needs.

"She's remarkably healthy for her age," the nurse's aide said as she led us down a hallway. "She can't drive and she can be forgetful—not dementia, just old age, if that makes sense—so living in a place where everything is provided and we distribute her meds is the best choice."

"That's fantastic," I said, feeling good about our upcoming conversation. "So did she select the facility herself?"

The nurse's aide nodded. "She did. And she could leave at any time, if she chose to. Like I said, she's in really great shape. You would never know she was almost a hundred years old. Honestly, I didn't believe it when they told me. I would have put her at twenty years younger. I'm glad she's having visitors. She'll enjoy that."

"She doesn't have many?" I asked.

"None. But then she's been overseas most of her life, so I suppose anyone she knew when she was young has passed already."

"No family?"

The aide shook her head. "Said she was in the system when she was a kid. I figure that's why she never talks about her childhood—only her time in France."

"France?"

The aide nodded. "She's a hoot to talk to. She keeps the other residents entertained and is always checking on people and keeping spirits up when they have medical issues. I chat with her sometimes after shift. She's a really interesting lady. And here we are. Enjoy your visit."

I knocked on the door and heard a voice inside asking me

to come in. I opened the door and stepped into the living room of a tiny but nice apartment. Clotilde sat in a recliner facing the wall with the door. Light blue drapes with sheer panels were drawn back on a patio door, and the sunlight streaming in, combined with the soft white walls, made the room bright and cheerful. Matching blue pillows with embroidered seashells with pearl embellishments were at both ends of the couch. A television was mounted on the wall in front of her and another recliner and couch made an L-shaped sitting area.

Five foot five. A hundred pounds maybe. Definitely didn't look like a centenarian. Obviously no threat, but I couldn't help but assess.

She smiled as we entered and anxiously smoothed the front of her pretty coral dress with carefully placed pearls that tied her outfit in with the pillows. She might have been the same age as Mary, but she had much better taste.

"I'm sorry for not getting up," she said. "When you're my age, you conserve things like rising and sitting and only do them for food, sleep, or the restroom. Please have a seat. I have a pitcher of sweet tea ready on the coffee table if anyone would like a glass."

We all accepted the tea offer, more because it was the polite thing to do than because we were dying of thirst. Mostly, we just wanted answers, but there was a social structure that had to be observed.

She gave us a curious look as we poured. "Well, I have to say, I'm thrilled to have some new faces to talk to, but I've been overwhelmed with curiosity ever since the nurse said someone would be calling on me today. I've outlived everyone I knew from back when I called these parts home, so please, tell me what an old lady can do for you."

"Well, first off, thank you so much for seeing us," I said.

"We were thrilled to hear you were nearby and in good health. We'd like to talk to you about the past."

"It's not many that come to visit an old lady and ask her to get on her soapbox about her younger years. Now I'm really curious."

"Good friends of mine just purchased the Leroux estate," I said. "I understand you worked there."

She broke into a huge smile and nodded. "Oh yes. Of course, I wasn't more than a child myself when I went to live there."

"Why was that?"

"My parents weren't the responsible type, and one day I came home and they were simply gone. The days of computers weren't upon us yet, and I'd never met or known other family, so I went into the system. Back then, when you turned fifteen, you were allowed to go to work in a live-in situation, so I posted out and got a position as a housemaid at the Leroux estate."

"What about school?" I asked.

"No one cared much back then if women were educated," she said. "But Lucien was a kind man and saw to it that I was taught along with Celine. He wanted us both to have options, you see."

"That's great," I said, feeling some appreciation for the progressive Lucien.

Gertie nodded. "I was a schoolteacher, so I'm glad to hear that Lucien supported your educational efforts."

"He and Celine became my new family," Clotilde said. "Oh, I was an employee, of course, and I had my daily work that had to be done, but so did Celine. Her father didn't believe in just lying around, and that included himself. He did a lot of the custom woodwork in the home. He was very talented that way."

She stopped talking and studied me for a moment. "I don't mind telling you anything you'd like to know about that time, but can I ask why you're interested? I understand that your friends purchased the home, but I don't see how my old memories matter."

"They've had some trouble," I said, and gave her a scaled-down version of the fake ghost sightings and the unfortunate demise of Elijah Charitte.

She listened intently, her eyes widening from time to time, but didn't speak until I was done.

"It's like something out of a movie," she said. "Of course, I understand now why you want to know everything you can find out. You want your friends to be safe and happy in their new home, and so do I. It was a beautiful place and despite all the tragedy, it was a happy place for me for many years. I think it can be again. So where do you want me to start?"

"I think the burning question that everyone wants an answer to is what happened to Celine?"

She smiled again, a wistful look on her face. "Celine and I had an adventure. The kind you only read about in story-books. We left the US and went to Paris. Celine took after her father in the creative realm and was an excellent dress-maker. I was always good with math and people, so we had everything we needed to make a go of it. We established a set of clients very quickly and lived the life that only young women could lead in a city full of romance and wonder. Then we fell in love with charming young men who became our husbands. We both buried them years ago, and then I buried Celine two years back. We'd bought homes next door to each other when we married and still lived there when she passed. Celine was my sister in every way. I miss her every day."

We all sat, stunned. The story, while incredible, wasn't at all what we expected to hear. And my guess was we were all bursting with a thousand more questions.

Ronald pulled a handkerchief from his pocket and sniffed into it. "That's just beautiful. Best ending ever. I can't believe it."

"How come no one ever knew?" Gertie asked. "The local gossip was that Celine's life probably ended the way her mother's did except they just didn't find the body."

Clotilde nodded. "It was better that people believed such."

"So that they didn't look for her," I said. "We found Celine's journal. We know the sheriff was suspicious about Lucien's death."

Clotilde's face darkened. "The nerve of that man, bringing more grief onto a girl who had already had far more than her share. Celine adored her father and he adored her. Even through his decline and even with all the rules he imposed, she knew he was doing his best to protect and care for her."

"So you think he died of natural causes?" Ida Belle asked.

"The doctor said a heart attack," Clotilde said. "Lucien had been very stressed for several months—pacing and mumbling at all hours of the night—but he wouldn't tell Celine what was wrong."

"And do you think the doctor was right?" I asked because she didn't sound convinced of the heart attack theory.

"I don't know what to think," she said. "After that sheriff came by, Celine and I talked and we were both worried. What if someone had done something to cause Lucien's death? If so, then why? And would they come for Celine next?"

"I hadn't even thought of that," I said. "It must have been frightening. Can you think of any reason someone would have wanted to kill Lucien?"

"I'm sure some of the local men would have objected to the time he spent with their wives."

"That would have been about the time some started to return from combat," Ida Belle said.

Clotilde nodded. "And one would have thought that those silly women would have stopped their visits, but they still came to the house with their plates of food. They'd started coming alone by then—not wanting to compete with one another for his attention. There were days the poor butler would usher one in while passing another on the way out."

"And Lucien liked this attention?" I asked, still trying to wrap my mind around it.

Clotilde thought about it for several seconds. "You know, I'm not so certain that he did. Not toward the end. When he'd first started going into town after his mourning was over, he was happy, upbeat. He really seemed to enjoy his time out among the locals and their visits to the house. But as time progressed and he grew more...depressed, I guess, his interest waned. Toward the end, he never left the house. The butler was dismissed around that time, and I was the only one left."

"So what changed?" Gertie asked.

Clotilde shook her head. "I don't know. I suppose we never will."

"Maybe he was worried about finances?" Ronald suggested. "I mean, if he dismissed all the staff except you—and you were more like family anyway—he must have been worried about household expenses."

Clotilde nodded. "Our first thought was money issues as I'd overheard some talk among the other servants as their numbers dwindled. But then Celine discovered her father's secret."

"What was his secret?" I asked.

Clotilde's eyes sparkled. "He was a jewel thief."

CHAPTER TWENTY-TWO

WE ALL STARED AT CLOTILDE IN SHOCK. OF ALL THE scenarios I'd run through my head, this one hadn't even had a glimmer, but it made complete sense.

"What?"

"I can't believe it!"

"No way!"

"I did not see that one coming!"

We all responded at once.

"It's true," Clotilde said. "Celine caught him red-handed, so to speak. We used to sneak out of the house when we were bored, and one time we hid in bushes, watching a group of women at a birthday party. A woman was on the patio showing off her new necklace to her friends. It was a pretty setting with rings of silver and gold and an emerald in the center. A couple years later, that woman was one of the many who called on Lucien, and one night, Celine walked into his room without announcing herself and found him hunched over his desk. He was crafting a necklace exactly like the one we'd seen."

"The bracelet," I said and pulled it out and showed it to Clotilde. "We found this in the secret cubby in Celine's room.

It's a replication of one that recently sold at auction for a large amount."

Clotilde took the bracelet and turned it over in her hands. "I remember this piece. Remember when Celine hid it in her stuffed bear and tucked it away in the wall."

"So you're saying Lucien was flirting with these women in order to steal their jewelry," I said. "And no one was the wiser because he was replacing the original pieces with well-crafted fakes."

"That's exactly right," Clotilde said. "It was his job, you see, back in France. He was a top jewelry maker for Cartier. But he drew suspicion when he spent too much time with the local society wives. By the time people caught on that it was the jewelry he was after and not the women, he was quite wealthy from his take and fled the country."

"And he told Celine all of this?" I asked.

Clotilde nodded. "There was little reason to lie any longer. And by then, Lucien's mind had started to wander. He was often out of sorts, like his grip on sanity was vanishing. Once Celine knew about the jewels, she knew money wasn't the problem, not really. He needed only to sell what he'd stolen and could be quite rich again, but I think he was too far gone to follow through."

"You think he was ill?" Gertie asked.

"Yes," she said. "In today's time, I'm sure they would have diagnosed him with a mental illness. Paranoid schizophrenia perhaps, but the knowledge of such things was very limited then, and with the shortage of doctors and Lucien becoming a recluse, there wasn't much hope for a medical solution."

"So the rumors of jewelry hidden at the estate were true," Ronald said.

"I'm not sure what the rumors were, but Lucien definitely had a collection of very expensive pieces," Clotilde said. "Is that what this is all about? Someone believes the jewelry is still there and is trying to find it?"

"We can't think of any other reason for what's been happening," I said. "And I can't believe it's a coincidence that the intruder who was killed was a relative of Lovelie's."

"No," Clotilde said. "I wouldn't think it coincidence either."

"Did Lovelie know about Lucien? About the jewels?" I asked. "Did she ever contact her family after leaving New Orleans?"

"I don't know. Celine was young when her mother passed and wouldn't have known the answer to either question. I suppose anything is possible, but if the Charitte family suspected the jewels were still contained on the estate, why wait until now to try to find them?"

I put my hands up. "That's the same question we have. Something had to have set it all into motion, but we have no idea what it was. And then there's the issue of the tunnels as well. We have to assume Lovelie knew about them and if she had any contact with her family, then I suppose she could have told them. I assume Celine knew."

"Of course," Clotilde said. "Lucien kept them hidden for many years by simply not using them, but we discovered the access in the tutor's room one day. We were being naughty and going through her things, so we hid in the closet and knocked open the panel at the back accidentally. We immediately went in and followed them all around, but we never told Lucien, or anyone else for that matter."

"Is it true that Lovelie committed suicide? Because there are rumors that her father killed her," Ida Belle asked.

Clotilde frowned. "I don't know if it was suicide or an accident, but all I know is what the servants said and it was years after the fact when I arrived at the estate. They all said Lovelie had bouts of depression that were worse after Celine was born, but they also said she never learned to swim."

"So it could have been an accident," Gertie said.

"We'll never know," Clotilde said, "but Celine believed it was an accident and I believed it along with her because that's what she wanted."

"You were a good friend," Gertie said.

Clotilde smiled. "The best."

"So what happened to the jewels?" I asked.

"We sold them, of course," Clotilde said. "One of the boys in town—a nephew of that awful sheriff—warned me that the sheriff was going to get a warrant for Celine's arrest. We knew we had to leave soon, so we collected every piece of jewelry from Lucien's hiding places. Then Celine made a beautiful gown and went to the charity ball to find buyers."

We all stared and I started laughing. "Oh my God. It makes perfect sense."

"It really does," Ronald said. "And yet it's like a fairy tale."

Clotilde nodded. "Celine got the buyers and sold the jewels. We saw someone who could get us documents and then Celine disappeared. I stuck around long enough to report her missing and then we left for Paris, ready for our big adventure. And that's exactly what we had."

"Incredible," I said.

She sighed. "It was a good life. Better than we could have ever imagined."

"Did Celine ever return to Louisiana?" I asked.

"No. She was afraid, you see. There's no statute of limitations on murder and it wasn't as if you could call the police and ask if you were wanted without raising some eyebrows. And the reality is, there was nothing left for her here. Our lives were in France."

"But you came back," Gertie said.

"After Celine died, I found myself wistful for the bayous I'd left behind. I wanted to see the marsh grass and the alligators and feel the humidity and taste the food again. I wanted my life to come full circle. I think, if Celine hadn't been worried about the risk, she would have wanted it as well."

———

THAT EVENING, I FILLED CARTER IN ON OUR INTERVIEWS while I changed clothes and packed what I needed to spring our trap. He was floored by what Clotilde had told us.

"You think she's on the up-and-up?" he asked.

I nodded. "I didn't detect any dishonesty and really, why would she lie? Lucien stole the jewelry and he's long dead and even if he wasn't, the jewelry's long gone so how would you prove it? And if Celine was still alive, she could claim she didn't know they were stolen. Selling something you inherited isn't a crime. There's just no reason for Clotilde to make it up."

"Yeah, even our ADA wouldn't want to pursue charges against a hundred-year-old woman, even if he could. Well, it answers a lot of questions. Between the jeweler and Clotilde, we know where the jewels rumor came from, but it's strange that there was never a dustup when people started discovering the fakes."

"I mentioned that on our way home and Ida Belle and Gertie had a theory for it. They suggested that given the quality of the replacements, no one would have known unless they went to sell the jewelry. If it was a wife or children selling, then they would have simply thought the husband had passed off fakes as the real thing when they were gifted."

"And if the man went to sell them?"

"Then he'd assume he'd been taken by a clever jeweler.

Either way, none of those people would go around broadcasting what happened."

Carter nodded. "Because they'd be too embarrassed. The whole thing is ingenious really."

"Yeah, I just wish we had a way to spread the truth that the jewels were sold off a long time ago."

"Maybe when we catch our thieves, I can release a statement that says during the course of my investigation, information came to light that revealed that the jewelry existed at one time but that Celine sold it and used the money to move overseas, where she remained the rest of her life."

"That would work," I said. "Clotilde said that neither she nor Celine told their story to anyone, not even their husbands, so there's no one to contradict it. I think it was cathartic for her, finally telling someone what happened."

"I'm glad Clotilde was still alive to answer all our questions. This one would have bugged me all the way to the grave."

"Definitely. Are you ready?"

"Yep. I stored my stuff in the boat earlier today. What about the Trouble Twosome? I don't suppose you convinced them to sit this one out?"

"It would have been a waste of energy to even try. They're going to sneak out of their houses and meet Mannie near the park. He got an old truck with a camper cover on the bed so it will blend well with the locals and they can't be seen in the back. They'll pass the main road to the house, hide the vehicle in the brush, then cross the woods to stake out the front of the house. Right now, Cassidy and Harrison are having an early dinner at Francine's so they can be seen by the locals and spread the word about staying at my place until things are sorted at theirs. Scooter volunteered to put the word out at the Swamp Bar."

Carter laughed. "I bet he did. It's dollar beer *and* wet T-shirt night."

"And you know these things, how?" I asked, teasing.

"Whiskey lets me know anytime there's something special going on. That way, dispatch isn't surprised by the higher call volume."

My cell signaled an incoming text.

"Harrison and Cassidy are on their way," I said. "I've left a tiny crack in the blinds and Cassidy will move around the house, turning different lights on and off. With all our cars in the driveway, anyone watching will think we're here. Harrison will cover the tunnel entry in the woods and you and I will access the house from the tunnels."

"What about lighting?"

"Cassidy left some lights on inside in the main areas, so that will carry through some of the downstairs and the upstairs landing. The blinds and curtains are all drawn so no one should be able to see us moving around if we're not using light."

He nodded. "I figure they're going to enter at either the point closest to where they want to go or the first stop-off, so either the library or the south bedroom, if we assume they were going to search upstairs last time. Which do you want to cover?"

"I'll take upstairs. I've been in the house more and can maneuver the layout better in the dark."

"Sounds good. They're pulling in."

We headed downstairs and I opened the door and let them in, then we all traipsed out to Harrison's truck to grab some bags and leftover containers from their vehicle. If anyone had eyes on my house, then they had a clear view of all of us in residence. When we got back inside, Harrison, Carter, and I dispersed to change into black clothes and then we were ready to go. Nightfall was just minutes away. We could only hope that we got to the house before the intruder did.

We reconvened in my bedroom and I opened up the hidden attic access in my closet. Harrison gave me a nod of approval.

"Nice," he said. "I was thinking about something similar when we put in the contract on our house, but clearly, all the work was done for me. Unfortunately, I've got to figure out how to keep people from coming in instead."

"I think we're going to solve that problem tonight," I said and climbed up into the attic.

We crossed the attic, exited out the window and into the oak tree, then traversed the giant oak onto Ronald's roof. He'd been warned ahead of time not to open fire when he heard noise. On the other side of Ronald's house was another accessible oak and we scurried down, then made our way to the dock where the boat was stashed, dodging street and house lights as we went.

When we reached the boat, we all hopped in and took off, sans running lights and using only moonlight to guide us. The boat was a small aluminum model, so not the fastest thing we had access to, but it was small and easy to hide, plus we could row if we needed to remain silent. Since the tide was coming in, we could access the opening of the bayou behind the house and drift to our exit point.

I checked my phone as soon as we were off and saw a text from Mannie.

"B Team has secured the vehicle and is approaching the house through the woods," I said.

"How long will it take us to get there?" Harrison asked.

"About twenty minutes," Carter said. "This boat isn't the fastest, but the bayous provide more of a direct shot than the roads."

Harrison shook his head. "You know, I thought when Fortune came here, she'd be bored silly in a week's time and be begging to get out. When she said she was resigning from the CIA and staying here, I thought she'd lost her mind. Then I started thinking about taking life down a notch and enjoying it and decided maybe she was a genius and not a crazy person."

"Then you moved here and saw it wasn't boring after all," I said.

"Got that right," Harrison said. "Don't get me wrong—the enemy doesn't appear to be as well trained or equipped as those we faced overseas, but that's balanced out by having to follow the rules."

"Rules suck," I agreed.

Carter laughed. "I don't know how Morrow kept his sanity with you two paired up."

"Who says he did?" Harrison asked and chuckled. "He certainly didn't keep his hair."

"What are you talking about?" I asked. "He has hair."

"He has hair *implants*," Harrison said. "Got them shortly after you made operative. You might want to be prepared, Carter."

Carter shrugged. "I'll just shave it all off. Not like I haven't worn that look before. If I'd wanted safe and boring, I could have already been settled. Walter says I've been waiting for Fortune all this time. I figure he's right."

Harrison grinned. "I couldn't ever imagine Redding in a relationship before, but I've got to agree with your uncle. It was the same for me and Cassidy. Everything just fits, you know?"

I nodded. "Which is why we're going to get this jewel thief nonsense solved so you two can get on with your lives."

"I have to say, even though it's frustrating because it's my house, I'm kinda enjoying all this cloak-and-dagger stuff. Not so sure about the Scary Mary side of things, or that woman you guys talk about who boats naked. But it definitely isn't boring."

Carter turned into a bayou and cut the engine. "This is it."

We grabbed paddles and helped the boat along while keeping it off the banks. When we were nearing the house, we stuck fishing poles in the holders and made sure our hoodies were up. If anyone was close to the bayou, they'd think it was locals doing some night fishing. When we drew close to the location where we planned on hiding the boat, I spotted the orange reflector Harrison had put on a cypress tree earlier that day and pointed. Carter nodded and we started inching our way over to the bank.

We tucked the boat into a little cove created by cypress tree roots that was just down from the one that Elijah had used. That way, if his former partners came the same route, they couldn't see our boat from where Elijah had stored his. But if I was a betting woman—and I was—I would bet my nine-millimeter that the intruder was driving in and would enter using the tunnel entry in the woods.

Once we secured the boat, we made our way to the tunnel, all on stealth mode. The only sounds were the rustle of our feet on dead leaves and the night calls of insects. Storm clouds formed overhead as we went, and I hoped the impending storm didn't keep the intruder from trying their luck. We were ready to go through this routine every night if need be, but we were also hoping it didn't take more than one.

When we got close to the tunnel access, we slowed our walk to a crawl, making sure we provided no indication that we were present. We circled the woods around the entry and when we were satisfied it was clear, we checked to make sure the stick we'd placed across the opening was still intact, then opened the tunnel and Carter and I headed inside. Harrison would take up a post behind some brush with a clear view of the tunnel access and the trail that we suspected the intruders were using to access it.

As soon as the intruders entered the tunnel, Harrison would text Carter and me and then proceed down the trail and disable the intruders' car. If they managed to elude Carter and me, then they'd be on foot. It was a slim chance that anyone could best the number of professionals we had in and around the house, but we were still going to cover all bases.

Carter and I headed into the tunnels. When we reached the library, he exited and I continued up to the second floor and located a hiding place behind a chair that allowed me to see out of the room and down the hall but would be hidden from anyone if they used the tunnel exit in that room. Not that it mattered at that point. Once they were in the house, the objective was to take them down. Now that we knew the jewels were long gone, we didn't need to know where they planned to search.

Since I didn't need to hide until I knew someone was accessing the house, I plopped down in the chair and waited to hear from Harrison. We'd all agreed that if nothing had transpired by 3:00 a.m., we'd pack it in and try again the next night. With nothing to do but wait, I pulled out my phone and queued up the book I was reading.

I'd been reading about an hour when I got the text from Harrison.

Single target entered tunnel. Under six foot. Light build. Black pants, black mask, gloves, and shoes. No weapon visible.

I frowned. There were definitely two people the night we'd found the body because someone had cut the power to the house while I was chasing the intruder inside. And one of them couldn't have been Elijah because he was already dead. We'd planned on two people entering, but that didn't appear to be the case. Maybe the other two partners had a falling-out. Or one didn't want to take the risk of coming back after Elijah's body had been found.

Or one was now another corpse waiting to be discovered.

I sent a reply then turned off my phone.

Watch front for second target. Split and cover dock. Going dark.

Mannie would have to decide who covered what area, but I was guessing he'd send Ida Belle and Gertie to cover the dock and he'd remain on the front of the house. I got into position behind the chair and waited. I could feel the adrenaline pumping through my body and couldn't help smiling.

This was it!

CHAPTER TWENTY-THREE

THE MINUTES TICKED BY, AND I FOUND MYSELF COUNTING the seconds as my breathing and heart rate automatically slowed. I knew it was selfish, but I hoped they exited on my floor. I really wanted to be the one to take them down and had wrangled a bit with Harrison over getting the position in the house with Carter because he'd wanted it himself. Carter had convinced him to take the position with the car because he was a better mechanic than I was. I had to admit it didn't take much. I was a wiz at guns, but didn't really enjoy messing with engines, so that part of our missions had usually gone to Harrison. At least he wasn't aware of Ida Belle's prowess in that area. Otherwise, I probably would have lost my house slot and Ida Belle would be under the hood of a car about now.

It was probably fifteen minutes but felt like longer before I heard a noise in the hallway. I peeked around the chair and saw the door to the attic stairwell swing open and the figure in black that Harrison had described stepped out. They must have decided to enter in the attic, then hold position to see if they could hear anyone else in the house.

I watched as they crept down the hallway toward the stairs

and forced myself not to run after them. I didn't know if they were armed and I had no cover in the hallway. As they inched toward the stairs, I wished I could risk sending Carter a text, but the display would have lit up the pitch-dark room like a spotlight.

I deliberated another second as they got closer to the stairs. Why were they going down? Was the second intruder going to be let in the front door by the first? The house was covered front and back but that didn't mean there wasn't risk involved with making my presence known. When the intruder headed into the bedroom closest to the stairs, I decided to spring. They were cornered.

But as soon as I stepped into the hallway, they exited the room and froze as they caught sight of me. Then they broke into a run for the stairs, just like the time before. I yelled, "Incoming!" as I bolted after the intruder, figuring they would make a break for the library access. I was momentarily surprised when they tried the front door first, but we'd adjusted the dead bolt on the heavy door to stick so it didn't release fast enough to make it viable. They gave up instantly on the door and took off again down the hallway toward the library.

I knew Carter had heard me yell and would be guarding the tunnel entrance, but I had to get in place and close off their opportunity to leave the room. When I got to the bottom of the stairs, I saw the intruder run into the library and turned on the afterburners. I heard a shriek, which I assumed meant they'd encountered Carter, and as I ran to the doorway, the intruder slammed into me, knocking us both over a nearby table.

The drapes that Gertie had wrestled with were still on the floor, and as we rolled around, they captured us both in a tangled ball. Finally, I was able to get on top of the intruder and put my arm across their throat.

"Stop moving or I'll choke you," I said.

I didn't like that I couldn't see their hands because if they had a gun somewhere under that cloth, I was in the worst position possible even though Carter stood nearby and held a gun just inches from their face. I hoped their desperation didn't go so far beyond common sense that they took a chance.

"We've got more people outside the house and at the tunnel entrance," Carter said, letting them know that they had far more to contend with than just the two of us. "It's over."

The intruder slumped and I released their neck and used my one free arm to work the drapes off my other. Then I yanked the mask off the intruder's head and stared in shock.

"Do you know who this is?" Carter asked, cluing into my expression.

"Yeah. It's Karmin Blay."

I shrugged off the rest of the drapes and rose from the ground, then pulled out my own gun and held it on her while Carter unraveled her and handcuffed her. She never said a word the entire time and wouldn't even look us in the eye. I could see tears streaming down her face. This was the strangest takedown I'd ever experienced.

Then I heard yelling outside and a huge bang.

I bolted out of the room and ran for the front door, forced the sticky dead bolt back, and raced outside, trying to spot the source of the yell.

It didn't take long.

An unidentified person in all black was running across the front lawn toward the drive, trying to get away from the burst of fireworks chasing after him. Gertie was running and firing at the same time. As I took off after the intruder, the clouds cleared for a second and I saw Ida Belle round the other end of the house. I could only assume that Mannie was somewhere near the gate and that between the four of us, we'd have the second intruder surrounded.

But as we neared the gate, the intruder dashed into the woods and a second later, I heard an engine roar. He was going to get away! I was already running at max speed and Gertie, while closer, was moving to cut him off at the gate, but I had no doubt the intruder wouldn't be letting up on the gas. I saw her reach into her purse and hoped she let go of whatever idea she had in mind and moved off the road.

"Move!" I yelled, and pulled out my own gun, figuring I might be able to take out a tire. But with the distance and the lack of light, I couldn't be sure. And even if I did, the vehicle might careen right into her.

"Crap!" Gertie yelled as the truck barreled toward her.

I saw a burst of flame in her hand and realized she'd set her entire handbag on fire. She flung the whole flaming mess at the escaping vehicle before running into the woods, and it landed in the truck bed.

"Cover!" I yelled, and dived behind a tree seconds before the blast shook the ground.

I heard the sound of metal and glass shredding and then someone screaming. I jumped up and ran for the cloud of dust and fire and saw what was left of the truck perched on top of one of the entry columns. A man hung by his hoodie on one of the iron spikes.

Another vehicle raced toward the spectacle from the other side of the gate and slammed to a stop, headlights illuminating the entire scene. Mannie jumped out and ran for the gate, arriving at the same time I did. Ida Belle was right behind me and we scanned the area for Gertie, hoping she'd made it clear of the blast. Finally, we heard movement in the woods in front of us and saw her crawling out of an overgrown ditch that separated the end of the drive from the woods.

"I found a culvert," she said cheerfully. "Totally lost my glasses somewhere though."

Ida Belle and I stared at her in disbelief. She was covered with mud with branches sticking out of her hair and what looked like glitter and slices of lunch meat clinging to her bare skin. The woman had more lives than any cat.

I heard more footsteps behind us and turned to see Carter and Harrison running up. Harrison took one look at Gertie, then at the truck perched on his gate column and the man hanging there, groaning, and burst out laughing.

"I swear I thought you were exaggerating," he said. "Even though I'd seen some of the YouTube videos, but I mean, come on. And now here we are—I'm not sure I even want to know what happened." He looked at Carter. "Do I want to know what happened?"

Carter shrugged. "Sometimes it's better to know what you're lying about. Sometimes it's not. I already know the answer on this one, so..."

Harrison gave us a questioning look.

"Gertie's purse."

Mannie, Carter, Ida Belle, and I all answered at the same time and Harrison pointed a finger at Gertie. "You are never allowed to bring more than a container of food and a wallet into my house."

Gertie gave him an indignant look. "I caught the bad guy, didn't I?"

"I think Mannie would have made an easier and less destructive go of it," I said and gestured.

Mannie grinned. "It wouldn't have been nearly as entertaining though."

"It's hard to think clearly while running," Gertie said.

"Plus, I didn't know if Mannie would make it back to the truck in time to block. *And* I didn't even get to finish my sandwich before all this started up. It's hard to think clearly when you're hungry too."

"Well, you're not going to finish it now," I said and gestured to the slices of meat she was wearing.

She plucked one off her shoulder and popped it in her mouth. "My shoulders never touched the ground."

Harrison stared at her in dismay. The rest of us weren't remotely fazed.

"Did you catch the guy from the tunnels?" Harrison asked.

"Currently handcuffed to the stairs," Carter said. "But it's not a guy. It's Karmin Blay."

Everyone expressed different forms of disbelief, and then Harrison pointed to the guy on the fence. "Then who's this?" he asked.

Carter stepped closer to the fence. "He looks a little rough, but if I'm not mistaken, it's the disappearing Abel Charitte."

———

It took some effort and Mannie's truck to get Abel off the fence. He was a little beat up but didn't appear to have sustained any serious injuries. Carter handcuffed him and Mannie hauled him back to the house, so we could question him and Karmin before Carter called it all in and everything had to be official. Plus, we needed time to get our stories straight, as some of this didn't need to be on record or we were all in trouble of varying degrees.

When we walked inside the house, I saw Karmin sitting on the floor, handcuffed to the stairs. She gave Abel a curious look, but I didn't see even a flicker of recognition. But then, Karmin had spent her entire life finding ways around her mother, so at this point, she could probably lie as easily as tell the truth. After all, she'd gotten by me with her whole ghost story nonsense and I would bet the farm that she and Elijah were partners in the whole thing.

Abel barely glanced in Karmin's direction and huffed when he was told to sit on the ground so that Carter could cuff him to the other side of the stairs. His attitude was beyond strange. He appeared to be annoyed rather than worried. And in the blast, he'd apparently lost his ability to talk along with pieces of his clothes. He wouldn't even look at Carter when he asked him his name and to explain what he was doing on the property.

Karmin, on the other hand, looked as if she'd been the one who'd been in the explosion and she hadn't even been near it. Her face was pale and her body slack. She stared right through us and I wondered if she was going into shock.

"You want to explain to me what the two of you were doing here?" Carter asked Karmin.

"What?" she asked, shaking herself out of her stupor. "I don't know him."

"We know you had a partner," I said. "Because someone tripped the breaker the other night when I chased you."

She frowned but didn't deny anything.

"You can't lie your way out of this one," Carter said. "So you might as well talk."

"I paid someone," she said. "A local I found in a bar. I thought Elijah had flaked on me and I needed someone to work the breaker."

"You mean you needed to pay someone because you'd killed Elijah," Carter said.

Her eyes widened and she shook her head. "No! I didn't kill anyone. I swear. We were here that night, yes, and we scared the lady with the whole ghost thing and the red eyes, hoping she'd leave. But I didn't know that Elijah had cut the carpet until after she fell, I swear. Then her husband pulled up right after and we hid in the tunnel. I told Elijah I was leaving, but he said they might go to the hospital and he wanted to wait. I was too freaked out. I told him I was going and I did."

I narrowed my eyes at her. "You expect us to believe that?"

"It's the truth! I didn't even know he was dead until you came to my office. I thought maybe he'd gone back in and..."

"Found the jewels and ghosted you," I finished.

Her eyes widened.

"Yeah, we know about the jewels," I said.

Her shoulders slumped. "They were my ticket out. My real ticket—not the old man my mother insists I marry."

"Then if you didn't kill Elijah, who did?" Carter asked. "Who else were you working with?"

"No one. It was just Elijah and me."

I shook my head. "So you're saying Elijah was alive and well when you left and some other random person just happened to be here and killed him? Do you realize how ridiculous that sounds?"

"You sure you didn't have another partner?" Carter asked.

"No," Karmin insisted. "Well, except for that guy I paid the other night, but he never came in the house."

"Uh-huh," Carter said. "What was this guy's name?"

"I don't know. He was just some guy I met in the bar. He said he was from Sinful and I told him I wanted to play a prank on the new owners of the house and asked if he could help."

"Well, you had to pick him up and drop him off," Carter insisted. "Where was that?"

"I just gave him the money, told him where to go, and what time to turn off the breaker. He said he was using his boat because it was easier and then he could fish afterward."

Carter nodded toward Abel. "And you're telling me you've never seen this man before."

"No."

"You'll excuse me if I find that hard to believe, because this man is Elijah's cousin."

She whipped her head around to look at Abel, who just continued to glare silently at the marble floor.

"I don't know him and Elijah never mentioned a cousin. Well, I mean, except for the one who runs the voodoo shop and her sister."

"Elijah stole a book from her," I said. "Why did he want it?"

She glanced at Harrison, then Abel, and I could see her hesitation. I looked over at Carter and he nodded. He could see it too.

"Harrison," Carter said. "Would you do me a favor and secure Mr. Charitte in the library?"

I could tell Harrison didn't want to leave but knew it was the right call. We might get more out of Karmin if the current homeowner and her dead partner's cousin weren't glaring at her. Not that I blamed Harrison at all. I'd feel the same way if it was my house and my fiancé who had been injured.

As soon as Harrison had Abel in the library, Carter focused on Karmin again. "Tell me how this all happened—how you knew about the jewels, how you met Elijah, everything. I don't think I have to explain just how bad this looks for you."

She shook her head, her fear apparent. Things were finally starting to sink in.

"I've always heard about the jewels," she said. "It's like urban legend in New Orleans society, but no one really believed it. Then I got the listing, and I noticed this clause in the estate paperwork referring to the discovery of historical property belonging to the Leroux family. The document is enormous, so no surprise that no

267

one mentioned it—and I found it by accident when I dropped the folder with the documents in my office and they scattered. I was putting all the sheets back in order when the word *jewelry* jumped out at me. That's when I figured there was some truth to the legend, and since the clause was still included in the paper-work, that meant the jewelry had never been found."

"And that's why you never listed the house," I said. "You wanted access for as long as it took to find the jewelry."

"Yeah, but I screwed up there. I should have listed it. It had been available forever and no one had been interested, but I was foolish and thought I could get away with not putting it up, at least until I found the jewelry. That was my big mistake. If I'd still been the agent when your friends looked at it, I might have been able to dissuade them from purchasing it."

"So how did you hook up with Elijah?" Carter asked.

"I'd already spent a ton of hours searching the house and hadn't come up with anything. I figured if the jewelry had gone undiscovered all this time, then it was really well hidden. And if anyone might know something about the house, it would be people who were related to the Leroux. So I hired a PI who found Destiny. I went to her shop to feel her out but I knew right away she wouldn't help me. She's really bent on all that voodoo stuff and curses. I casually asked if she was any relation to Lovelie, and she went off on a rant about abandoning faith and family, so I crossed her off my list. She was more than a little scary."

"Destiny can be intense," I agreed.

She nodded. "So I went back to my PI and he tracked down Elijah at a side hustle he had bartending in the French Quarter. I knew he was already walking the wrong side of the law most of the time and needed the money. And he didn't buy into the voodoo stuff like Destiny did."

"I'm guessing he didn't need much convincing when he got a look at you," I said.

She looked down at the floor. "It wasn't like that. Not really."

"I'm sure it wasn't for you," I said and she blushed.

"Anyway, he said Destiny had an old journal—from her great-grandfather's time," she said. "Elijah had never paid much attention to Destiny and her sister when they brought up stuff like that, but we figured if there was going to be information about the jewelry anywhere, it would be in that journal."

"And was it?" Carter asked.

"No. But he talked about tunnels. Lovelie and her father made peace at some point and he worried about her safety, especially living so far out among people of differing beliefs, and with a man of questionable reputation and obvious amounts of money. Lovelie reassured him that Lucien had provided them a way to escape the house without detection if the need should ever arise. I had made copies of the keys when I lost the listing, so Elijah and I had been getting in that way. But we knew we had to find another way inside in case Travis sold the house."

"So you looked for the tunnels," Carter said. "How did you find them?"

"By accident," she said. "We were checking the cubbies in the library and I banged my foot on a chair and fell into the wall with the hidden panel."

"So you continued to access the house even after my friends moved in," I said. "And you played on the ghost story to try to scare them away. You know my friend could have died from that fall she took down the stairs."

"I didn't want to hurt anyone, I swear. I just needed the

jewelry so I could get away from my parents. Elijah needed a way out too."

"Then why did you kill him?" Carter asked.

"I didn't. I swear. He was alive the night I left."

"Then who else knew what you were doing?" Carter asked.

"No one! I didn't tell anyone."

"Then why was Elijah's cousin here tonight?" Carter asked.

She frowned. "I don't know."

CHAPTER TWENTY-FOUR

ONCE WE'D GOTTEN EVERYTHING WE COULD OUT OF Karmin and nothing out of Abel, Carter faced the problem of having to call the whole thing in. The issue of civilians setting a trap to catch an intruder wasn't really a problem because the homeowner had been part of the plan and in general, what we'd done wasn't against the law. But the truck perched on top of the entry column presented a unique problem, and one the ADA wouldn't want to hear about.

Mannie had found registration papers for the truck and it was one of a fleet of work vehicles for a petroleum company based in NOLA. When Carter voiced his concerns about the ADA and Gertie's purse, Mannie told him to hold off a little longer and let him call in some favors. Within thirty minutes, two men arrived with a crane on a trailer and lifted the truck off the columns and onto a second trailer that two more men had pulled up with.

While the first crew got the truck off the fence and onto the flatbed, the second crew picked up all the scattered truck parts, leaving no evidence that the truck had ever existed. None of them had said a word—simply gave Mannie a nod, did their work, then left. When they were gone, Mannie said he'd clear out as well and told us to call if we needed anything.

"I've seen special ops missions with less precision than that," Carter said as Mannie drove off with Ida Belle and Gertie.

Harrison nodded. "I'm just glad he's on our side."

Carter decided on being mostly honest about the setting a trap part and who was involved. Karmin and Abel had seen everyone, so there was no point in lying about that part or it would just make our entire story look sketchy. The ADA wasn't going to pat anyone on the back for the move, but it didn't change the facts that we'd apprehended two suspects in the murder of Elijah Charitte. And it wasn't likely Abel would bring up the explosion or the disappearing truck since it had been stolen and there were already warrants out for him for parole violation and for two other crimes. He was more likely to claim he was just taking a stroll in the woods and had been arrested for being in the wrong place at the wrong time.

It wasn't the cleanest of stories, but it would work.

The state police showed up to take Karmin and Abel into custody, and Carter's forensic team arrived shortly after to pick up the truck Karmin had parked at the old homesite. She claimed she'd borrowed it from her parents' landscape manager, but I figured that wasn't the case. I also figured that the manager would support her story due to his employment.

Regardless of the time and the messiness of a suspect with society connections, Carter got a judge out of bed who agreed to sign a warrant to search her Mercedes and apartment, and the two of us headed back to Sinful in the boat so he could do just that. Harrison had called Cassidy and filled her in as soon as things had settled down at the house and she'd headed that way. The forensics team would be taking photos and gathering up evidence for probably another couple hours but had indicated there was no problem with Harrison and Cassidy occupying the areas of the house that they didn't need to document.

Ida Belle, Gertie, and Ronald were already at my house with coffee and cookies ready when I got there. It took a good thirty minutes of all of us talking and Ronald interrupting before we finally got out the whole story, each of us throwing in our angle to fill in all the gaps. Then we all sat completely silent for a bit before Ronald blew out a breath.

"So do we believe her?" he asked. "Not the jewelry hunting stuff—obviously that part is true—but I mean the not-killing-Elijah part?"

I slumped back in my chair and shook my head. "I don't know. She didn't give any indication that she was lying, but then, she didn't the first time we talked to her either when I asked if she knew Elijah."

"I would imagine Karmin is a very skilled liar," Ronald said. "She'd have had to be to survive living in that house."

I nodded, but something about Karmin's story bothered me. Well, a lot of somethings, but one thing in particular.

"She said that she and Elijah argued over staying the night Cassidy fell and that she left," I said, talking out loud more for my own benefit than anything else. "No big deal because Elijah was squatting in the camp nearby and had come by boat, not with her, right? So it's not like she left him stranded."

"But something about it bothers you?" Ida Belle asked.

"Yeah. Something Big said, about people like Elijah being followers not leaders, and that followers rarely got shot because they'd go along with whatever leaders asked."

"That sounds right," Gertie said.

"But according to Karmin, Elijah argued with her about leaving the house and that doesn't fit with his character," I said.

Ida Belle nodded. "I see what you're saying, and I agree that it probably didn't go down exactly as she claims. But I think her reason for lying is different than you think."

"What would it be?" Ronald asked. "What am I missing?"

"That Elijah was in love with Karmin," Ida Belle said. "And Karmin knew it."

"Ah," Ronald said. "That's how she roped him in. It wasn't his overwhelming desire for money."

"I don't think so," I said. "Don't get me wrong, he wanted money too, but I think he wanted Karmin more. Remember what Brenda said—that Elijah had a hot one on the line? I think he was referring to Karmin, not the jewelry."

"So you don't think there was an argument?" Gertie asked.

"I wouldn't be surprised if there wasn't," I said. "It's more likely that Karmin got spooked after Cassidy fell and ran. When it comes down to it, she's a privileged society girl, not a professional criminal."

"I have to admit, I'm hoping it was Abel who killed Elijah," Gertie said. "I know Karmin still broke the law, and Cassidy could have been seriously hurt with that stunt they pulled, but I kind of feel sorry for her. At least for the situation she's in with her parents and marrying some old guy they picked for her."

"Yeah. That whole thing grosses me out," I said. "But I feel sorrier for Elijah, who fell for the wrong girl, which led to his own tragic end."

Ronald sighed. "A beautiful woman has been the ruination of many men."

I nodded. It was like a Shakespearean tragedy but despite all evidence pointing that direction, I really hoped Elijah wasn't killed by the woman he loved.

My disappointment was overwhelming when Carter recovered the murder weapon from under the back seat of Karmin's car.

———

CARTER SLUMPED INTO A CHAIR AT MY KITCHEN TABLE. Everyone had gone home after he'd called with his gun announcement. I'd tried to sleep but I tossed and turned for the little amount of time I was in bed. It was still better than Carter, who hadn't even been to bed yet. He passed on coffee because he was planning on going home for a shower and a couple hours' sleep before he had to go at the case again, and I heated up some pastries from Ally's to go along with sweet tea. If nothing else, the sugar might help knock him out.

"Were her fingerprints on the gun?" I asked.

He shook his head. "It had been wiped clean, but it was wrapped in her scarf and under the seat of her car."

"Anything on the rounds?"

"Yeah, three different sets. They were reloads. But none of them popped."

"Crap."

If Karmin had purchased reloads, the fingerprints of the original shooter and anyone who created the reload could be on them.

"And I'm guessing the gun wasn't registered."

"Originally, yes, but it was reported stolen about fifteen years ago."

"So another dead end. What is Karmin saying?"

"That it isn't hers. That she left the top down on her car all the time and anyone could have put it in there."

"Well, that's not untrue. It was down the day we followed her, but I can't imagine that the ADA is buying it."

"Ha! Exactly the opposite. The ADA has a long-running

beef with Karmin's mother—some zoning issue they fought over—so he's practically foaming at the mouth."

Worst possible scenario for Karmin, that was for sure.

"But if we believe Karmin is capable of murder, then why didn't she have the gun on her last night?" I asked.

"I put that very question to the ADA because I see it as a plot hole a defense attorney will drive a bus through. But the ADA says killing Elijah probably wasn't premeditated and she scared herself, so therefore left the gun behind so nothing could go wrong again. I get the impression he's thinking her lawyers might go for an accidental discharge defense."

"But even if it was an accident, she left him there to bleed out. That wouldn't work out any better for her."

"No, it wouldn't."

I shook my head. I knew Karmin needed money to rid herself of her mother's control, and I absolutely believed she had used Elijah by convincing him they were in a romance, but I still couldn't quite picture her in the role of a killer. Not even with all the evidence stacked against her. But then, I'd been wrong about Karmin twice already, and of all people, I should know that the deadliest among us took on all forms.

"What about Abel?" I asked. "He was on-site and has the record to back up this level of violence. Maybe all three were in on it and he took Elijah out to increase his take. Maybe he was going to eliminate Karmin next."

Carter nodded. "And I'd bet that he wouldn't have an issue with doing so, but the thing is, Abel was headed to the back of the house carrying a crowbar. He must have dropped it in the lawn when Gertie set the fireworks on him, but his prints are all over it. If he was in on it with Karmin, then he would have known about the tunnels. Or even if they were approaching from different avenues, Karmin could have simply opened the door and let him in."

"But if they're not partners, then how did he find out?"

"I don't know and unless Abel starts talking, we might not ever find out. I'm sure Karmin's attorneys will be all over the theory that Abel killed Elijah and planted the gun in her car, and they'll have a good shot at reasonable doubt because we can place Abel at the house on two different occasions when he had no legitimate reason for being there."

"He must have clued into Elijah being onto something," I said. "Maybe he followed them before they started using the tunnels."

"Or maybe Elijah let something slip. Bottom line is he found out and was making his own play, but there's nothing to tie him to Karmin. Only Elijah. And all evidence points to Elijah being shot in the woods and retreating into the tunnels, but if Abel didn't know about the tunnels, he wouldn't have known where to find the exit in the woods."

"Maybe he never found it," I said. "Maybe he followed Karmin one night and figured she was going to the house, then when she went down a different road, he hung back and waited so she wouldn't see him, then went to search the area when he thought the coast was clear. Maybe he never saw them go in or out of the tunnel. Maybe he found the boat Elijah stashed and waited for him there."

"It's possible, but that's quite a hike for Elijah with a gunshot through the stomach. Not saying he couldn't have made it. We've both seen what adrenaline can do, but..."

I nodded. It was thin. Really, really thin. And compared to the case against Karmin, it was laughable. Everything indicated that Karmin was the one who'd pulled the trigger, and she'd already proven herself to be a professional liar. But something still bothered me.

"So what's your directive?" I asked.

"Document it and call it closed."

"I don't like it. Even with all the evidence."

"I'm not completely sold on it either, but the reality is Karmin has lied about everything. She's got motive and opportunity, and all the evidence points right at her. Sometimes a duck is just a duck."

"Did you talk to Destiny?"

"Briefly. I told her about the arrest and what Elijah had been involved in. I told her I'd see her later today to explain how things would proceed."

"How did she take it?"

"Stoic. She seems to be more worried about purifying the body for burial than anything else."

"Murdered on the Leroux estate during the commission of a crime. She might set his casket on fire."

"It wouldn't be the first time."

I stared.

"Well, I need to run," he said. "Thanks for the sugar high. I'll call you later. Maybe now that this is wrapped up, I can throw some steaks on the grill and we can sit in that hot tub with some beer."

"Sounds like a plan," I said.

But I was already making different ones.

CHAPTER TWENTY-FIVE

IDA BELLE, GERTIE, AND I MUNCHED ON COOKIES AS IDA Belle drove down the highway. It was early, but I was hoping to talk to Destiny before she opened her shop. We hadn't slept much and although we were all happy that Harrison and Cassidy's troubles were over, none of us were thrilled with the way things had played out. But the facts were the facts. The ADA had a strong case against Karmin, and it was far more likely that she was guilty than not.

But that didn't stop me from wanting to fill the gaps.

Abel Charitte was still on the table as far as I was concerned, and if I was right in my suspicions, the trouble at the Leroux estate might not be past us. Abel was probably set for a return to jail given the transgressions he already had warrants for, but they wouldn't keep him locked up forever. Carter intended to tell Abel that we knew what had happened to the jewelry and that it was sold years ago, but would Abel believe him? Or would he press his luck and return to the house at first opportunity?

I'd read his rap sheet, and Abel Charitte was trouble—real trouble. Violent and serious trouble. If he was a murderer on top of all that, then it was an even bigger problem. So I wanted to talk to Destiny to see how she felt about her other cousin's involvement and if she thought he'd prove to be a problem in the future once we told him about the jewelry's history.

I could see someone moving around in the shop but the Closed sign was still on the door. It wasn't due to open for another fifteen minutes, which was enough time to find out what I wanted to know, assuming Destiny would talk to me. Because we'd used Gertie as the decoy the time before, she had to stay behind. If Destiny saw her and realized she'd been played, she wouldn't talk to us at all.

So Ida Belle and I headed to the shop and I rapped on the door. Destiny looked up from the cash register and frowned, but she did walk our way. She pushed open the door but didn't invite us in.

"What do you want?" she asked.

"Some answers," I said. "It will only take a few minutes."

She stared at me, her lips pursed, then finally stood back so we could enter.

"My cousin is dead and the woman who killed him has been arrested," Destiny said. "I can't change the fact that your friends purchased a property so cursed it can't be fixed, so what could you possibly want from me?"

"I want to know if your other cousin will continue the trouble for my friends," I said. "I want to be certain this is over."

She frowned. "The curse on the house is forever, so in that way, it won't be over for them until they leave that place of evil. But that is a different kind of trouble than my cousin. Abel is a loose cannon who strayed from the family long ago. I was not even aware he was back in town. The deputy who informed me of the arrest tells me this was all over the jewelry that Lucien was said to have hidden in the house, and that he has proof that it was all sold years ago."

I nodded.

She held her hands up. "If there is nothing to be gained, then Abel no longer has a reason to go there. Abel serves only himself."

"And you're certain it wasn't Abel who killed Elijah?"

"He wouldn't dare kill a Charitte. Abel is an immoral man but he's also a coward."

"Was Abel raised with the same beliefs that you were?"

"Of course."

"But he had no problem going into the house."

"Abel would sell his soul for money," Destiny said. "It has always held too much power over him, and the less he had, the more powerful it became."

"But couldn't you say the same thing for Elijah?"

Anger flashed across Destiny's face. "Elijah was led astray by the woman who betrayed him. He should have known better."

"Know what, exactly?"

"That a woman like Karmin Blay doesn't dally with people like us except to use us for something and then dispose of us when done."

"What do you mean 'people like us'?"

"Poor people, uneducated, not Christian or connected with New Orleans society."

"So you think all of this was Karmin's idea and Elijah just went along with it without even thinking? Was he that weak? After all, he stole the journal from you and used it to help him find a way into the house."

Her jaw flexed and I knew I'd made her angry. "I think she led him down a dark path...like Lucien did Lovelie. Money is the great corrupter. But so is love.

When you're offered both, it's a hard temptation to resist, especially for a young man who left the protection his family offered. If you'll excuse me, I have things to do. They're releasing Elijah's body today. I have to prepare what I need for the purification. The evil that infected him can't be allowed to spread any more than it already has."

We headed out and climbed back in the SUV. I watched as Destiny exited the shop and locked the door behind her. She carried a box of God knows what, and I assumed it was all needed to treat the corpse before another curse descended on the family.

"So?" Ida Belle asked as she started the car.

"Home, I guess."

I wasn't sure if I'd accomplished what I wanted there. I hoped Destiny was right about Abel not pursuing the jewelry any longer, but ultimately, that remained to be seen. As far as Destiny was concerned, it was all over except for the curse protecting part, and I suppose for her, it was.

I slumped back against my seat and closed my eyes, both my body and my mind tired from everything that had transpired in the last couple days. I must have lapsed into a state of light sleep, because I could see Destiny in front of a coffin, holding sticks of incense and chanting.

He thought our culture outdated and fanciful.

The evil that infected him can't be allowed to spread.

His lack of belief was his end.

It's my responsibility to be the spiritual guide for the family here.

Abel serves only himself.

He would never kill a Charitte.

He's also a coward.

I jolted awake, my heart racing. I whipped around toward Gertie.

"That bag that the bath salts came in? Do you still have it? Crap! Never mind. Your purse blew up last night."

"That was my waterproof purse that exploded," she said. "It was supposed to rain so I changed handbags. I still have the bath salts bag right here."

She held up her purse.

"You thought of something," Ida Belle said to me.

I nodded. "I thought of a *lot* of something. We have to get that bag to Carter right now. I think Destiny is the one who shot Elijah."

What?

No way!

They both responded at once.

"Where the heck did that come from?" Ida Belle asked.

So I took them down the rabbit hole—Destiny's deep belief in the Leroux house curse and the risks Elijah took by going there, her knowledge of where he was living, her insistence that both Lovelie and Elijah were led astray by love then corrupted by evil, and the things Destiny had said about Abel.

"She was practically disgusted when she said Abel wouldn't dare kill a Charitte," I said. "It felt odd when she said it, but I couldn't put my finger on exactly why."

"But if Destiny killed Elijah to protect the family, then it makes sense," Ida Belle said.

"You really think she's that deep into what she believes?" Gertie asked. "That she would kill over it—and a family member? One who lived with her during his childhood?"

I nodded. "I think Destiny absolutely believes that what Elijah was doing would bring the wrath of the spirits onto the family. My guess is when Karmin first approached him, he started asking questions about the Leroux estate and that made her suspicious. That's about the same time as Big says she started paying the rent late."

"She thinks her financial problems were because of the curse Elijah had brought onto the family," Ida Belle said. "I suppose anything is possible, but how did she know how to find him that night?"

"Remember she made that comment about being led astray by love in regard to Elijah and Lovelie. But none of us ever suggested there was any romantic overtures involved with what was going on, and Carter wouldn't have either. So there was no way to know unless..."

"She was following him," Ida Belle said. "And saw him with Karmin, who was playing up the romance angle to keep Elijah doing her bidding."

I nodded. "Remember how guilty she looked at the house last night when I questioned her about that?"

"Oh yeah," Ida Belle said. "She was definitely playing him."

"But if Destiny figured out what they were up to, then why not kill him in New Orleans at that sketchy motel?" Gertie asked. "Why would she risk going there when she thinks the house is evil?"

"I think she would have killed him at the motel, but I'm guessing by the time she figured out what they were up to, Elijah was squatting at that camp," I said. "Remember, they had full access with a key before Harrison and Cassidy moved in. That changed everything. Someone needed to be on-site to know when the house was empty."

Ida Belle nodded. "The timing makes sense. When Harrison and Cassidy made the offer, Elijah started asking questions about the house, trying to narrow down where the jewels were before they moved in. Destiny knew something was up because Elijah didn't have any interest in their family history and only contacted her about money. So she followed him and saw him with Karmin. But before she could get to him in NOLA, he bounced."

"That's what I think," I said. "And I don't think she ever went into the house or ever would. When Elijah disappeared from NOLA, I think she followed Karmin and saw her meet him in the woods and go into the tunnel."

"And she would have known about the tunnel from her grandfather's journal," Gertie said.

"Exactly," I said. "So she just waited, hoping she could get Elijah alone. And she got her chance because after Cassidy fell, Karmin left—whether she fled or they argued and he refused to go, we may never know but at some point, Elijah decided to clear out as well."

"And Destiny was waiting for him when he came out of the tunnel," Gertie said. "That's cold."

"She wouldn't see it that way," I said. "As the eldest, she sees it as her responsibility to protect the family."

"So she shot him and he ran back into the tunnel to get away, because he figured Destiny wouldn't follow him there," Ida Belle said. "But what if he hadn't died? Wasn't Destiny worried that he'd get away and identify her as the person who shot him?"

"I think Destiny believes she was on the side of right- eousness and doing the spirits' bidding, so they would take care of the rest," I said. "Remember, she said Lovelie wouldn't tolerate a traitor in her midst."

Gertie nodded. "And even if Elijah had managed to get to the hospital, I doubt he would have given up his cousin when he'd have to admit what he was doing as well."

"So why hide in that tunnel room when he ran?" Ida Belle asked.

"My guess is he couldn't make it up the ladder. He'd lost a lot of blood and would have been in shock on top of it. I mean, his cousin had just shot him. He was probably in panic mode and figured he should hide, just in case Destiny came after him."

"That would also explain why Karmin didn't know Elijah was dead," Gertie said. "Because although she denied knowing who he was, her shock at a body being found there looked genuine."

"And it explains why she didn't bring the gun with her into the house last night," I said. "That one has really been bugging me."

"I would have never put that together," Ida Belle said. "But it tracks—in a Destiny sort of way. So what's up with the bath salt bag?"

"I'll tell you all inside," I said as she pulled into a space in front of the sheriff's department.

I ran inside and grabbed the arm of a startled Carter, who was talking to the dispatcher, and pulled him back to his office. "I need you to lift and run some prints."

"What prints?" he said.

I motioned to Gertie and she pulled the paper bag out of her purse.

"It will have Gertie's prints, of course, but I want you to lift others off and run them against the prints you pulled off the rounds in the murder weapon."

I felt my chest tighten when without question, Carter put on gloves, took the bag from Gertie, and started lifting prints. A couple minutes later, he loaded them into his software and I clutched Ida Belle's shoulder as we all bent over the desk, waiting for the results.

It was a short wait.

"There's a match," he said and stared at me in disbelief. "Who do they belong to?"

"Destiny."

———

CARTER SHUFFLED INTO MY KITCHEN LATE THAT EVENING and plopped into a chair at the table. He looked as though he needed a shower and to crawl in bed for the rest of the year.

"Rough day?" I asked in my best sarcastic voice as I got him a beer.

"Ha! You don't even know. First, I debated on do I approach the ADA first or Destiny. I mean, a volcano couldn't blast either from their beliefs, so it was a rough call. I figured I'd just get in my truck and start driving to the city and I'd figure it out on the way, but when I hit the city limits, I got a call from the NOLA medical examiner."

"You had the body transferred?"

He nodded. "The local ME had an issue with his cooler."

I cringed. "Gross."

"Could have been...hence the transfer. But anyway, apparently Destiny wanted to do some incense and prayer thing before the body was moved out of the building. The ME said she couldn't access the body because it was stored with others so she'd have to do her thing outside the freezer door. He left her in the hallway to arrange transport to the funeral home and you're not going to believe what she did—"

"Tried to burn the building down."

Carter blinked. "I don't know why I'm surprised anymore. How did you know?"

I shrugged. "Destiny, voodoo, curse...fire is a traditional purification method in many belief systems. And since you smell like smoke and accelerant—lighter fluid?"

"Are you sure you don't want to be a detective? Because your deduction and observation skills are off the charts."

"I'd be a liability as a government employee."

"You spent most of your adult life as a government employee."

I grinned. "And look how that turned out."

"Good point. Anyway, I got to arrest Destiny and that stunt got me a pass with the ADA for not closing the file on the case."

"So he's dropping the charges against Karmin?"

"The murder charge, yes, but he won't let it go completely. She'll be looking at everything from trespass to criminal mischief because of Cassidy's fall. There's only her word that Elijah cut the carpet, and honestly, I'm not convinced. It seems too active a role for the person everyone described."

"Well, without Elijah to say differently, Karmin can claim whatever she wants. She's a professional-grade liar so it will probably play out well for her."

He gave me a curious look. "I thought you were disappointed when she was arrested."

"Because I couldn't convince myself she'd killed Elijah. Not because I think she's a stellar human being. But there's still a big gap between playing people to steal something and murder. And while I absolutely think that whole marriage thing her parents are pushing is archaic and gross, the reality is, if she hadn't taken advantage, Elijah would still be alive."

"True. Well, at least it's finally all over. I can write this up and close the file."

I just nodded. I didn't have the heart to tell him that Karmin's whole arranged marriage thing had sent me off on another avenue of thought—one even thinner than Destiny being the shooter—but one I thought I was equally right on. I'd just have to make sure I was right before I tossed another curveball at him.

"I'm going to get out of here," he said. "My plan is to take a long shower and then go to sleep for at least twelve hours. Rain check on dinner?"

"Of course."

He gave me a kiss and headed out. I waited until I heard the door close before picking up the phone and placing a call to Morrow.

"I need a background check—former military. Just a date and battle location of death."

Morrow didn't even bother asking me why because he was always better off not knowing what I was up to. And since the request seemed innocuous enough, he simply tapped in the information on his keyboard and a couple seconds later, confirmed what I'd already suspected.

My second call was to Clotilde. I gave her a brief description of everything that had transpired since we'd visited, and she was amazed at all that had happened over jewelry that had been sold long ago. Then I got around to my real reason for calling.

"The day Lucien died," I said, "did any of the women from town bring food?"

"Yes," she said immediately. "That strange woman brought those horrible fig cookies. I remember because we always joked about her obvious crush on Lucien."

"What woman?"

She told me.

CHAPTER TWENTY-SIX

IDA BELLE LOOKED OVER AT ME AS WE PULLED INTO MUDBUG just after midnight. Ida Belle had told Walter that we were having a girls' case-solving celebration at my house and since our plan was to indulge heavily in both food and drink, they were going to stay over.

"You sure about this?" she asked.

"No," I said. "If I was sure, I'd have told Carter. But since there's no evidence to get a warrant, we need a fact-finding mission."

"I get it, but if Mary comes out that back door with a gun, we're getting the heck out of there," Ida Belle said.

"It's pitch-black," Gertie said. "She won't be able to see where to shoot."

"And you think that somehow makes it less dangerous?" Ida Belle asked as she parked at the curb a couple houses down from Mary's.

We pulled on our gloves and grabbed flashlights and trowels and headed off. We dipped into Mary's neighbor's backyard and crawled through the azalea bushes until we reached the stretch of roses at the edge of the lawn. I pulled out a couple of glow sticks and placed them under the bush. It gave us just enough illumination to work with. I looked over at Ida Belle and Gertie.

"Here goes," I said and we started to dig.

About twenty minutes in, I heard the clink of a trowel striking something hard and solid. I looked over and saw Gertie staring back at me.

"I didn't want to doubt you," she said, "but this one was out there, even for me. I should have known better."

Ida Belle nodded. "Rambo has his work cut out if he's going to beat you at finding bodies."

I heard the sound of creaking hinges behind us and cringed when I heard the neighbor's dog come barking into the lawn... and the barking was headed straight for us. The owner started yelling at the dog—an enormous German shepherd—to come back inside but he'd barreled into the bushes and latched onto Gertie's foot. She was trying to shake him off when the voice of the one person I was praying slept through the night boomed out.

"What's going on out there?" Mary yelled. "If you Jesus people are in my rosebushes, I'm going to send you off to meet him."

I heard the sound of a shotgun pump and flattened myself just as shot peppered the bushes above me. I'd had Gertie bring fireworks in case we needed a diversion but we were well beyond that point. What we needed now was divine intervention. The only plus was that the shot had scared the dog into letting Gertie's leg go and he'd run off yelping.

"Dial 911!" I heard the neighbor yell. "Mary's shooting again."

Another blast tore through the bushes and I felt shot hit the bottom of my shoes. We didn't have time to crawl back through the bushes. Not without catching a load of shot in our backsides, so I did what any good soldier would do in that situation.

"Run!" I yelled.

We scrambled up into half crouches and took off through the bushes, me bringing up the rear so I could cover. When we burst through on the neighbor's side, the German shepherd got us in his sights and broke into a snarling run. We made a hard turn and ran for the front of the house, and I was praying the cops showed up before Mary made it out the front door and onto the street.

The dog was barking as he ran, and I knew there was no way we would make it to Ida Belle's SUV.

"Throw a sandwich or something!" I yelled, because there was exactly zero chance that Gertie didn't have something to eat in her purse. Or her bra.

As we barreled through the hedge that separated the front and back yard, I saw Gertie fling something off to her right... where it hit an approaching Harrison right in the face. The dog shifted direction and jumped, slamming into Harrison so hard he knocked him down, then the dog grabbed the coveted item off Harrison's chest and took off running to his backyard.

Harrison scrambled up and stared at Gertie. "Did you just throw a human hand at me?"

"When Mary started shooting, I panicked and took off with it," Gertie said, wheezing as she talked.

"A human hand?" Harrison demanded. "And a dog just left with it."

"Don't worry," I said. "I know where you can find the rest of him."

———

No one wanted to risk going after Mary with her sitting on the front porch with her shotgun, so we just waited behind the bushes with the cops until she fell asleep, then Harrison disarmed her and two other deputies sat with her in her living room to make sure she didn't move. Harrison brought in the forensics team to finish what we'd started and by the time Carter crawled out of bed and got over there, they'd unearthed the entire body.

When Mary saw them carrying the body bag down the driveway, she collapsed and the paramedics collected her and took her to the hospital. The Mudbug deputies dismissed Ida Belle, Gertie, and me with the condition that we show up the next day to give our statements. They also decided we could do that in Sinful—for our own convenience. Harrison just smirked. Everyone knew they didn't want any part of what had gone down here and were tossing it all back to Carter.

So we headed back to Sinful and our respective homes, showered, and all went to bed. Now, it was 9:00 a.m. and Ida Belle, Gertie, and I were in my kitchen, on our second pot of coffee, and I wasn't going to count how many of Ally's croissants we'd consumed because we hadn't done nearly enough running last night to compensate.

I heard the front door open and Carter appeared in the kitchen and slumped into the empty chair. Ida Belle, Gertie, and I hadn't really discussed everything from the night before —mostly because we'd been busy with coffee and croissants— but now that Carter was here to give us the wrap-up, we could delve into everything.

"So?" I asked as I poured him some coffee and pushed a croissant in front of him.

He gave me a grateful smile and took a bite of the croissant. "You were right—it was Mary's husband. They tested the hair, and it looks like poisoning. I got an order to exhume Lucien Leroux with the expectation that we'll find the same."

Ida Belle shook her head. "I still don't know how you put it all together."

"I wasn't certain," I said, "which is why we had to get the evidence ourselves. No judge was going to issue an order on my feelings."

"They would if they were smart," Gertie said. "I'm beginning to think the only paranormal stuff going on in all of this is you."

Ida Belle nodded. "You do set a bar. So spill."

"Well, it was a combination of things that just came together and brought me to that conclusion. It all started with Karmin's parents basically trying to arrange her marriage. It made me remember Mary's comments about her own marriage, which weren't exactly complimentary. Things like 'My daddy met a strong young man when I was of age' and 'I made a good marriage to a decent man like you're supposed to.' If Karmin's back was against the wall today, then where was Mary's eighty years ago?"

"Women definitely didn't have as many options back then," Gertie said. "But how did you make the leap to her killing her husband? And why would she kill Lucien?"

"Because she was in love with Lucien," I said.

They all stared.

"Think about it, she said Lucien was Hollywood charming and handsome. Those descriptors didn't sound like something the usually hyper-religious and chronically negative Mary would say."

"But she also said he philandered with ladies in town," Gertie said. "Wouldn't that bother her?"

"I'm sure it did," I said. "But she was determined to catch him for herself, which is why she was always bringing his favorite fig cookies over to his house. My guess is Mary had a good piece of jewelry that Lucien was after, so he played her like he did all the other women he'd stolen from."

"But Mary said her husband died in combat," Ida Belle said.

I nodded. "I think what happens is Mary's husband came home and since Mary was head over heels with Lucien by then, and her husband was the duty that had been forced on her, she poisoned him, buried him in the backyard, and told everyone he died in combat. Remember, she was very protective about letting anyone work in her garden. And she said that when her husband passed, she started growing roses to fill the time and had won the state fair several years after."

Gertie's eyes widened. "Her husband's body was fertilizing the ground, making those roses grow better than the norm."

"So I called Morrow and asked for the date of death and combat location for Mary's husband," I said, "and found out that he didn't die in combat and should have arrived home just a week before Lucien died."

"Where he expected a reunion with his wife, but was instead poisoned and buried under rosebushes," Gertie said.

"Exactly," I said. "But Mary miscalculated. After she announced her husband's demise, she thought that freed her up to become the next Mrs. Leroux."

"Which Lucien never intended," Ida Belle said and whistled.

"And since the dallying with others didn't stop, and Mary didn't want to see it, she poisoned Lucien," I said.

"The ole *if I can't have him no one can* adage," Ida Belle said.

"I called Clotilde and asked if anyone had brought food over right before Lucien died," I said. "She confirmed that Mary brought the fig cookies."

"And she knew no one else in the house would eat them," Gertie said.

"Remember she said something about Lucien's death being a man's choices catching up with him?" I asked. "I think she somehow saw her actions as justified because of Lucien's deceit."

"Then after that, by all accounts, Mary got hyper-religious," Gertie said. "Guilt?"

"I'm sure that's part of it," I said. "But there was also something Ida Belle said—'some are so invested in dishonesty that the lies become their truth'—and I think that could apply to several people in this case."

Gertie threw her hands up. "That's it—you're magic."

Carter smiled. "I agree."

"I bet the ADA doesn't," Ida Belle said. "How's all this hitting him?"

His smile turned into a grin. "Like a hurricane. He has no idea what to do with Mary. He doesn't want to prosecute her or lock her up but she's probably committed two murders and likes to shoot at people. It's not safe to leave her alone. I'm just glad it's not my job to figure it out and that Mary lives in Mudbug and not Sinful."

"And you're enjoying his discomfort," I said.

"Oh, definitely!" Carter agreed.

"Well, now that this is over, maybe we can take a break," Ida Belle said. "Do some fishing."

Carter clasped his hands together like he was praying. "I can't tell you how much it would mean to me if the three of you took some time off."

"We could go to my camp and eat snacks and watch movies," Gertie said.

"You found a dead guy the last time you three were there," Carter said.

"True," Ida Belle said. "Between Fortune and Rambo, you might never have another day off."

Carter gave her a pained look and we all laughed.

"At least we're wrapped up for now," Ida Belle said.

I nodded, but I still had one more thing left to do.

CHAPTER TWENTY-SEVEN

CLOTILDE WAS IN HER FAVORITE CHAIR WHEN I POKED MY head in. She beamed when she caught sight of me and urged me to sit. I placed the box of Ally's cookies on the coffee table and sank onto the couch, admiring the pillows again as I sat.

"I'm so glad you came to visit me again," she said. "When you told me everything that had happened when you caught the thieves, I just couldn't believe it. And then your call this morning—well, I can't even tell you what a jolt that was. Hit me harder than an entire pot of coffee. Do you really think Mary killed Lucien?"

"Yes. I think she used the same poison to kill both her husband and Lucien, and since she can't exactly deny knowledge of her husband's body under the prize-winning roses that she planted, I don't think anyone can challenge the evidence."

"But why did she do it?"

I told her my theory and she listened intently, then shook her head. "So much tragedy over one man's lies. If only Lucien could have led a normal existence, then maybe none of this would have happened."

"I don't think he was capable," I said. "Some just aren't

geared for the daily grind and if they also have less of a conscience than the average person, it can lead them down a questionable path."

She nodded. "I suppose if Lucien had wanted normal, he would have stayed in Paris and continued making jewelry. It wasn't like he didn't have a well-paid and respected profession."

"But he wanted to have a royal title and live like it."

"And a returning soldier and now two young people paid for it all. Oh, I know those kids were up to no good, but death and prison seem high prices to pay for trying to steal some baubles. And what of the other cousin?"

"There's no evidence that Abel was involved other than trying to capitalize on Elijah's find. But the cops were already looking for him for other things and I'm sure he'll go back to jail. Hopefully, he'll believe Carter when he tells him that the jewels were sold long ago and won't make any more trouble when he's free again."

"And Destiny?"

I blew out a breath. "Where do you even begin on that one? I'm positive her attorney will go for an insanity defense, which given the things she's done, might work."

"Do you not think she's insane?"

"From the perspective of someone like us, then yes, it all appears to be the actions of someone not dwelling in reality. I truly believe that Destiny is one hundred percent invested in her beliefs and thought the actions she took were her obligation. I'm also certain she knew that killing him was wrong by law or she wouldn't have framed Karmin. What a jury makes of all that, I don't know."

"I would hate to be on that jury because I don't know what I make of it either. It's a complex problem, but then, seems everyone involved in this sad tale was working with complex problems."

"There were definitely a lot of variables at play, and when the two accelerants are money and love, well, you can get an explosion."

She sighed. "If only I'd known those jewels would cause even more tragedy all these years later. I wish...well, I wish there was a way I could have prevented it. Told someone the truth maybe."

"I doubt you would have been believed without all the other things to support your story. And Elijah and Karmin were desperate. Even if they'd heard your story, I think they still would have taken the chance that you were wrong or simply lying."

I lifted the box from Ally's bakery and opened it.

"I brought you some cookies from my friend's bakery," I said. "Your favorite."

She peered into the box and smiled.

"Sugar cookies were Celine's favorite."

I nodded.

She stared at me for a moment, then sat back in her chair.

"How did you know?"

"The pillows and matching curtains for starters, and the dress you were wearing that day, and today for that matter. Ronald, my friend you met, has been teaching me about fashion—against my will—but a lot of it still sticks. The fine fabrics and skill level required to create something of that quality is that of a superb professional and none of those items came off an assembly line. Plus the aide here said you never talk about your childhood but you tell stories all the time with employees and other residents. At first, I figured that was because Clotilde's childhood wasn't all that grand, but then I realized you couldn't talk about it because you weren't

Clotilde. You only know about her life after she came to live with you."

"So my sewing and my lack of rambling about my childhood gave me away."

"That and returning here. I know Clotilde considered the estate her home, in a way, but it wasn't really. Not so that she would leave Paris and come back here. She wasn't born here... didn't bury her parents here. But you couldn't return as Celine because you were worried there was a warrant for your arrest. And since one silver-haired lady looks enough like another..."

"Everything you said is true, but everything I told you about Clotilde and me running off to Paris was also true. I suppose now that Mary's treachery has been exposed, I could tell the truth..."

"But you don't want to?"

She stared outside for a good while then finally shook her head. "I don't think that I do. My mother and father brought a lot of tragedy to this place and it's still affecting the Charitte family. I don't think my existence would be a welcome thing. More likely it would cause them more mental hardship."

"I understand."

"I don't have much—this place isn't cheap and I've lived long beyond what I thought my savings would have to carry—but I don't think I'll need everything I have before I pass. Could I pay for the funeral, anonymously, of course?"

"I think that would be a wonderful thing to do. I imagine Destiny's sister is worried about how to handle everything—her sister's impending trial, the store that's been in their family for generations, and all the publicity that will come from this. One less thing to have to manage would be a blessing."

"I can't imagine how difficult it all must be for her."

"Carter said she was overwhelmed when he talked to her and explained what had happened. He said she was a really nice woman—a nurse, actually. She said she'd always been concerned about Destiny's stringent beliefs but that she'd never imagined things would go this far. She's got a lot of grieving and responsibility ahead of her, I'm afraid."

"Then it's settled. I'll trust you to let me know how it can be arranged. You're an interesting person, Fortune. You have compassion for people, even when they've done the wrong thing."

"I do for those who aren't truly evil, but evil is where my compassion ends."

Celine nodded. "I wish I had time to hear your story, because I have a feeling it would be even more exciting than mine."

"Well, given that I mostly work part time, I don't see why I can't visit and tell it. That is, if you'd really like to know."

Her face lit up and her smile stretched to both sides of her face.

"I would love that."

As I drove back to Sinful, I thought about all the years of secrets that had been uncovered in the span of a week. It was incredible, really, and I was feeling blessed to be the one person who knew all of it. I'd asked Celine if I could let Ida Belle and Gertie in on her secret because I knew they'd enjoy visiting with me and it would be easier if they knew everything. I didn't figure she would mind—and she didn't—but I wasn't about to share without asking. I'd also told her that Ida Belle and Gertie had their own secret adventure stories to share and she was excited for our next chat. I was too. Celine was as good a storyteller as she was a dressmaker and I figured we'd only scratched the surface of her life story.

My phone rang and I saw Carter's name come up in the display.

"The sheriff is in the hospital," he said.

"What happened?"

"He fell off his horse."

"Did he break anything?"

"His heart. He had a heart attack. He's stable, but I think this one scared him. He called me in and told me he was stepping down as sheriff."

"Holy crap!"

WANT TO SEE WHAT HAPPENS WHEN SHERIFF LEE RETIRES? You'll hear all about it in the next Miss Fortune mystery.

Made in the USA
Middletown, DE
03 January 2023

21172966R00176